Gaia Codex

Sarah Drew

METAMUSE MEDIA

Gaia Codex
By Sarah Drew

Editing: Maya Rock and Jannon Stein
Cover Illustration: Damon Za
Book Layout and Design: Benjamin Carrancho

Original illustrations in the Illuminated e-book edition of Gaia Codex are by Atelier Sommerland.

Library of Congress Cataloging-in-Publication Data

Drew, Sarah.
Gaia Codex / Sarah Drew.
p.cm.
1. Women–Fiction. 2. Goddess–Fiction. 3. Priestess–Fiction. 4. Dystopian–Fiction.
5. Evolutionary Biology–Fiction. 6. Libraries–Fiction.
Library of Congress Control Number: 2014908124
ISBN-13: 978-0-692-21166-3 (pbk.)

Metamuse Media
38 Miller Avenue #438
Mill Valley, CA, 94941
www.gaiacodex.com

Ordering Information: Quantity sales. Special discounts are available on quantity purchases by corporations, associations, and others. For details, contact the publisher at the address above.

PRINTED IN THE UNITED STATES OF AMERICA
First Edition

For Nicole, Page and Greta ... and all Dear
Sisters connected through time.

PROLOGUE

THROUGH THE FLOW of ages and the rise and fall of cultures, a secret codex has been inscribed with tales and stories, the rites and rituals of priestesses who are emanations of the Eternal Goddess, caretakers and guardians of our Mother Earth, Terra Gaia.

In India, China, and ancient Sumer, in ancient Greece and Egypt, in the Serengeti and the Amazon, and in the Celtic wilds, there flows a timeless tradition amongst those who have walked the Earth, who revere and remember the Circle of Life. Passed from grandmother to mother, daughter to sister, aunt to niece, held safe in the hearts of sisters who have incarnated through the ages, this text is not written on pages, paper, or papyrus. Instead, it is inscribed in holograms of light, in the leaves of trees, the hum of bees, and in the codes of spiral DNA. Hidden from many, the Codex is known to those with the eyes to see, the ears to hear, and the heart to feel that which lies just beyond the veil.

It is said that the Gaia Codex contains jewel seeds of planetary destiny for all beings and life on Planet Earth. These women, the Priestesses of Astera, have sheltered and protected the Codex and, when necessary, kept it hidden and ready for those moments of extraordinary crisis and transformation when it will be needed once more for the nourishment and regeneration of humankind.

PART ONE

Beginnings and Endings

CHAPTER
ONE

We incarnate through ten thousands lives,
but few are those who remember
that in the beginning and in the end
we are everything and we are nothing.

Gaia Codex: Node 34.25.81

Birth ...

"LILA SOPHIA," MY mother whispers into the soft curves of my ears as I suckle sweet milk at her breast. "Lila Sophia, may you be strong and wise. May you remember all of your lives." Mother caresses me with her chant and song, the ancient blessing passed down through generations, lullabies our mothers sing as we grow in the womb and as we take our first breath. The protective cloak of all good things— love, courage, honesty, strength, insight, kindness, and good fortune—blessings given as I am wrapped in my mother's arms.

Lila Sophia.

My mother kisses my tiny toes, fingers, and the tuft of silken hair on my head. She takes in the sweet smell of my birth, and I take in her aroma: warm, sweet, Mother. Nourishment flows in.

"Daughter, know and remember your name. *Lila* is Sanskrit for the divine play that creates worlds. *Sophia* is Greek for the Goddess of Wisdom. Lila Sophia." Mother speaks my name out to the sea, setting it free on the winds. Mother sings my name to stars in the cobalt sky as the sun melts like fire into the horizon on this, the first day of my birth.

"Most humans are born into this world not knowing whence they have come or where they will go," Mother gently reminds me as I take my first steps, as I learn the names of the trees and bees. "They have forgotten the ancestor's wisdom. But we are different, you and I. We remember. Our sisters remember."

My sisters. The fabled women my mother calls the Priestesses of Astera, who populate the tales of my mother's imaginings. Women revered and often feared for their practices of magic and healing, for their knowledge of herbs, midwifery, and alchemy. Women celebrated and scorned for their uninhibited sensuality—their primal connections to the forces of nature: water, fire, earth, and wind. Sisters who carried the ancient wisdoms. These are the tales my mother tells me as I turn one, two, and three.

CHAPTER

TWO

Our mothers are many: Mothers of Blood, Mothers of Lineage, Mothers of Spirit, and our Mother Earth. Our Mother is the doorway into this world and through her we each will pass.

Gaia Codex: Node 76.29.3881

HOW TO DESCRIBE my mother? How to describe someone who expresses herself in a thousand and one ways?

My mother, Dominique Haydn-Nataraj, a patron of the arts, the sciences, and of revolutionary causes, is a most exquisite piece of art. Her intellect is scintillating and lush, her words seminal. A superb hostess, Dominique is a muse whose dulcet tones in intimate conversation plant seeds of masterworks in fertile minds, over sips of vintage wines. Her salons are legendary.

That I am my mother's daughter is dually unsettling and intoxicating, for Dominique's presence is heady, like when you sink your face into star lilies still dripping with pollen and nectar. Mother is leonine and solar. She has the uncanny ability to make people in her presence feel that they, too, are magnificent—most of the time.

But I am aware of the whispers behind her back: "Muse, magician, sorceress—dangerous." This is what many call my mother, Dominique.

My father, Raj, is my mother's complement, an ethnobotanist who has documented our planet's rich legacy of life as it has been preserved in myth, legend, ritual, and custom by indigenous cultures.

His great love—besides my mother—is something he calls the Metamorphosis Project. My father is obsessed with finding correlations between embryonic cellular development in different species and the evolutionary patterns of biological change as they are found in our planet's geological record. My father often says: "If we humans as a species do not learn how to dynamically adapt in resonance with our rapidly changing environment, we will not exist."

My father is passionate. He is obsessed. Many say he is too brilliant for his own good.

Legacies and my parents' Midas touch bestow our family with fortunate circumstances. Thus, I grow up in such places as Buenos Aires, Mumbai, Morocco, Rio de Janeiro, and London and on the steppes of Mongolia, the high desert plateaus of the American Southwest, the lush fertile jungles of the Xingu in the upper Amazon, and the savannahs of the Serengeti. We live in villas, longhouses, hogans, yurts, teepees, igloos, manors, and proper brick townhouses, and we sail on teakwood sailing

vessels as we track and set our course by the stars, the wind, and the ocean currents for months on end.

In my early years I am wrapped in the cocoon of my parents' world, but soon this changes. I remember life with my parents as happy, yet time often softens blows and adds honey to those cuts that pierce so very deep that we think they will never heal.

CHAPTER

THREE

There are Priestesses of Astera whose bodies and minds have been dedicated as Temples of Memory. Into these women's bones, flesh, and organs, into their very cells, are poured historical events and knowledge for safekeeping. In these women, these Memory Keepers, are stored jewels of revelation, boons for healing and creation. Some say the true gift of these women is their ability to seamlessly connect with all Life itself—to read the ancient records in the tiniest grain of sand, in the veins of a leaf, in a constellation of stars, or in the softness of a kiss upon the lips. These Memory Keepers are both empty and full as they carry wisdom through the ages.

Gaia Codex: Node 444.54.281

A S I GROW older, Father seems particularly interested in my experiences: How do I perceive the subtle hues of a rose? How do I react when I see a dragonfly mating or deer running through the shadows of the trees? The questions seem random, but for us, they are a game. He is always scribbling notes in his journals as though my every experience and observation were important. I do not think this is strange.

Mother is in charge of my education. I am not sent to schools. Instead we explore the great museums and libraries of the world: the Bibliotheca Nazionale Centrale di Firenze, the Bibliothèque Nationale de France in Paris, the National Library in London at the British Museum, and the New York Public Library in America.

"It is not certain how long these libraries and museums will be here, Lila. The world is changing quickly." I am seven. My mother is kneeling down next to me so that her deep cornflower blue eyes are looking directly into mine.

"It is important that you take in all these artifacts of past civilizations. Remember what you see, hear, touch, and smell. Store it away for future reference."

"You are a Memory Keeper, Lila. Our Earth has many histories. Some histories are remembered, and some are not. There were many civilizations with stories that ceased to exist when the last of their people died." My mother gently pushes a loose hair from my face as she speaks. My wavy, honey, autumn-colored hair is in two neat braids I wear a little skirt, a blouse, and knee socks.

My mother continues, "Our sister-priestesses remember the various histories of Earth—and we compare these histories side by side. For you see, daughter, there is a hidden history of women and of our Mother Earth that has been mostly forgotten. And it is because it has been forgotten that people no longer revere Life, and so our planet is slowly dying. If things do not change, human beings will also die."

Caught in the enchantment of my mother's words, I cry as my mind is filled with visions of a dying planet. For a moment my heart feels the pain and suffering of people who have so carelessly destroyed that which gives them Life.

"Do you understand, Lila?" my mother asks.

I nod my head. "Some of it is clear, Mama," I say slowly. "Some of it is not."

Mother smiles. "So it often is. Never forget that there is always something you do not know."

Through Mother's charm and connections, we have access to the rare books and special library collections. Together we roam through cloistered halls and winding labyrinths, discovering dusty tomes and ancient relics, inspiration for my voracious mind. My mother lets me scramble up narrow mahogany ladders to explore volumes bound in faded red Moroccan leather and illuminated medieval manuscripts written on vellum. I leaf through tomes written in Latin, Greek, German, and various forms of English on subjects ranging from the hummingbirds of the Americas to the architecture of sixteenth-century Firenze or the origins of Western alchemy.

Donning white cotton gloves, I am allowed to gingerly inspect papyrus scrolls marked with Egyptian hieroglyphs and parchment notated with Phoenician script. I examine books from China made out of bamboo. They fold out over several feet and contain the faded black brush strokes of ideograms—tens of thousands of ancient *hanzi* characters. I touch the textured wood blocked texts of thousand-year-old Tibetan sutras, bound with carved and painted wood, and inlaid with coral and turquoise, printed long before Gutenberg invented his press.

"Every object holds its history. All the information is here. Where the object has been, how it was made, who has touched it over the years," my mother instructs me as we look at the texts.

Under my mother's direction, I look at an eighteenth-century hourglass or the gleaming brass of a polished Celtic mirror and receive vivid images, snippets of conversations, or a flow of images, pictures of people long dead and experiences long past—information attached to these objects.

That I might not know how to read these texts, written in so many languages, glyphs, and scripts does not bother my mother. "Let it soak in, Lila. Let it run and flow inside you, and perhaps you will remember what you already know, what you have always known." Thus, she gently encourages me as I finger those pages of ancient texts, many dusty and fragile with time, many exuding odors of decay, reminders that nothing is permanent even in these hallowed walls.

Ashes to ashes, dust to dust. All eventually comes tumbling down.

Naïve, indeed ignorant to the fact that it might be impossible, as the years pass, as I begin to lose my child's body, I easily learn to understand Italian, French, Tuvan, Japanese, Sanskrit, and Urdu just as easily as English. These languages become part of how I understand the world. Every language, when spoken, gives us a slightly different experience of the world, a different texture, a different hue and nuance. As I hear and speak these different languages, I imagine taking on different skins, eyes, ears, tastes, and feelings that shape and flavor my experience.

Most central to my education is the richness of the living library that is our Mother Earth: climbing the peaks of her mountains, swimming deep in her streams, rolling in her rich black soil on volcanic islands, sinking deep into the barrenness of her deserts, the wetness of her oceans. Growing up, I spend many a night under open skies, counting stars to fall asleep.

"When a civilization forgets that we live under a roof of stars, we have forgotten who we truly are. From whence we came and where we will go." Or so a craggy, wizened Mongolian shaman who saw the birth of the last century tells us as we camp in yurts across the green fields and shifting sands of the high plateaus.

As we travel, Mother and I often stop to pray at velvet moss hollows in centuries-old trees, at flowing water falls or in ancient temples that hold wooden statues of Black Madonnas, their bellies kissed with prayers, or marble statues of a beatific Kuan Yin, fragrant with incense, or at the looms where a pattern of Spider Woman is being woven into a rug by a Navajo grandmother.

As Mother kneels and brings her hands together over her heart, I follow her lead.

Goddess Mother, Mother of Earth and Stars, protect and guide us. May we be your hands and eyes in the world. May we nourish the abundance of gifts you give us: clean water, fresh air, rich black soil, and food for our children. May we share your wisdom that flows through us. May we remember that we are born of you, Mother, and we return to you at our death as the cycle turns.

Sometimes my mother and I simply sit in silence, listening to the wind in the leaves or the gentle fall of a stream flowing down to meet the ocean.

"The Goddess Mother speaks to us in many ways if you know how to listen," Mother says as we sit in the rustled quietness of

an ancient Aspen grove, the eighty-thousand-year-old Pando deep in the Rocky Mountains.

"Daughter, listen to the Goddess, and she will help you remember how to speak. She was here before the rise of Rome, Greece, and ancient Egypt, and she will be there when these civilizations are gone."

When my mother prays, sometimes for a moment, she appears to become the Goddess we evoke: ancient and luminous in the depths of darkness. The many forms of the Goddess flow through my Mother, filling her as liquid light.

"Our bodies are vessels, Lila," my mother says quietly. "Do you see Her reflected in our eyes, daughter? Do you feel Her?"

I nod my head or hug my mother tighter and sometimes I am filled with Goddesses' light. I shake and quiver. Tears come to my eyes. I bow down in the beauty. I am transported.

"The Goddess will not leave your side, daughter, when you carry her in your Heart."

Mother's words are reassuring.

Mother does not speak of our prayers to the Goddess with most of the people we meet.

Instead, it is something secret and sweet that she and I share.

Such are our family stories as we trace our meandering and tangential course across the globe.

CHAPTER
FOUR

Life and Death are as One.

The Ouroboros bites its tail.

Gaia Codex: Node 33.21.543

THERE ARE CLUSTERS of hummingbirds and scarlet macaws, pink dolphins and sloths, howler monkeys and piranhas. It is two days past my twelfth birthday, and we are in the upper Amazon. We are here for Father's work. He is looking for a rare undocumented form of morpho butterfly that he feels is a cornerstone for the Metamorphosis Project, but there have been troubles and clashes between locals and scientists and company heads arriving from Europe, America, and China.

High stakes. Big Money. What happens when a species is dying?

The tension in the air is palpable, and for the last few days I have heard my parents talking behind closed doors in quiet, fervid voices. I shouldn't be eavesdropping, but I am. The walls of our thatched roof hut are thin.

"The findings will break everything open, Dominique, and

that is what they're afraid of. It redefines what a human being is. *Homo sapiens* are destroying themselves and their natural habitats. We must evolve. This is the natural order." My father is speaking low, but I hear the passion in his voice.

"Raj, many of my sisters have understood the importance of species evolution and variation for millennia. Many cultures have known the simple wisdom that what we call a human being is ever evolving, but the Priestesses of Astera, my sisters, have survived only because we know how to work behind the scenes when it's too dangerous to show our faces. We don't push our knowledge upon a culture that is not ready."

My mother is pacing the floor. She does this when she gets worked up.

She continues, "The situation is beyond urgent, but it is best to take our time and be certain with our findings before we make any claims. Lila must make it to maturity for us to understand the full effect of what we are doing. Plus, darling, I have a bad feeling about you dealing with these people. They would eat your flesh, if they thought it would give them what they want and what you have."

"Surely, you joke, Domi," my father replies. I smell the rich tobacco of his pipe wafting through the woven walls.

"Not entirely," my mother says quietly. "Be careful, Raj. You are pushing our good fortune: the protection we have enjoyed for our family and our work. I don't want to lose you, my love."

"Nor can I imagine life without you, Domi," my father says softly to my mother. There is a silence on the other side of the thin wall, and then the sound of my parents passionately, softly kissing—as they often do.

I sigh, roll over in bed, and look up at the ceiling as a

blue-black tarantula slowly makes its way across the ceiling. *I like spiders.*

That was one week ago. Now my mother is standing before me, her golden hair disheveled as tears stream down her cheeks. There is blood splattered across her crisp white linen shirt. She holds me tight as she rocks me back and forth.

"Raj has been killed, Lila. Your father has been killed, my love." Mother's delicate shoulders convulse as tears stream down both of our cheeks. I have never seen my mother like this. Fragile. Vulnerable. Exposed.

My handsome father, with his caramel-colored skin and black wavy hair torn apart by gunshot wounds, lies on the jungle floor. The scene sears my mind. I often see images when Mother speaks. It is something we share, a language that is more than just spoken words—images and sensations that penetrate deep beneath the skin.

Mother cries for days and nights. She holes up in her room.

Guests come to pay their respects. I serve tea and biscuits as a parade of tribal leaders, uniformed officials, well-meaning friends, and acquaintances come to ask too many questions. I tell them that Mother is not available–at least not now.

In a strange way, I am enjoying having to be the adult. I wear a cotton dress with embroidered flowers and have my hair tied neatly back into a single ponytail with a satin bow and at night, after everyone has left, I fall in my mother's arms and hold her tight. I am in shock, I am in a trance. I can only let myself feel a little bit of the pain.

CHAPTER
FIVE

A woman's womb is sacred. It is the center and source of creation.

Gaia Codex: Node 444.3221

ONE WEEK LATER, we are packing Father's belongings: the writings, experiments, and specimens. "They can kill your father but they cannot destroy what was inside him—inside you, Lila. Our work will continue," my mother says as she methodically wraps up all of my father's precious belongings and places them into leather trunks and wooden boxes.

A few days later we bury my father, Raj Nataraj, at the roots of a sacred *ceiba* tree. There are three female tribal elders who pray in a litany of songs as they burn *palo santo*. They have given us permission to bury my father here. "He was a guardian—a protector. He belongs here," the women say.

Mother sings in an ancient language I have never heard

before. The sounds are beautiful and textural, like the ten thousand colors in the first bloom of spring.

"Your father knows how to make his way back home," my mother says softly, after the last notes of her song had been offered to the earth and the sky above.

What I didn't realize was that my mother, Dominique Hadyn-Nataraj, also buries a part of herself there by the roots of that ancient *ceiba*—or so it seems, for after my father's death Mother changes. Her effervescence subsides, her easy manner becomes severe, and she now wears her long golden hair bound back into a tight bun, accentuating her aquiline face. She can still be charming and sensual, but now there is also a danger about her. She is a mother lion; she will easily kill any who cross the line. As we continue our travels, and as Mother increasingly takes on work that had once been my father's—the collection of specimens, the cellular analysis, the charts, and the formulas—a warrioress emerges that some fear, and many, it seems, cannot resist. Mother flirts with men with a cool calculation, leaving them with hope but without satisfaction, usually getting whatever she wants in the process.

"You are cruel to them, Mama." I am beginning to observe my own effect on boys, and I am watching Mother for cues and guidance on how it is all done.

"I can't fulfill their desires in the way they want, Lila. No one can replace my Beloved—not now." Nine months have passed since my father's death. We are riding horseback across the high plateaus of the Himalayas, looking for a particular moss, reputed in the Tibetan Buddhist pharmacopeia to be a panacea—able to heal all manner of ills.

"Daughter, a woman's sexual energy, her *Shakti*, is precious. It is never owned by a man, although men in many cultures have been mistaken about this." Mother laughs for a moment looking up at the sky. "Our Shakti is our direct relationship with creation, Life, and the Mother. If you share this energy with a man, it is your choice alone—not his. Remember this. Lila, soon you will be receiving your menses moon, and all these things will become more real to you and more precious." As my mother says this, I notice that she gazes at me wistfully, as though I am a treasured thing she doesn't want to lose.

We ride on for some time before she turns to me again.

"Know that time is much more fluid than we imagine, Lila. It has many textures and dimensions. Know as well that there are those not bound by time."

The statement sounds strange to me, but I know my mother wants me to remember her words. Her blue eyes pierce into me. I shudder.

"*Shakti* moves inside you. She is a powerful force to be reckoned with and to use. She is the Goddess alive inside us." Mother lets out a yelp, digs her heels into the sides of her horse, and gallops up ahead of me.

The yellows and purples of the high plateaus, the sharp thinness of the air —all of this sears my mind as I feel murmurs of movement at the base of my spine while Mother rides ahead.

CHAPTER
SIX

There are stories of sacred habitats where flora and fauna have existed for hundreds of millions of years. Some say that such places exist outside of common time. The hidden valley of Shangri-La, high in the Himalayas, the habitat of a lost tribe deep in the Amazonian rainforest, a fabled underwater city in what was called the Mariana Trench— the deepest part of the Pacific Ocean. Some say these are portals between the worlds, places of genesis where the world is born ever anew.

Gaia Codex: Node 3334.221.8

I HAVE JUST TURNED fourteen. Despite the best predictions, I am a late bloomer. I have yet to get my menses moon, and my breasts are barely developed. "You will flower fully when it is time," Mama assures me.

Perhaps, but right now I am lanky and odd angled—suspended somewhere between child and woman. I have creamy skin and my hair is a riot of abundant honey autumn curls. I'm told that my mercurial hazel-gold eyes shift with the changing light. Mother says I am beautiful. Although lingering, hungry looks of boys and full-grown men inform me that I am striking, unsettling, even desirable, I still feel half-formed and unfinished. I'm not yet comfortable in my skin.

I am restless, ready for my life to change. For the first time, I am tired of always being with Mother. I daydream of when I will be off on my own, but in the meantime we are in the Congo living in a mud hut.

Governments and communication systems are collapsing. Air travel has become increasingly difficult. Food shortages are common. Weather patterns grow increasingly chaotic. Thinking about it makes my body ache, my head hurt, and my heart feel a sorrow that lies too close to the skin.

The Congo was once one of the largest rainforests in the world, but it has been ravaged for diamonds, rare minerals, and petroleum. Terrain that once was habitat for over tens of thousands of species has been torn asunder. My mother is here to document the flora and fauna that still exist in an interior rainforest valley called the Crevice. By all accounts, the valley has been miraculously left untouched; accept by the Pygmy inhabitants for millennia.

My father had talked about this valley for years. "There are butterflies the size of a big man's hands, primate populations who seem to have unique tool-making abilities, flora and fauna that at first sight may look familiar, but are indeed species undocumented in other regions. There are clues here that point towards what may be possible for human evolution—for the collective evolution of all species on the planet. And beauty ... Lila, it is a place of unprecedented beauty. You will remember much when we are there."

I miss Father asking me questions and taking notes in his journals. I miss our laughter, his passion, and the strength of his presence. I miss his strong hand in mine.

Today, Mother wakes me up early. "We are going visiting," she says.

The sun is high in the sky, the air hot and still when we arrive at the village of clay huts where Mother and I are invited to share a simple meal of peanut soup and *fufu* (plump cassava) with a circle of local women.

After the meal, the chattering subsides and the Grandmother of the clan, an old woman, whose well-oiled ebony skin hangs loose from her bony frame, whose eyes see stars, the wide savannahs, and the secret architectures of time, takes my face in her gnarled hands:

"Know you are strong, child. Know we are built to weather the storms of sorrow when they come," she says to me in her native tongue. Her daughter translates as I look across the circle at my mother. Silent tears fall down my mother's face as the Grandmother speaks. Although my mother is often moved to tears of joy or empathy, these are tears of sorrow. I feel them, and they startle me.

"Tears are our healing rivers. You understand," Grandmother continues. When I do not answer, Grandmother asks more softly, her gnarled hands grasping my face tighter, "You understand?" she says with sharp exhale of air. *Ptawth.*

I nod my head as Mother watches closely. The scent of grass and earth, the musky charcoal of the embers in the fire, and the

lingering tanginess of the peanut soup permeate the air as each woman in the circle places her hands on my head, on my heart, and on my belly.

My body is shimmering. I feel the energy of burning fire, liquid stars, and sweet honey pouring down my spine. I am being cracked open—until there are only stars—inside and out. I gasp and then bow as my mother has taught me with my hands over my heart. I bow to the Mother who moves through each of us.

There is singing, chanting, and then, as suddenly as it started, it is done.

"Thank you, Mother," Dominique says as she looks into the Grandmother's eyes.

The women are chattering as we leave.

Dominique says nothing as we walk back to our temporary home. I probably should have asked Mother why she cried, but the moment is tender, and I am afraid my questions will only bring more tears.

Now, as we sit by the fire and the moon rises outside, Mother sketches the Grandmother's face with charcoal on paper. My mother's drawings are vibrant with Life as though one could easily step through the pages into the world depicted and touch the flesh of the person who is being drawn or painted.

"You can embed all the senses into a single stroke of color, Lila. It is a technique practiced by many of the great masters. A painting is a doorway into a world," Mother often says to me as we practice painting and drawing together. I have inherited some of her talents. I keep my own notebooks that I fill with sketches, stories, and visions of places I have never been, but that haunt my mind: cities, people, and schematics for elegant technologies from some future or past, all rendered in ornate detail. Places I know like the back of my hand, but that I have yet to see.

This evening I am reading two books. The first is the *Amduat*—a map of the underworld and step-by-step guide of what the ancient Egyptians believed happens to you after you die. The second book is an illustrated version of the *Bardo Thodol*, the Tibetan Book of the Dead. Like the *Amduat*, the *Bardo Thodol* is a guide written by the ancients to help your soul to move through the stages of the afterlife and hopefully have an auspicious rebirth.

I am obsessed by the topic: how we move from one world to the next and what happens between death and birth. It was comforting to know that someone had mapped it out. Although I remember the moment of my birth—I know this is unusual— yet I only have the faintest memories of the womb. Nonetheless there is something ancient inside me that remembers our planet and our people, that knows the ancient songs. I am searching for a thread that connect it all.

The third item I am sporadically reading is a copy of *Vogue* magazine from the 1990s that I picked up in a second-hand col- lectibles store in London. My interests are eclectic. I like fashion, especially vintage, and even out here in the wilds, I try to put together intriguing outfits. This is a passion both Mother and I share.

"Lila, do you think this is a good likeness of the Grandmother we visited today?" Mother asks, holding up the charcoal sketch.

"The drawing is good, Mama," I answer as I turn back to my books.

It is hauntingly good. The eyes in the charcoal sketch make me shudder.

My mother looks out into space as though she is listening for something unseen. She often does this now, since my father died.

"Lila, I know this is not where you want to be right now," Mother says as she continues sketching the shape of the Grandmother's face.

"You're right," I reply. The words are unkind, but I feel on edge. She probably thinks I am being testy, but I too am lost in thought, remembering the dream that I had last night: I am falling off a cliff and never hitting the bottom. I scream, but no one hears. I am alone. I don't tell my mother of the dream, but I have been thinking about it all day.

My mother watches me carefully but says nothing. I do not notice the glowing skies outside or the rising crackle of fires in the distance as the hours pass into the night, but I feel my mother's restlessness and my own unexplained discomfort. "They are coming," she says suddenly.

A moment later there is a sharp knock at the door. One of my mother's assistants is here, sweating and breathless. "They are burning the Crevice. We have to go and see what can be saved," the young man's words come pouring out. He is in shock.

The burning jungle, the screech of parrots scattering, bonobos grabbing their newborns as their skin is being scorched. I see this, and I feel my father's sadness, my mother's urgency, as the treasure trove of rare DNA samples they have been accumulating is destroyed—as the possible cure for our species is going up in flames.

"I am coming with you," my mother calls to the aide as she

rapidly places her gear into a backpack: a pistol, a buck knife covered in a leather sheath, a rope, a compass, night vision glasses and a water bottle. She leaves the room for a moment and puts on her trekking trousers and a warm jacket lined with many pockets. Her long, wavy, blonde hair is tucked under a cap with wisps and curls escaping at the temples.

"Where are you going?" I call after her, but she does not answer. *Details that sear the mind. Details we remember when we see someone for the very last time. This time, it is different. The quality of time is different—like the dream where you try to scream, but there is no sound. Real, but not real. I have been here before. I am frozen.*

"Lila." My mother comes back and kneels down beside me. My copy of the *Amduat* clatters to the floor. She places her hands around mine.

"Lila, I need you to look at me." Her voice is surprisingly soft.

I look up slowly. I feel the blood rushing to my face. My breath comes in gasps.

If I had known then that it would be my last chance to look upon her beauty, to look upon my mother's face, I would have held her tight. I would have buried myself in her arms and kissed her cheeks a thousand times.

But instead I look at her impatiently. "What Mama …"

"I have been meaning to give this to you so you have it for safekeeping." Dominique slips a ribbon around my neck. On the ribbon are three items: an old-fashioned brass key, a small cylinder, the type you can put a rolled up piece of paper in, and an ebony pendant, dark as night with a single star diamond at the center. The three items fall cold against my skin.

Everything is falling, slowly, slowly.

"Keep these with you at all times," Dominique continues as she places her hands gently on my heart. "Lila, if I don't come back—"

She continues, "The information written on the note in the cylinder will give you instructions: where to go and where I have left resources for you." My mother leans in closer touching her forehead to mine—an ancient gesture. I feel my mother's tears streaming down my face, their salty wetness falling on my tongue.

My mother's words startle me.

"Lila, you are part of a larger family—a larger clan. You have sisters who are waiting for you. It is important that you find them. I have told you of these women, your sisters—the Priestesses of Astera. Now it is your time to join them."

The Priestesses of Astera. My heart and head explode as I hear the name.

"Lila Sophia. They are waiting for you. They are your family—our family."

My mother's tears continue to fall into my hands and lap as a knot of nausea rises in my stomach.

"There is one other thing I must tell you." I feel my mother's hesitancy to speak. This is so unlike her. This hesitancy.

"I want you to hear it from my mouth. You have been an experiment." My mother's cornflower blue eyes look intently into mine. I feel her asking for my forgiveness. "Our hope is that this experiment will serve you and our Mother Earth well."

An experiment? I have no idea what this means.

My mother's warm hands grip me tighter.

"Why are you telling me this now?" I ask, finding my voice.

"Because it is time, my love," my mother answers.

Again the nausea rises.

The explosions. The rage of fire. The fire of fear. The land is burning.

"Lila, you have everything you need, you have been trained well. It is important that you remember this. Do you understand, Lila?" my mother asks.

"No," I answer. There is panic in my voice. My throat is dry. I bite my lip. Now I am crying. *The explosions, the light, the screams of terror in the night.* This time it is different.

"If I don't return in five days, you must leave the Congo. Understand?"

"I will go with you now!" I say as I start to put on my shoes.

"No!" My mother's voice is firm, and I sit back down. She lifts my chin up so that I am looking into her eyes. "Lila, you are born of love, this is your legacy. Remember this, for when everything else is gone it is only love that remains."

She gives me one last hug, and then she is gone, out into the fiery night.

CHAPTER
SEVEN

Touch the rawness of your fear and you will know your greatest strength.

Gaia Codex: Node 3221.841

Day One:

THE MEN ARE drunk and boisterous. They speak in a language that sounds strange and rough to my ears. I hear their boots muddy the research papers scattered on the floor. I imagine them grabbing bags of grain, my mother's soft, silk, summer blouses, and scientific instruments. I have left enough in the room for them to leave satisfied, but I did not leave everything for their looting. I have the gold coins and currency my mother always stashed away for emergencies, neatly tucked into a pouch belt at my waist. I am hidden in a small cupboard in the wall. Girls and women have been raped and tortured in this land. I know this. I will not let this become my fate. I listen carefully, and I am very still.

They do not find me.

Day Two:

I slowly sip the water I brought with me into hiding. I do not cry for fear of making sounds. In the darkness, it is hard to tell the difference between day and night—the only indicator is a sliver of light that pours through a small crack.

Day Three:

"Child." It is a woman's voice. "Child, you can come out now."

I do not answer. After some time, I hear the woman sit down in the middle of the room and start to sing a little song—a song that winds round and round the room. She waits for me patiently. One hour. Two hours. I see the sun set as light from the sliver crack in my hiding place disappearing. When I finally come out, I am shaking.

"Child," she says simply. I recognize her as one of the women from the village of the Grandmother.

I am dusty with cobwebs; my pores are filled with the stench of sweat. The woman, unmoving, lets me approach her as though I am a wild animal that needs to be tamed.

When I am close, she gently puts her arms around me.

"She is gone, child. The place your people called the Crevice is gone—all burned up."

"And my mother?" My parched voice cracks.

The woman takes me gently by the shoulders.

"Dead, everything is burned—too many bodies. My husband was there. He saw your mother run into the fire. He held her charred body in his hands. Everything is gone. You

understand?" She looks deep into my eyes. I shudder. My body is convulsing without tears.

The woman takes me back into her arms.

"No, no, no." It is all I can say in response, as I bury my face into her chest.

"We knew no good would come of travelling into that valley. It is not made for humans," the woman says softly.

I remember Mother telling me that we can tell when a soul passes from the body.

"You will feel it, Lila, if you are connected to that person: even if you are in a different part of the world. You will know of the passing. We priestesses are trained in such things, and you have the gift." I had felt my father's soul passing. The shimmering threads that connected him to his bodies dissolving as he passed through the realms. It had come as a dream, but I had seen this passing with my father.

I finger the talisman, cylinder, and key around my neck and for a moment close my eyes. I quiet my mind as Mother had shown me. I have not felt her soul pass—it is strange and yet she is not here with me. This I know. I feel my heart tighten. Gasping. Grasping. *I am alone.*

"Your mother asked that I help you leave," the woman says.

We leave the mud hut that night, in the back of a truck, in a wood box, hidden under a flatbed of produce. It is rare and expensive to find a truck these days since gas is so hard to find.

"You can't look back child. You must go forward." The woman whispers as we make the long journey to Kinshasa—the crossroads city on the Congo River.

As we ride the bumpy roads, she sings a soft melody into my ears and holds me tight. I don't understand the words, but

I imagine it is an ancient lullaby that she sings to her children when they can't sleep. The chaos is our cloak and protection.

People should have noticed the girl with silent tears, the tears that won't fall, but people are busy with their own problems. Riots, burnings, and lootings. Cities are going down.

Miraculously, I make it through all the border checks. Ten days later, after giving officials some money, I am free to leave the country.

"Travel safe, child." I feel the woman's prayers as she says goodbye. I sense she is at risk in this city, and yet she travelled with me.

"I don't know how to thank you." My voice is hoarse as I speak. I am fragile and scared.

"Sister, it is what we do for each other," she answers. "Sorrow is our doorway," she adds as she places her hand on her heart.

Once on the airplane, I collapse. I was lucky to get a flight. So few planes are flying these days. I am exhausted and alone. I bite my lip so I will not cry. Through the night, the tiny airline pillow remains dry. *Our tears become the rivers that heal our broken hearts.* I remember the Grandmother's words but I know it will be some time before the deluge roars.

CHAPTER

EIGHT

The ancient art of illuminated manuscripts was the art of bringing a page to life with color and sound, with the texture of words. It is said that the true illuminated manuscripts were doorways into other worlds.

Gaia Codex: Node 34.521.97

IT HAS BEEN six weeks since Mother's death. My fear, my aching, and the crippling sorrow has transformed into a numbness that penetrates my very bones. I am frozen. I am alive but dead. I am not ready to be left alone. I am here in Paris out of duty—following the instructions in the golden cylinder that Mother placed around my neck.

Paris. The grand houses of couture, the cafés, and the confectionaries are for the most part boarded up and closed, here on the Boulevard Haussmann. In their stead is an abundance of little pushcarts that carry belongings and goods for sale: fresh-baked bread, herbs gathered from parks, pieces of cloth and old clothing, baskets made of willow, and jugs of made of clay. There are eggs and fresh milk. In the streets, people feed the flames of bonfires with Empire style tables made of cherrywood and old magazines from the last century. Word on the street is that the effects of the Crash are echoed in New York, London, Tokyo, and Shanghai. Some people say it is only temporary: a glitch in the system.

"Things will soon get back to normal." This is the hopeful refrain of many, but I smell people's fear.

I keep my eyes down as I walk towards the once elegant marble quarters of the centuries-old bank. As I step inside, I see cracked art nouveau glass. There is dust on the mosaic marble floors, yet this revered financial institution is still tenuously open.

The guard, satisfied with my identification, leads me to a private viewing room. Inside the room there is a table upon which sits a brass safe deposit box. I sink down into the chair. I slip the key off from around my neck and fit it into the brass keyhole. It opens easily.

Inside are three items: a book bound in wine-colored leather, a letter written on thick ivory paper stock, and a velvet bag. I open the letter.

Dearest Lila Sophia,

If you are reading this, it means that both your father and I are no longer with you. We are either dead or there has been an unfortunate circumstance of separation. This manuscript is my bequest to you, my daughter. My prayer is that it will lead you to your destiny. Within these pages you will also find information about my work with your father on the Metamorphosis Project. I have also left you

some of my gemstones. You may find the large one, the
Phoenix Stone, of particular interest.

The letter goes on about logistics: accounts that had been set up at banks in various countries and the locations of small deposits of gold that had been buried in case those banks were no longer functioning. Also included are signed papers for legal emancipation, if necessary. There are no contact numbers for relatives, friends, or next of kin.

My parents never mentioned direct relatives. As we travelled the world there were many tribes, clans, colleagues, and acquaintances that welcomed us into their homes, but I never met grandparents, cousins, aunts, or uncles, although I had met hundreds of women, men, and children who were introduced by my parents as "extended family."

The closest hint of clan I had was from my mother's mentions of the Priestesses of Astera—but sitting here in the bank, these stories feel distant: sweet tales from childhood. Reawakened by my mother's recent strange request.

I hear the guard pacing outside. I put the letter down and carefully pick up the manuscript. It is bound in a deep burgundy leather cover, beautifully engraved with lush vines that encircle a spiral labyrinth. As I hold the book up to the light, the labyrinth appears to transform into a luscious blossom of many layered petals. Hanging from the vines are stars—as one looks closer, they seem to break into a wealth of constellations disappearing into the horizon.

So very curious—and for a moment, I am transported. I look up at the walls of this small, official room. *Yes, I am still here.*

I run my fingers over the cover of the tome. Something

tingles. I slowly open it up. The pages are made out of an unusually strong material that is oddly also translucent. They too seem to tingle with a certain energy, like matter transforming into its oscillating atoms.

The title page is written in my mother's beautiful hand—writing that bespeaks of another era, when beautiful, clear penmanship was key to communication.

Priestesses of Astera

EXPLORATIONS INTO THE SCIENCE, MAGIC, AND RECORDS OF THE

Gaia Codex

Next to this first entry is a beautifully detailed painting, revealing nuanced shadows, depth, and color. The painting depicts a circle of thirteen women beautifully robed in vibrant jewel tones of rich ruby, emerald, sapphire, silver, and gold. The women appear to be fusions of different ethnicities, beautiful hybrids that display a genetic coat of many colors. It is hard to place them in time. Are they from the past or from the future? In the center of the circle, the women hold a babe, a girl-child holding a brilliant star.

I recognize my mother's artistry, and for a moment, I smell star lily and hyacinth—her scent. I blink my eyes. I let my fingers run across the pages, but only the first pages of the book are accessible to view. The rest—at least for the moment—are sealed shut. *Curious.*

The first entry is dated on the day of my birth.

Our daughter, Lila Sophia, was born today. She is healthy. She is beautifully formed. Soft skin. Bright eyes. Thankfully, it was an easy birth—a blessed birth. After carrying her for nine months, I am grateful to finally hold her in my arms, surrounded by my closest sister priestesses.

I dedicate this child, Lila Sophia, to the Great Mother—she who sustains our Mother Earth. I dedicate her to the sisters of the stars. May her life benefit all Life.

As I look closer, the scent of nutmeg, lily of the valley, sweet grass, and sweet spring waters, ocean-salted winds, and amber waft from the page. *How curious.* My mother's words bring forth vivid images that sear the mind. I miss her. I continue reading. I feel the book wrapping itself around me and seeping inside me.

The words on these pages are for my daughter, Lila Sophia. They are not my words alone but are also the words of my sister-priestesses, those who have remembered and cared for our Mother Earth through the ages—the inscriptions and teachings of the Gaia Codex itself.

These writings are also here to shine a light on the

*experiment that my beloved Raj and I created, the
Metamorphosis Project.*

The experiment … my stomach drops as I continue to read
my mother's writing.

*A note of caution for those who proceed to read the words
on these pages: the code of the Gaia Codex is known to
transform one's perceptions, relationship to time, birth,
and death. It can change the very structure of our DNA.
To read it is to know death many times in one life. This
is not a path for everyone, for you will be shown your
deepest fears, and you may have to relinquish what you
hold most dear. Yet the rewards are great, and our mission
is deep: to continue the teachings of balance and the
rejuvenation of Life on our Mother Earth.*

*Know that you do not walk alone. Choose well, my
sister-daughter. My prayers, our prayers, are with you.*

I hear the guard's raspy cough outside the door. I put the
book down on the table. I am shaking. The words I read are intimate, as though my mother is here speaking to me. I let my fingers run across the pages of the book one more time, hoping to
see what else it might contain.

This time the pages fall open like a fluttered fan. Interwoven
with the entries in my mother's hand are drawings, diagrams,
formulas, and notations that reference different times and eras.
These are in such a beautiful script—a combination of calligra-
phy and symbols that I do not recognize. After many of these

entries, there is a notation indicating it stems from something called the Gaia Codex. The entries have such titles as: "Time," "Earth Histories and Guardians," "Medicines," "Star Travels," "Architecture and Alchemy," and "Pharmacopeias." There are also excerpts from what seem to be the personal diaries of women; each one seems to have a different nuance and flavor, like the women themselves. The pages scintillate. I am mesmerized.

My eyes fall upon a page with a brilliant blue morpho butterfly. Underneath the butterfly is the title *The Metamorphosis Project*.

> *At this juncture, human beings must accelerate their ability to adapt and successfully mutate. It is our analysis that if this does not occur, we will not be able to sustain Life on this planet. We are a species out of balance. In our observations of the record of species evolution laid down over millions of years in the Earth's geology, and through our understanding of the cellular differentiation and formation that occurs in the early stages of embryonic development, and through the isolation of certain factors we have observed in the development of imaginal cells (those cells that instigate and distinguish the body of a butterfly), we have come to the conclusion that the traits of the imaginal cells can be successfully synthesized with human RNA by utilizing the potential of what has been called junk DNA—the portions of the DNA sequence whose function were not accounted for in early studies.*
>
> *This experiment cannot be completed by science alone. It will take knowledge of alchemy and the arts of*

magic developed by the Priestesses of Astera over multiple
generations to complete it.

Together, Raj and I believe that we may be able
to create a new hybrid species that potentiates a
turning point for human beings and for Earth. The
Metamorphosis Project's first test will be on a human
embryo—our daughter, Lila Sophia.

I let the book drop onto the table in front me. Suddenly, the room is too small. I do not know my parents. I look at my hands for a moment. I do not know myself.

Who am I? What am I?

I could get up and walk away. I could leave the text in the safe deposit box, but it is the only link I have to my mother, to my parents, to the life that once was mine. It is the only clue I have that might shed light on how I might find the sister-priestesses my mother said I must find. My wounds are still too tender and my curiosity too great to leave this door unopened.

I will take the manuscript with me. This decision gives me an unexpected sense of relief.

As I leave the room, I place the manuscript, letter, and velvet bag into my backpack and leave the deposit box empty on the table.

"Mademoiselle, did you find everything?" the guard asks as I come out.

"Yes, thank you," I reply.

"I won't be needing this." I hand him the old-fashioned brass key.

"But, Mademoiselle, the box is paid for at least another decade," the guard answers, trying to hand me back the key.

"Good. Thank you. If we need to use it again, we will let you know." I push the key back towards him.

The guard looks at me carefully and then gives me a strange smile. He continues speaking in a hushed tone. "You are probably right, Mademoiselle. It is likely that this institution will be able to service your needs in the future. These are uncertain times. And Mademoiselle ... a small suggestion—treat yourself to a good meal. It is best to keep your strength up for what is ahead."

"Thank you," I answer quietly.

The guard bows slightly as I walk out of the building.

I feel fragile as I walk out onto the Boulevard Haussmann. The backpack that carries my mother's manuscript feels surprisingly light, as though I am carrying a bundle of silks and not an oversized book. A pack of dogs race by me: grungy poodles and bichon frises, who look like they have been without their owners for months—their once white coats are now mottled yellows and browns. I barely see the boarded over or broken shop windows or the strings of ragged laundry hanging out of once elegant apartment buildings.

Given my state of mind, I am surprised that I notice him, but it is hard to ignore the intensity of the young man's eyes. He is in his late twenties, casually but well dressed, with jeans and a wool sweater that shows the cut of his broad shoulders, and luxuriant wavy brown hair. He gazes at me with that look I often feel from men and boys—the hunger, the desire, the need to possess—but there is something else. His eyes make my heart melt–sweet like honey.

Heat rises to my cheeks.

I am waiting for you. The voice inside my head startles me. It is not my own. It is male.

He smiles, and my legs began to shudder.

I turn away quickly. *I want you, too.* I say softly to myself— surprising myself. *Why would I say this about someone I don't know?*

Remembrance. Recklessness. The comfort of his arms around mine.

I cannot go up to him now, but I feel him watching me as I quickly walk the other way.

As I am about to turn the corner, I look back one more time, but he is gone, and a street vendor's cart selling various odds and ends is parked where he was standing, only moments ago. *Strange.*

I walk forward. The door has closed on the life that once was mine. Or so it seems, on this early spring day, before the first chestnut trees have broken their buds.

CHAPTER
NINE

*The Goddess descends to the underworld. It is a known
tale, an old tale, woven in veins of rhyme and time. It
is the memory of how a woman, a priestess, is born—
and how she dies while she is still alive. She who is light
returns to the darkness. Persephone. The young maiden
of spring is stripped, shorn, and torn. She meets with her
deepest fear and sorrow. She loses youth and innocence.
She is Inanna, who has learned the lessons of Persephone,
and this time leads the king into the underworld. She is
the Inuit shamaness, who is torn into ten thousand pieces
by a bear or a whale, and must—with the help of Mother
Creator—weave a new body to return to the realm of the
living.*

*She is Isis, who gathers the pieces of her Beloved Osiris
so that once more she can enjoy him as her lover. She is
Cybele, who holds the baby Dionysus in her arms before
he is torn apart by the Maenads.*

She is the young girl who will always lose her

childhood. She dies to what was so she can be born anew into womanhood.

When you descend, dear sister, and you face your deepest fears, know that the many women who have travelled to the underworld before you are holding you with love. Know that when you feel the call of death and you are filled with anger and desperation and when you are sinking in the swamp of tears. Your sister-priestesses are with you.

Gaia Codex: Node 4445.621

CHAPTER
TEN

She of many deaths: a priestess must die many times to learn to truly live.

Gaia Codex: Node 444.87.921

London:

RENTED ROOMS AND the hidden backsides of parks, makeshift cafes, and random bazaars: the next week is a blur as I make my way about London. I am tender. I am raw. I am broken. I am the wounded animal, easy prey for the predator. Instinctively, I know I will be taken down if I spend too much time amongst the crowds or with the roving bands of children, who—like myself—have lost their homes and families. At this time, I am unable to defend myself.

I could have stayed in the guarded sectors of town. Places that still have electricity and modern conveniences. My parents provided me the means to do this, but I prefer to live more simply. I don't want to answer the questions of strangers. I don't want to take a bath or brush my hair. My passion for fashion has degenerated. I wear rugged black trousers, layered t-shirts, a sweater, a jacket, and a cap to cover my hair. I look like a scarecrow. I don't care. I want to hide.

Following childhood memories, I make my way to Hampstead Heath, the nearly eight-hundred-acre forest and park close to Trafalgar Square. When I stayed in London as a child, Mother and I would often take long walks in the park, meandering from ponds to forests, and through open fields.

I seek a balm for my wounds—for this ache so crushing that I can barely breathe. I have my mother's illuminated manuscript. I have the memory of the young man who took my breath away in Paris. But the manuscript will not open for me, its wine red covers are sealed shut. As for the young man, he is not here, and I would not want him to see me like this. I am breaking into ten thousand pieces—caught in an undertow that pulls me down beneath the surface.

I shed no tears. I am dry and parched. I seek the comfort of the earth. There are places in Hampstead Heath where I can set up my tent and stay well hidden. In our travels to Madagascar, the Canadian Rockies, and the high crystal lakes of Patagonia, my parents taught me the ways of the woods—how to trap a bird or a rabbit, how to find a local water source, and how to gather edible plants.

"If you learn to live close to the land, Lila, you won't have so far to fall when we can no longer live in our cities," Father had often told me. It is because of this training that I am not worried about my material sustenance.

I know there are dangers for a girl alone in a city wood but I am reckless—a soul in limbo. I have nothing to lose. I tell myself

I do not fear death. Indeed I might welcome it—anything to stop the pain that is slowly consuming me.

I lie upon the earth as days turn to nights and nights turn to days. Spontaneous prayers to the Goddess well up from within, shaking my body and hijacking my lips. She is the only one who can comfort me now.

> *Dear Divine Mother, protect me in your arms. Please reveal to me what I cannot see. May your love guide my thoughts, words, and actions. May I be nourished so that I may best serve all Life. Please protect me, Mother, as I journey through cycles of day and night—protect me as I descend down into the depths, for there is no other place I can go.*

There is wisdom in those ancient cultures whereupon the death of a beloved we join with our sisters, all dressed in black, and we keen and cry, letting forth a trail of tears that continues for days, weeks, or months, until the tears are done. But I cannot cry. My parents are gone. The life I had no longer exists and the well is dry.

Holed away in my tent in a hidden forest hollow, I am unaware of the epidemics that are sweeping through London. All I know is that my heart, my whole body is searing with pain. My organs—my liver, heart, kidneys, and lungs—feel as though they can barely function. My throat feels like it is covered with blisters, and my head is exploding with headaches. The daylight is too bright; all I can do is lie perfectly still. I am suspended.

The fever rises, racking my body, sucking out the very marrow of my bones and with the fevers come visions of descent. I am crushed by my sorrow and terrified by unknowing, as I feel hundreds of millions of people who are simultaneously suffering from loss, fear, hunger, and unknowing. I feel those who will experience the pain of early death and those who will be witness to the death of human civilizations. I feel the heat and sickness of our Mother Earth, the result of human carelessness and greed. I feel this inside me, and I break open—I am broken.

In certain moments, as I fall further down, I feel circles of women and sisters holding me—those who pray with me and for me. These women are the arms and hands of the Goddess—sisters I feel as kindred spirits I have yet to meet. In those rare moments when I feel their presence, I feel a modicum of comfort before I descend again, crushed by physical pain.

Death in her darkness beckons. Each breath I make is difficult and a miracle.

A dry, arid desert filled with millions of people in different stages of death, starvation, dehydration, and desperation. In the distance is one lone tree reaching to the sky, a reminder of once fertile Life. The tree is dying, and the people are climbing on top of each other—as if this could save them from the fate to come. In a forgotten corner a girl cries. Her tears are the only water left in the land. They create a meager pool that reflects her shining eyes. There is hope. With her tears, rains fall from the sky.

When the Goddess finally comes to me, she is dressed in white robes lifted by the softest of perfumed winds. Her face is beatific; she carries a vase of nectar—nectar she pours upon my lips. The Goddess Kuan Yin with her healing nectar. As I awaken, a single tear rolls down my face. The fever has broken.

CHAPTER
ELEVEN

Specific families of priestesses have been guardians of the land for ages. In a particular area they ensure that the streams are clean and the wildlife nourished, that trees grow strong, and the prayers are given to give thanks for the cycles of Life. The role is passed on through the generations from mother to daughter, so that the necessary knowledge accumulates and deepens with time.

Gaia Codex: Node 976.310.31

WHEN MY EYES finally open, fresh water and apples have been placed in my tent. I drink deeply. The water soothes my parched throat. The apple is too much for me to eat. "You are cooler now. Not so much fever." The voice comes to me as if from afar—an echo within an echo. I open my eyes, but the light is bright. When I finally focus, I see a figure leaning over me, a girl who appears younger than me, maybe eleven or twelve. She places cool rags soaked in water on my forehead.

"Thank you," I say as I close my eyes again. The darkness is soothing.

Later when I open my eyes again, she is still there, looking at me intently. She is slight. Caucasian-Asian, her hair in cornrow braids. Like me, she is dressed in layers perfect for those who sleep outside.

"I am Teal," she says, answering my unspoken question.

"How did you find me?" I ask.

"I live here in the park too—for right now," she says simply.

"Where are your parents?" I ask, for she looks too young to be alone.

Teal pauses for a moment. "My parents are gone. I live with my auntie, but one month ago she said I should come and make camp here."

"Alone?" I ask, surprised.

"Yes, I have started my training in woodcraft and herbs. The women in my family have been guardians of the forests and wildlands of the Heath for many generations. We care for the land, the plants, and the animals." I notice Teal's wrist. She has a tattoo, a star, not unlike the one I wear around my neck, on the inside of her forearm. Teal watches me take in the tattoo and smiles. Her eyes are intense, beautiful, and wise beyond her years.

"My auntie said I was also to look for you, since I saw you in the Dreaming."

"You saw me?" I ask, surprised.

"Yes. I saw you," she laughs. "We priestesses often communicate with each other in the Dreaming and through telepathy. It has been our way in those times when it has not been safe to speak aloud or when travel was impossible."

I close my eyes, suddenly overcome with weakness.

Mother had told me of times when it was not safe for many women and priestesses to speak aloud for fear of death. "But there are many ways we priestesses communicate," Mother would say as she filled my mind with vivid sensations and images.

"The Goddess Path is not easy. She devours those who are not ready," Teal says quietly. "That you are still alive is a testament that you have passed one of her initiations."

"How do you know such things?" I ask. My eyes are closed as I speak. It is easier this way. My body still aches.

"Like you, I am being trained," Teal says.

"I don't think I have been trained," I reply.

"If you are Dominique's daughter, you have been trained," Teal laughs.

"You knew my mother?" I ask surprised. Hearing my mother's name, I touch the pendant, the Star of Astera that I wear around my neck. *I wish she were here.*

"Not personally, but she is well known amongst us," Teal answers carefully. She is carefully observing my every reaction.

My head hurts from too much information. I sink back down into my sleeping bag and blankets.

I notice that clean blankets have replaced the soiled and dirty ones I had before.

Very thoughtful of Teal. I am raw. Nowhere near healed.

"You are the one who can read Dominique's writings. The information in the manuscript is meant for you."

"You know about the manuscript?" I ask as I reach over and touch the backpack.

The manuscript is still here.

"It was not a secret amongst many priestesses that

Dominique was preparing an illuminated text for you. It is as much a part of you as your own skin, Lila Sophia—or so they say."

"What do you mean?" I ask.

Teal speaks slowly. Like she is explaining something to a small child. "In our tradition, the Gaia Codex is rarely accessed through a written book. Out of necessity, our sisters have found others ways to store and share this knowledge so that it could remain safe from those who might misuse it. We priestesses read the Codex in the trees and leaves. We see it in our visions and dreams. This has been our way. We have not needed manuscripts to do this."

"Your mother though was adept at creating illuminated manuscripts that were said to connect the reader to their soul's destiny and to the Codex itself. They say Dominique was able to weave elements of the codex into the words and images to create a spell, the 'true spelling' as they say. Lila, from what I know, the manuscript is your personal legacy and an activation."

"An activation for what?" I ask.

Again, Teal looks surprised at my ignorance.

"Here is what I know," Teal continues. "Your mother was engaged in an alchemical experiment with the potential to either help restore human beings' balance with the Mother Earth or wreak even more havoc. That is what the stories were, anyway."

"How do you know so much about my mother's manuscript?" I ask. Teal looks at me with her steady eyes. She is slim and frail, and she appears a mere wisp of a girl, but her voice is strong and clear. The effect is disconcerting. I wonder if I am still in a fever dream.

"Your mother came from time to time to see my mother,

grandmother, and auntie for council and to share her knowledge. She came to pray with us and to circle with our clan. Our female kin, like your female kin, Lila, are sister-priestesses in a larger circle of women. You should also know," Teal leans in, "that there are some priestesses who believe that this book and perhaps even you yourself should be destroyed. Not everyone agrees with your mother and her experiments."

Instinctively, I reach over and draw the manuscript closer to my body.

Who were my parents? I am one of my mother's 'experiments,' an experiment I don't understand.

Teal watches me carefully. My body suddenly feels heavy. I am very tired. The fever still pulses through my veins.

"Sister, the women of my family have a deep kinship with Dominique and thus with you, Lila Sophia." Teal looks at me with her intense aquamarine eyes. "We are your allies."

Such a little girl. Such a big presence.

"We are all vessels for the Goddess, Lila Sophia."

I feel the call of my sister-priestesses. I feel a deep love for our Mother Earth and for these women who would bring me back again and again. And I am a fourteen-year-old girl starting a journey with many unknowns.

"You need to leave London. Go to where we priestesses have kept sanctuary for millennia," Teal says pointedly.

"Where is that?" I ask. Although my body can barely move, the thought of travel gives me an odd sense of relief.

Teal pauses for a moment, listens to the wind, and then answers.

"Open your mother's manuscript after I leave. Let her words guide you."

Teal stands up and pulls her long wool jacket closely around her body.

"Will I see you again?" I ask. Teal's presence comforts me.

"With good fortune we will meet again, Lila Sophia."

Evening is falling. Before she leaves, Teal fixes me a bowl of watercress and mint soup. She stays with me until I fall back asleep. When I wake later that night, she is gone.

CHAPTER
TWELVE

Water Wells are considered portals between the worlds viewing glasses into the past, future, and the realms of dreams.

Gaia Codex: Node 3321.98.21

TODAY I TAKE my tent down. I braid my hair. I wash my face.

Goddess Mother, thank you for bringing me to the other side. Thank you for giving me Life.

I kiss the ground with this ancient prayer welling forth from inside. My body no longer aches. The fevers no longer rage.

I pull Dominique's manuscript from my knapsack. It has remained closed since I first opened it in Paris. Teal said I would find guidance here. Hopefully I will find some answers. I pray that it will open.

I run my fingers along the spine and cover. *Once, twice, three times.*

A gentle wind licks the leaves in the trees. As the pages of the book open, they shimmer. I read my mother's words:

I first received the vision of our daughter in Glastonbury at the Chalice Well. It was at the turning of the seasons, when the crocuses were just breaking the frozen ground, and before the first buds of the apple blossoms had broken open. I was wearing the cloak of many circles—the web of infinite creation—a symbol of our lineage that my sisters had woven for me. This cloak, woven of silver and gold threads, also allows the wearer to easily meld with the vibrations of the land.

Sitting there that day, I looked into the Well's waters— the silver mirror that reflects back to us visions of the past and what might come.

It was in this moment that I saw her: a child, a beautiful creature, who would also be an alchemical vessel for specific evolutionary codes. She would hold them, carry them, in order to pour them forth into our Mother Earth. In this vision of a beautiful newborn, I saw a sister and an ally, who had travelled with me far and wide through the many cycles. We would come here together to give our offerings for the birth of what was to come for our Mother Earth.

I put the book down. My mother's deep love touches me and I am struck by the question: *who am I?* I look at my skin and feel my changing body. My breasts are fuller. I feel a bit more like a woman, no longer just a girl.

Glastonbury, this is where I need to go. Five days later, I am travelling to the county of Somerset, following my mother's footsteps.

PART TWO

Old Woman

CHAPTER

THIRTEEN

*The menarche, the first flow of blood, this is a girl's
initiation into the Moon Lodge—the cycles of the moon,
the rhythms of the oceans current. This is our counting
calendar, from times gone past, based on the number
thirteen.*

Gaia Codex Node: 33321.89

IT IS TWILIGHT when I arrive. The cloistered gardens
that protect the ancient Chalice Well are quiet. No one else
is here. Dominique had told me of the changes to come,
the transformations that all women are initiated into as they
transform from girl to woman. My belly and breasts are swollen,
and there is a sharp ache in my side. My blood is about to break
the surface on this full moon night.

I follow the sound of running water, past ancient yews and
winding springs, to a well not too wide in diameter, and I am
able to place my feet on either side of its open mouth, straddling
it wide, letting the rush and the flow of waters, the ancient spirits

of place, move energetically up through me. It is healing and comforting.

It is said that each natural spring, river, and lake, and even the ocean herself has her own Goddess who ensures her continual sweet flow, so that all Life is nourished. We humans—like our Mother Earth—are made of seventy percent water.

Gaia Codex: Node 44321.314

Standing over the well, my tears come first as a single drop that falls down my cheek. *As our blood flows, our waters flow.* Drops run into torrents like the rain that washes the land. As the land rests, in these final moments of gloaming, the deluge of my sorrows rushes and pours. Tears for the loss of my parents, long held in, fall and mix with the healing waters of this ancient well.

"Child, why do you cry?" Her words come to me as though from across a chasm, an echo from far away. I slowly turn.

She sits there, perfectly still in the darkness, blending seamlessly with the night, carrying a staff of yew. I cannot see her, but I feel her. She is ancient and rooted, her face hidden deep within the folds of her black cape.

I try to form my mouth around words, but I am unsuccessful. Words cannot express my rupturing heart.

"I cry for so many things," I finally answer.

"Let it flow, child. Let the waters receive you." The Old Woman's sonorous cadence echoes the water's flow. My belly

aches. My new breasts are tender. The moon rises, full in her splendor—shining silver onto the waters and still-life gardens of rose, hollyhock, and ancient oak. Moonlight falls upon the woman's face, revealing it. Her eyes are the deepest black, a universe unbound with searing light at its center. She is ancient. I am naked under her gaze, exposed but also deeply seen, as if she fathoms that which burns without form—the flame of the soul. I shudder.

The sound of night crickets rises, while the waters continue in their rhythms. I have stopped crying. I am simply looking into her eyes. We are perfectly still as the moon moves across the sky, lighting the garden. We remain so for some time.

"Come, child, your journey has been long. You need nourishment," Old Woman finally says as she gets up, leaning on her staff of yew. She begins to walk and I, not unlike a young doe trailing after its mother with legs still wobbly and unsure, follow her through the moonlit gardens, into narrow, winding side streets where the houses are closely stacked together.

We don't walk far before we arrive at a small wooden gate set into a thick sod wall, which encloses a garden and a small cottage with slanting roofs. The garden also houses a tool shed, a root shed, and a small hothouse for winter vegetables. Flowers, herbs, and vegetables are planted, and a golden apple tree that still looks like it will bear fruit for many seasons. An ancient yew looms behind the cottage—indeed, it may be older than the house, for yews can live thousands of years. This is Old Woman's house, but I don't see all of it on this first silvery moonlit night.

Instead I follow Old Woman through the sturdy oak door to a small main room with a fire crackling on the hearth and two overstuffed chairs.

"Sit, child," Old Woman commands, and I sink down into one of the chairs.

A large, round iron pot of stew bubbles on the fire, filling the quarters with savory aromas.

"Tender rabbit with shallots, honey, ale, olive oil, sage and thyme. Rosemary and potatoes, carrots. And cider. Salt and pepper to taste. Let the juices seep, savor, and mix with each other. The secret: is to cook it very slowly. And to taste it as you go. The recipe is always just a little different, depending on who will be eating it. Tonight you are the guest, and the stew has been made for you."

Old Woman spoons the stew out of the cauldron and into two earthenware bowls and then places one of the bowls into my hands.

"Bread?" Old Woman asks.

"Yes, please," I nod my head. The bread is hearty and homemade. The butter is sweet and freshly churned. Following Old Woman's lead, I tear off chunks and dip it in the savory stew.

"It is delicious, thank you," I say as I savor bite after bite. Old Woman smiles and continues slowly eating. For the first time in months I feel relaxed.

"Would you like more, child? " Old Woman asks, as I scrape the last of the stew out of the bowl. I nod my head, and she fills my bowl up again. I am ravenous. It has been months since I have had a proper meal.

"Don't worry, child. Eat as much as you need. We have plenty here. Plenty of everything."

When I am finally finished, Old Woman takes the bowls into the kitchen. She brings me a mug of drinking chocolate, rich with creamy milk, sweet honey, and nutmeg. Old Woman then sits down and takes out a long pipe and fills it with herbs. We sit in silence, as puffs of smoke slowly twirl up into the rafters of the cottage. Such companionship and comfort after so many months alone is a sweet balm indeed. Old Woman continues to put logs onto the fire. I am beginning to nod off to sleep when Old Woman gently places her hand on my shoulder.

"Come, child. It has been a long day. Time to rest your body. Time to enter the Dreaming." She says this ever so softly. *Words that whisk and whisper softly into the ear.*

I get up and follow Old Woman up the narrow stairs. It feels good to have someone watching over me, taking care of me. My body unwinds and relaxes.

At the top of the stairs, Old Woman opens a small door: "This is your room."

Inside the room there is a small fireplace and a four-poster bed of good size nestled under the low eaves. The room is small but cozy. I pull off my clothes, pull on a soft cotton nightgown waiting for me on the side chair, and then crawl into the big, high featherbed, dressed with linen sheets dried by the sun. They feel freshly smoothed, as if an iron heated on the fire was just lifted away, and smell of lavender and fresh summer grasses. The bed is topped with a blanket of fine Shetland wool, and soft goose down pillows envelope my head. My eyelids are heavy with sleep. Old Woman kisses me on the head.

"Thank you," I murmur to the Old Woman as I close my eyes.

"Sleep well and remember your dreams so you can share them, when morning comes," Old Woman says.

As she leaves, she throws a handful of dried herbs on the fire and then closes the thick wooden door, leaving me to the subtle movements of night.

CHAPTER
FOURTEEN

They say that if you are young and you meet the Crone,
she who has swallowed the full cycle of Life—both birth
and death and the fullness of seasons—she who eats time
and is time, that she will bestow you with a simple grace.
But only if you meet her with a full embrace.

Welcome the Crone with love and the ancient soul
inside your supple body of youth will break through the
surface, revealed—shining, radiant, and bright. This is
a secret we priestesses know. Mother Time and Mother
Earth consume us all in the end.

Gaia Codex: Node 333.45.21

CHAPTER

FIFTEEN

There are stories of creatures that change with the seasons.
A feat of illusion, or a communion with Creation itself.
Creatures that are fluid in their form. Chameleon,
Shapeshifter, the Goddess Maya herself.

Gaia Codex: Node 333.45.8541

I WAKE UP THE next morning basking in the golden light of dawn. The window looks out onto the ancient Tor, emerging from misted light. As I turn over in my bed, I feel something unfamiliar, sticky, and warm between my legs, accompanied by a throbbing ache in my belly. There is blood. My moon flows.

An hour or so later, I make my way down the narrow staircase to the small kitchen. Smells of breakfast waft up as I descend: freshly baked cinnamon rolls, bacon and eggs. The copper kettle whistles on the stove.

"You are up. Good. Now the day can begin," Old Woman says as I enter the kitchen.

In the daylight she looks more human. Her eyes are a sparkling blue. Her grey hair is tied back firmly and covered by a blue kerchief. She wears a long blue cotton skirt covered with an apron and a neatly pressed gingham blouse that matches the kerchief.

"These are for you." She hands me small sea sponges, clean white rags, and a small package wrapped in bright red silk and tied with pink, red, and white ribbons.

"What are these for?" I ask.

"For the blood. And for your auspicious start on this full moon at the Summer Solstice. We will have a small ceremony later, in the garden, to mark the day, to celebrate your passage, to mix the blood with the earth."

"Thank you." I am blushing as I answer. *How odd that she knows.*

For a moment, I think of what my mother had told me about the menses moon ceremonies of the Priestesses of Astera.

*Amongst our sisters we honor the passing with gifts
and sweets. We mix earth with blood and we paint our
bodies and braid our hair to show that you are now a
young maiden: full, lush, and beautiful in your fruit. The
menarche is the doorway into the deeper initiations, into
the cycles of the moon and the wedding of our bodies with
the Mother Earth.*

Gaia Codex: Node 23.4321.1

I am sad that my mother is not here to share this day with me. "Child, our menarche comes in its own timing, and we make what rituals we can where we can. The earth and the moon are always here to receive us, even if all those that we love are not."

Old Woman places the steaming hot cinnamon rolls on the table as she speaks.

"And your dreams child—tell me of your dreams. The dreams of the first blood are important. They foretell of things to come."

I am shy to speak, but Old Woman asks kindly. I take a deep breath and begin to tell Old Woman the dream:

"I dreamt I was pregnant, but when I looked closer at my belly, instead of a child, it was the orb of our Mother Earth—her oceans and mountains, her rivers and trees. I held it with the care and nurture that I would a newborn child. I could take my hands and run them over continents and feel the rough edges of high mountain peaks, dip my fingers into rivers and feel the expanse of oceans under my palm."

It feels good to share my dream with Old Woman. As I slowly open my eyes, Old Woman is looking at me kindly.

"So it is, child, you dream of things to come and those things that have been. As for you holding our Mother Earth in your womb," Old Woman looks directly at me, "this is the *Anima Mundi*—the Spirit and Soul of the Earth—and this is a very auspicious sign of what may come, if you follow your path and destiny. Our women's wombs are not only for birthing children but also for birthing new worlds. Yes, this is true, but it has been forgotten by most women."

I let her words sink in. I am happy to be here with Old

Woman. It has been so long since I have shared simple pleasures with another human being.

"Raspberry leaf tea, good for soothing the cramps. Drink, child, I put a bit of honey in there for you so it would not be so bitter." Old Woman pours the tea from an earthenware pot into a large handmade mug. The tea has been steeping as we talk and is a deeply brilliant ruby red.

"Thank you," I murmur as I gratefully drink the tea. I still have slight cramps and the aroma of the tea is soothing. The morning light pours in through small double windows open to the breezes. As I sip my tea, I casually look down at my hands.

That's strange. They appear a different color—a dark chocolate brown. Perhaps it is the light in the room. I look again. My hands are definitely more brown than crème. And my hair …

I feel my hair. It is heavy, black, smooth, and well oiled, scented with jasmine and sandalwood. It is very different from my wavy, honey-colored, autumn hair. "I don't understand," I gasp as my tea mug clatters to the ground.

"Do you often remember your dreams?" Old Woman asks, not acknowledging my shock and even more disturbingly, not seeming to take any note of my physical changes.

And for a moment, I wonder if this was indeed the dream.

I remember when I was with my mother and an ancient Tibetan lama in the highlands of Ladakh. As we sat enveloped in the pungent scent of thousands of burning yak butter lamps, the lama explained to us about dream yoga—milam as they called it—and how, in that ancient practice, the dream world and the waking world are one and the same. I remember the lama instructing us to look down at the top of our hands when we want to orientate

ourselves in a dream. This helps anchor our waking selves inside our dream bodies so we can willfully navigate within the dream.

I look again at these hands that are mine but not mine. They are slender and pretty, hands of the warmest chocolate brown with soft pink fingernails neatly manicured, all quite nice. But they are definitely not mine.

I look up at Old Woman. I am in shock.

"May I look at your hands?" she asks.

"Yes." My voice is barely audible as I hold my hands out, palms upraised.

Old Woman gently takes my hands. She slowly inspects them, back and then front. As she does this, she slowly nods her head and makes small clicking sounds with her tongue.

Finally she places my hands gently onto the well-polished table.

"There are tales told of those who frequently change their skins. It is significant that this is happening in these times. And to you, child."

I reach up and grab again at the dark, heavy, silky hair. *My dark, heavy, silky hair.* The idea of a new skin, a new body, is so improbable, so inconceivable, that it is exhilarating. Like when you hold your breath to the point of passing out, but instead you explode into brightness.

How can this be possible?

I am taking in this thought when I am suddenly aware that my belly feels bloated, and I have cramps that pierce my side. My breasts are still tender, and I feel the sticky flow of blood.

"We do not always choose our medicines, child, but they say that ones that come to us are exactly the ones we need. You will have time to take this in—to let it all settle. You are welcome to stay here with me as my guest."

"Will I always be like this?" I ask helplessly.

"I think not," the old woman laughs as she gets up to wash the dishes, but her laugh is not unkind.

Later that day, a small cup of my blood is poured into the garden under the yew.

"With this blood that falls, with the blood of your womb, you are—sweet child—connected to our Mother Earth. May your womb be Her womb. May you follow the Mother Moon in her cycles. May you offer your Life force in her protection of those who have come before and those who will follow."

Old Woman looks deep into my eyes as we do the rites together, as the blood falls onto the rich black earth. I am not the first to stand here, nor will I be the last.

That night, I open the red-wrapped gift. Inside is a chocolate ball scented with roses and filled with brandied cherries. I eat the chocolate before I go to bed. I give thanks for sweet comforts and ask for protection for the future. My body is still the color of chocolate brown as I fall asleep.

CHAPTER
SIXTEEN

In the Hindu Tantric tradition, Mahadevi is the Goddess expressed through her many forms:

She is Kali, goddess of time and death, Lakshmi, goddess of wealth and good fortune, she is Saraswati, goddess of learning, writing and music, she is the fecundity of beautiful milk laden breasts, she is the universe, she is emptiness, she is the Lover. Fluid, ever changing, she appears in the form that best answers the prayers of those who call to Her.

Gaia Codex: Node 321.54.83

AFTER TRAVELLING AND unknowing, life with Old Woman in the sweet thatched cottage—in the garden filled with butterflies, bees, and abundant trees—soothes me.

A slender Asiatic, an ebony-skinned Nubian, a golden-blonde Scandinavian, and a broad-cheeked Inuit. My form changes from one day to the next. I am tender and open, I am born anew, all the cells in my body are healing and strengthening. The DNA in my body is reconfiguring with each metamorphosis, each change of form.

Every morning when I wake, I run my hands over the curves of my body: my breasts, belly, legs, and arms. I run my fingers through my hair to feel its weight and texture. The only constant is that I am always a young woman. I do not turn into a zebra, a tree, an old woman, a newborn, or a man.

Dark brown almandine eyes, creamy white skin, kinky black hair, hazel-flecked round eyes, olive skin, cornflower blue eyes, tall and willowy, plump, lush, and round. Each body I experience has its peculiarities—a different way of experiencing the world, subtle, distinctive ways of smelling, tasting, feeling, hearing. Each body has different genetic memories and innate knowing. Some love to eat, others pick delicately at their food. Some move like hummingbirds and others like sloths. Some are nimble with their hands, others quite clumsy. It is peculiar, yet no matter what body I am wearing, I am very aware that I am still myself, Lila Sophia. My soul is thankfully firmly anchored inside these changing forms, as I wear this coat of many colors. Sometimes I think of when my mother and I would pray to the Goddess, and she carried the shifting forms of Kuan Yin, Kali or Spider Woman, Lakshmi or Tara. Just for a moment.

Every morning Old Woman greets me warmly with a smile and a delicious breakfast: apple pancakes, French toast as light as a feather and drenched with vanilla crème, sliced summer peaches, coddled eggs with home-cured bacon and creamy cheeses. There are always fresh breads and muffins, marmalades and jellies, fresh yogurts, and homemade mueslis.

And every morning, like the first day, she invariably asks, "Tell me of your dreams, child."

I tell her my dreams of pomegranate seeds I have eaten, labyrinths I am caught in, soaring dreams of flying, and terrifying dreams of unspeakable loss. I share with her my visions of ancient Grecian *asclepeions*, healing dream temples, and future cities of crystal turrets that lie beneath the sea.

Old Woman asks me questions and guides me in the practice of navigating these dream realms. She gives me herbs such as marigold, rose, bracken, and mugwort to aid in the lucid dreaming process, and she instructs me how to see more clearly in the waking day.

"It is all part of a continuum—the dream world and the waking world are one and the same. When we have the eyes to see. Dreams are a communication to us in the deeper language of symbols—a message from your soul and from other realms. Listen closely, child," Old Woman gently instructs.

I keep some things hidden. I do not speak of my Mother, my past, or the illuminated manuscript I carry. I never say my name. I do not ask about the Priestesses of Astera. Nor does Old Woman ask, but even with the strangeness of my ever-changing form, I am finding a momentary peace.

CHAPTER
SEVENTEEN

We nurture and teach the arts and crafts of culture through the generations—sister to sister and mother to daughter. What if we forget how to shape clay into pots or weave fiber into mats?

What if we forget the midwifery of our own children? What happens when we forget how to grow our own food? When a civilization loses these skills, it loses its vital connection with the Mother Earth. At some point, it will collapse. The wheel turns.

Gaia Codex: Node 3321891.003

EVERY DAY AFTER breakfast, the work begins. Old Woman and I tend to the cottage gardens of peas, carrots, squash, and tomatoes. We weed, trim, water, and plant. We pick sweet apricots and pears from the trees and berries from the vine. Produce that we don't eat is processed and canned in glass jars stored in the cool of the root cellars. It becomes my job to milk the goats in the morning and evening.

Old Woman and I both drink the warm, frothy, slightly pungent milk and use it to make delicious cream cheeses laced with dill, mint, or rosemary.

The grounds of Old Woman's cottage appear small and humble from the outside, but from the inside they are ever expanding. There are many nooks and crannies, unexpected root cellars, hidden herb gardens, and a deep fishpond fed a by a two-pronged stream.

As the days grow warmer, Old Woman and I shear the small herd of sheep and card the wool so that it can be later spun into cloth.

"When the days are short and the nights long, I will begin to teach you how to weave the patterns of the land," Old Woman says. It is evening. Although we sit inside, the windows are open, letting in the warm summer air.

"What do you mean by that?" I ask. I am in the body of a plump, pretty, young woman with a freckled face, blue eyes, and dark brown hair. This one is nimble with her fingers, and I am making good time carding the wool.

"Every region has an energy, a pattern, a vibration that is distinct. Those who know how to listen to the land can paint or weave these patterns into their cloth and art. We also sing the tones and vibrations of the land into the cloth we weave. It is part of the weaving process."

"How does one learn about such things?" I ask Old Woman.

My question makes Old Woman smile.

"Listen and use your full perception. There are many layers of perceiving," she answers.

As she says this, Old Woman gently places her fingers on my

forehead between my two eyes. "This eye is the doorway into true insight and perception."

As Old Woman touches me there, it tingles and softens–and my pineal gland begins to open. Everything around us glistens. I perceive the energy flowing from the trees, plants, and bees in the garden.

"This, child, is the natural warp and woof of the land. Do you see it?" she asks.

"I do," I murmur. *In this moment there is no separation between inside and outside.*

As the days pass, as we harvest lavender and summer squash, Old Woman tells me stories of Glastonbury and Avebury, of the ancient stone circles, the rites of moon and sun: stories of a hundred years ago, a thousand years ago, ten thousand years ago. Old Woman tells the tales as though these events—the tales of Druidic priestesses and Roman legions, of Christian nuns and starry-eyed shamans—happened only yesterday.

"The land keeps all our memories, child, never forget that. It knows every one of us who has walked on top her with our bare or booted feet. Mother Earth remembers our ancestors and the ancestors of the plants and animals who have fed us. This is why we thank her every day when we arise. It is why we thank the sun for her warmth, the water for her sweet healing, and the food from the plant and animal world that fills our bellies."

"How long have you been here?" I ask Old Woman.

Old Woman stops cutting the squash from the vine for a moment and looks at me.

"As this land lives so do I. When she dies or when the weaving is done, then it will be my time to go."

"I don't think I understand." I put down my handwork of cleaning beans.

"Child, some souls are bound to the land as guardians and caretakers. I am a caretaker and weaver. We each have a different purpose, child—a different service to give."

"And what is my offering?" I ask.

"Child, asking is the first step. Yours is a path of high consequence." I shiver under her words, yet the day is not cold. For a moment, I feel a restlessness; the question of who I truly am brimming inside me.

As days and weeks pass, I notice that Old Woman has no other visitors. It is as if the little thatched cottage is separate from the life of the rest of Glastonbury. I, too, forget the world outside the garden walls. But then, this changes.

"I would like to go into town," I say one morning as I eat a breakfast of apple fritters drizzled in honey that Old Woman has prepared for me. I am in the form of a lithe, flaxen-haired young Norwegian woman with snow-white skin.

Old Woman continues kneading the dough she is preparing for bread.

"You can go, child, but know that you are in a delicate time—a tender time. If you go, your return to our little home is not certain." Old Woman's voice is gentle but firm. "It is your choice, of course."

I take Old Woman's warning, and I do not go into town.

CHAPTER
EIGHTEEN

*The Gaia Codex is always with us, waiting to reveal its
secrets. It is in our veins, our breath, and in the Mother
Earth herself.*

Gaia Codex: Node 3322.851

I HAVE NOT OPENED my mother's manuscript since my
arrival at Old Woman's cottage. It has been a comfort to
let the past rest, but tonight I am curious. Old Woman has
gone to bed and I am alone in my room. There is a sliver of new
moon in the sky and I have a large beeswax candle to provide
just enough light for reading. I pull my mother's journal from
under the bed. It is tied up with a silk-braided cord, wrapped
around a silk cloth cover embroidered with enchained circles of
gold and silver. The cloth was a gift from Old Woman. "To wrap
your special possessions," she had said knowingly.

I gaze at the glimmering star tree cover on my mother's red
journal. What a strange legacy I have been given—this experiment. Is it fate or a curse?

Daily my skin and features change—it is heady and strange, but also strengthening. With each body I experience, I also receive its dreams and ancestral memories that pulse through DNA: highland Peruvian, Basque, and Hadza of Tanzania, Siberian Yupik, and African Mbunda.

That I am a part of my parents' science experiment, their alchemical dabbling, this Metamorphosis Project, evokes a mixture of emotions: fascination, betrayal, anger, and curiosity. Why didn't my parents tell me earlier? Why did they abandon me to deal with consequences of their creation? What possessed my parents (especially my mother) to think it was okay to manipulate the DNA structure of her child in the womb?

I exhale deeply. Under my breath I make a small prayer that my mother's manuscript will open for me tonight. When it is scaled shut, the manuscript is inert—a beautiful but rather ordinary book that simply will not open. I try once, but nothing.

I inhale and then under my breath clearly ask, "Dominique, Mama, please let me see."

It is the texture of the manuscript that changes first. I feel the vibration on my fingertips as the pages come alive, luminous as they flutter under my touch.

I open my mother's illuminated manuscript and turn to a page with a beautiful morpho butterfly and the title *The Metamorphosis Project*. I flip through the pages written in my mother's hand: the drawings, graphs, notations, equations, and the entries about my development through the years:

The vision was to have a child able to fluidly shift between all human ethnicities. Perhaps even, as necessary, between other species. This would be coded into the essence of her

*DNA. A child who will be acutely adaptable to changing
environments, not only through her wit and skill, but also
through her ability to physically transform—quite rapidly
if necessary.*

*We priestesses have, of course, practiced types
of shapeshifting over millennia. Our efforts for the
Metamorphosis Project would in essence be a wedding
of science and magic to create a sacred technology with
the potential to rejuvenate Life and restore balance on
our planet by reestablishing Homo sapiens' affinity and
connection with all Life. Our hope is to seed these traits
into the human species as a whole.*

*Some of my sister-priestesses do not agree with these
methods. It is risky. I agree. The outcomes are uncertain.
We will have to share and release what we have kept
hidden for so long: hidden histories, our knowledge, and
magic. Yet I know that if we wait much longer, human
beings may no longer be able to flourish on our Mother
Earth and much of Life will be destroyed. The human
species cannot continue as is. If we do not change, we will
destroy ourselves and many other species with us.*

*As a mother, I worry of course for the fate of my
daughter, Lila Sophia. My prayer is that our efforts will
benefit all beings—that the outcomes benefit all Life.*

I put my mother's journal down. The beeswax candle burns
by my bedside and for a moment, I rest in the comfort of Old

Woman's home. My skin pulses as though the DNA is mutating and changing as I breathe.

What am I? Who am I?

CHAPTER
NINETEEN

A Priestess of Astera is initiated over many lifetimes. She walks in all cultures. She wears the skins of many races. Trained to hold the thread of memory, she is said to carry the seeds of wisdom as civilizations are born and die. A priestess may play many roles in a culture. She may not be recognized—except perhaps, for the kindness of her heart or for an unusual ability to comfort, nourish, and heal those wounds no one else can heal.

The Priestesses of Astera have been artists, lovers, and courtesans. They have been queens, scientists, alchemists, poets, scholars, mothers, medicine woman, muses, and shopkeepers. You will find some priestesses in deep forests or in high mountain caves, where they are yoginis, saints, and oracles. Priestesses who are in seclusion are dedicated in prayer and blessings to the larger energies of our Mother Earth: to the forests, the plants, the trees, and the animals, to the collective soul of a species, or to the planet herself. Some priestesses have merged with the Goddess in her forms as Lakshmi, Oshun, Aphrodite, Kuan Yin, or Tara, or Mary.

They walk the Earth as her living embodiment. All priestesses have taken a vow to sustain and rejuvenate Life, to plant and cultivate the seeds of wisdom in the hearts of human beings and in the soil of Mother Earth, as civilizations are born and die. The way of the priestess is not easy, for you must die a thousand deaths to be One with the Goddess—she who flowers ten thousand times.

Gaia Codex: Node 3332.841

CHAPTER
TWENTY

Old Woman appears to the priestess when the bud of
womanhood is breaking open, in order to remind us of
what we have been and what we will someday be.

Gaia Codex: Node 44.321.83

I WAKE UP EARLY the next morning. Hot porridge with plump currants, walnuts, and freshly ground nutmeg has been left on the stove. Old Woman is nowhere to be found. The day is warm: a burst of sun before the coming cold. I eat breakfast and then go outside to read. There is a willow tree shading two tall wicker chairs filled with comfy cushions. I leaf through my mother's manuscript, looking for more clues. The pages open easily as I read of Indian princesses leaving behind kingdoms to become ecstatic enlightened poets on the shores of the Ganges. I read of Japanese geishas practicing the arts of beauty and healing, praying every night to become the Goddess and take the form that will ignite the souls of those they touch. I read of wise German women, herbalists and midwives, who practiced in times when our kind were burned at the stake for our knowledge. I take in the lives of women like Hildegard von Bingen, Queen Elizabeth the First of England, and Veronica Franco of Venice, women who held power and influence, who practiced the ancient arts in times when it was a man's world. I read of women who helped to keep the ancient practices alive unseen to the common eyes. I read of power misused and kindnesses offered. I read of a deep devotion and dedication that runs through lifetimes.

"The day is going well, child?" Old Woman asks as she walks into the garden a few hours later. I put down the manuscript but make no attempt to hide it.

"I am sorry I was not there to help you this morning with our work," I apologize.

"It is good that you have time to think and dream. It nourishes the spirit," Old Woman replies as she sits down beside me, placing berries, hard cheeses, freshly made bread, and ice-cold pints of mead on the table. Old Woman and I had brewed the mead together the first week of my arrival, stirring up and measuring out the honey, water, and fermented mash. Now it is ready to enjoy.

Old Woman casts her eyes upon the pendant around my neck.

"You are wearing one of the Stars of Astera," she says matter-of-factly.

Instinctively my hands go up to touch the ebony and diamond pendant given to me by Dominique. I have worn it every day since my arrival and yet this is the first time that Old Woman has taken notice.

"There have been times when it was best to keep such things

hidden. Do you remember those times?" Old Woman asks gently. Bees flit through the garden, amongst the fennel, nettle, and roses, drifting back to the bee skep made of dry coiled rye. They buzz and hum.

"Not fully," I reply. I have read my mother's writings and I have had visions—but these are distinct from personal memories. "What can you tell me of the Priestesses of Astera?" I ask.

"The Priestesses of Astera are both your past and your future. They are your deepest kin, Lila Sophia." As Old Woman speaks my name, I feel a spark of light at the very center of my Being. I feel the shape of her words calling me forth, and I see the faces of my sisters. Priestesses who have lived and died, who have born and buried children, who have both been worshipped and killed for being female. These women who took vows to carry the seeds of life through the birth and death of worlds—women who dedicated themselves to the Goddess and to Life itself. I feel our lives connect though the ages just as my shifting form connects me with the roots, traditions, and DNA of so many women who have walked the Earth.

"Do you see a bit clearer?" Old Woman asks as the bees buzz around us.

"Yes," I say softly, adding, "you know my name."

"I do," Old Woman answers simply.

"Did you know my parents, Dominique Haydn and Raj Nataraj?" I ask.

Old Woman smiles and slowly blinks her eyes, not unlike a cat in deep relaxation.

"Your mother, Dominique, is dear to my heart." Old Woman answers.

"Has she stayed here with you?" I ask.

"Yes, many times. She was my apprentice when she was a younger," Old Woman replies.

"And my father?"

"I never met your father, but he was, from my understanding, your mother's passion—and her fate. Many women have a fate that comes to them in the form of a man who captures their heart. Such a man can shape a women's destiny."

I flash back to the young man in Paris. I have not forgotten how his words felt inside my head or the longing that for a single moment captured the rhythms of my Heart.

Old Woman continues, "What I know of your father is from the weavings of the cloth and what is written in the Codex."

"Can you tell me more?" I ask.

"Your father is an old soul, who usually incarnates as a man. Driven by ambition and vision, passion and power, he is mercurial—a sorcerer and a scientist. He has the potential to create great benefit for the planet but also great harm. This is what I have seen in the lines in the Codex and in the weavings," Old Woman says.

"This man is my blood," I say quietly.

"Yes, he is in your blood, Lila Sophia, but you have sovercignty of your soul. The changing forms should teach you this. Your soul is your own, no matter what body or form you wear."

"Your mother was known as a very powerful priestess with a certain mastery of time, the elements, and the hearts of both men and women," Old Woman says as she pours me a bit more mead. "She was a visionary and many called her a sorceress."

"I knew her as quite loving. She was protective of me," I say as I shake myself from the vision.

"As she should be," Old Woman smiles.

"What do you know about me?"

Old Woman laughs gently. "We are all learning who you are, Lila Sophia. You are written in the records of the Gaia Codex. You have lived many lives. You have the potential to give deeply, love deeply, and to bestow great gifts upon our Mother Earth and humanity in this life—but all in good time, after you have fully ripened. You also have a secret that you keep even from yourself. Find this, and you will be free. This is what I know."

The bees are returning to the skep, and the sun is going down.

I watch the last rays of sun flicker on Old Woman's face. She is human and she is cosmic. She is ancient.

Old Woman. The Weaver. Witch of the Waters. The information flows through me as pictures. *She who with her sisters weaves the worlds. Mother Spider.* I smile, and Old Woman smiles back at me. I am remembering her names.

"Remember, child, the Gaia Codex is all around us, always here for us to read—if you have the eyes to see the ever-evolving translucent Mystery. It is in the rocks, the leaves, and trees, and it can be accessed like this, as the web of infinite dimensions." Old Woman touches my arm again and a glistening multidimensional web appears. At every cross section of the web is a pearl that reflects back every other part in the web into infinite dimensions. Along each node of the net, there are sequences of numbers such as 4444.85.321 alongside an image or symbol, inviting me to dive deeper.

"The Priestesses of Astera have used and have had access to the web for millennia," she says quietly. "Although we are not the only ones. The Buddhists reference it in their text, the *Avataṃsaka Sūtra*, as Indra's Net. A net of infinite dimensions

where each node holds a pearl that reflects another pearl. There are also legacies of this in Greece and Egypt and in many Earth tribes. Its existence is as sure as the elements, but many present-day human cultures have forgotten how to access the web directly, without the mediation of technology. This forgetting is to their detriment, for once you experience the Gaia Codex, the web directly, you know we are deeply connected with all life. This then shapes our actions. Why destroy something that is part of you?" Old Woman asks.

The sun fades from the land, and Old Woman and I continue to sit in silence, breathing in the darkness.

CHAPTER
TWENTY-ONE

He is the Stag King, the Green Man, and the King who is
the Divine Consort to the Queen who sits on her throne.
The Sun to her Moon. He is Osiris to Isis. Shiva to Shakti.
We humans are both male and female. One cannot
sustain without the other. Balance is essential.

Gaia Codex: Node 555.98.61

THE SKIES TURN the palest of blues; the air becomes cold and crisp before the onset of greying hues. With the change of seasons, I notice the appearance of distinct markings on my skin. If one looks closely at a morpho butterfly, there are subtle markings on the wings. Circles and spirals that appear when viewed in particular angles of light. My new markings mirror the markings of a morpho butterfly— delicate, shifting tattoos that appear and disappear on my temples, at the nape of my neck, on my forearms, and at the crest of my belly.

Along with these new markings I begin to receive a stream

of information from the plants and the trees, from the black soil of the earth and the skies above. The information moves through my blood. I receive visual flashes of movements occurring in my mitochondria, the matriarchal metabolic engines of eukaryote cells that instigate life, death, differentiation, and transformation.

This is all happening within the temple of my body. That I can both see and feel the adaptive features of my DNA and the response in my cells is startling. It feels as though veils have been lifted and that this is something that every human being could have access to. This discovery leaves me breathless and ecstatic.

The changing of my form has settled ... somewhat. I no longer change every day. Instead a form (whether I am an Eurasian, Basque, or Inuit) will last for a week or two before I become, once again, someone apparently different, at least from the outside.

I do not feel like a monster, and oddity, or mishap. Perhaps I should. Instead I feel like a deciduous tree, shifting through the seasons, roots stretching to the center of the earth and branches high to the stars in the sky. In the center, my heart continues to beat. I feel steady and yet it is all a mystery.

"Do you think I will ever settle back into my natural form?" I ask Old Woman as we stack wood for winter fires.

"Every situation is different, child. Best to listen to your own rhythms to find the answer." As Old Woman speaks, I hear the rush of my blood, my breath, the expansion and contraction of cells, strangely in harmony with the movements of these late autumn days. It is comforting.

The last summer squash, pumpkins, potatoes, corn, and beans have all been harvested. The apples have been picked from the tree. Together, Old Woman and I light the Samheim bonfire as autumn passes into winter.

"Take care to note the winter dreams, child, for they portend of things to come. Tend the hearth, for the home fire is the heart fire, that which burns within us—a soul fire that continues through cycles of birth and death."

As the days shorten and the winds of winter blow, my body, in each different form, becomes more voluptuous and womanly. My breasts are fuller, and my hips now have gentle curves. At night when I rub my belly, legs, and breasts with the rose attar Old Woman and I made in the summer sun, I think of a man who might admire my limbs, and as I do a sweet sap stirs inside me even though the night is cold.

Thick winter eiderdown quilts have been put on the bed, and as I fall asleep, I see myself plucking stars from the branches of trees as I fall deeply into the dream. It is on the Winter Solstice, on the longest night of the year that I first dream of him.

The Dream ...

I am in an emerald forest glen that opens up into a shaded clearing. The grass underneath my bare feet is soft and fresh. In the center of the clearing is a looking-glass pool with a hexagonal stone border. When I look into the gazing pool, I see my own face—the wavy, autumn, red-golden hair, the freckles, and green-gold eyes. I have the morpho marks, but they look like beautiful tattoos.

A leaf falls onto the water, and as I reach to pluck it from the surface, I see him. He is a young, perhaps in his late teens or early twenties. He has dark, wavy hair and intense, green-brown

eyes that draw me in. His face appears at the exact place where moments before I had been gazing at my own reflection. I recognize him and pause. *He is the man from Paris.* I look up to find him, this young man casting the reflection—but there is no one, only a persistent image in the water. I hold his gaze as the image transforms. He is the same young man, but now matured into the fullness of his life. He is muscled and strong. He takes my breath.

"Who are you?" I ask. My voice is throaty as I speak.

He does not answer. *Honey rises inside me.*

Three more oak leaves fall into the water. They are the color of autumn. He now has long white hair that is slightly yellow. I watch his face become gaunt, his eyes milky, and his skin fill with puss, as though it is being eaten from the inside out.

"I need your help, Lila Sophia." As he speaks the pool fills with light, and then he is gone.

He who passes through the Ages of Man cannot be reborn without his Goddess Lover.

The snow is falling on the ground, and I wake up. Tears stream down my face, and I am filled with questions. I am filled with longing.

CHAPTER

TWENTY-TWO

*The Goddess heals the wounds of the King so that the
Earth can be reborn.*

Gaia Codex Node: 3334.84.21

THE DAY IS grey. There is a heavy blanket of snow
outside. Icicles hang from the windows, and ice
patterns cling to the thick glass windowpanes. I sit
by the fire with Old Woman as she wraps lavender from last
summer's harvests into bundles. I help her, but my fingers move
slowly as my mind replays the dream from the night before. *His
face. His plea. His strength. His beauty.* My heart aches.

"What is it, child?" Old Woman puts down the lavender.

"I miss him," I blurt out. It may not make sense to miss
someone who I have never met, but this is how I feel.

"I see," Old Woman answers softly, reaching over to gently touch the soft flesh on the inside of my arm. The contact
of her warm, gnarled fingers jolts me, and I see an incandescent web of jewels in which each jewel reflects the whole. I am

becoming used to this manner of accessing information, under Old Woman's guidance. My attention zooms into one of the diamonds on the net as then it opens into a flow of images:

Deep inside a forest, long forgotten, is a tree that has seen the many ages of man. The room, fire, and Old Woman fade away, and I am again in an emerald forest glen with the young man in my dreaming. He stands in front of an ancient tree with a trunk as wide as a small house. The tree stretches to the sky. The young man stands with his back fully against the tree. His chest rises and falls as he breathes. The rhythm of a tree that lives for thousands of years is much slower than our human rhythms. Time is dilated. I watch the young man breathe, and I breathe with him as scintillating greens of the forest soak into our skin. The air begins to vibrate. Slowly the young man with dark, wavy hair and brown-green eyes transforms. His skin becomes the rugged bark. His arms become branches, and his leaves hands. He becomes the tree, and I watch as he lives tens of thousands of years in this deep forest glen.

Suddenly there is a high-pitched scream and yellow smog descends. The streams in the forest turn sour, the ancient tree branches begin to wither. I watch the man in the tree begin to shrivel and die.

"It does not have to be like this, my Love," his voice speaks in my ears.

As the high-pitched sounds of machines increase, I let out a scream. Old Woman gently pulls back her fingers. Once again we are in the room together with the fire burning on the hearth.

"He has contacted you." Old Woman picks up the lavender and continues bundling.

"Who is he?" I ask.

"He is an ancient soul tied to the Earth. Long ago, before the civilizations of Sumer and Egypt, he was born of a human father and a Priestess of Astera. The Priestesses of Astera keep detailed records of such times."

"What is his name?" I ask.

"He goes by many names: Green Man, the Stag King, Dionysus, or Osiris, the Wounded King. He holds great power, and is bound by a vow to protect the Mother and to absorb the folly of man into his blood and bone and into the cells of his body. The Goddess—she who comes to him in human female form and approaches him with unconditional love—is said to be the only one who can heal him. When one world dies and another is born, it is said that they must partake in the divine act of Hieros gamos—the alchemical union of male and female that is said to birth the world anew."

"Has he chosen me?" I ask. His face, the depth of his eyes, his power, and his pain—I feel the longing of my heart and a primal ache that wishes to be fulfilled. I desire him—his hurt, his strength, and his suffering.

"Perhaps," Old Woman answers. "The priestess who meets him is not a child. She is a woman who has awakened into her body, her mind, and her spirit. This takes time and training. Your heart and your desire may call you now, child, but know that such a rite will ask everything from you. If you are chosen and if you choose him—for you, priestess must also choose—you will walk into his chambers naked, bare, and exposed with only your soul to offer. They say such a rite offers the greatest bliss, but in return, you must surrender everything to gain everything, and so it goes."

"What I feel for him right now is a profound love and care. I want to help him."

"This is a good start, and you do have the gift of training in many lifetimes, but nonetheless it will take the proper initiations with your sister-priestesses to prepare—if you are to be his partner and consort. Nothing is certain."

I must be with him.

"Do not let your desire blind you, child," Old Woman says. She can read my thoughts.

As the snow falls gently on this cold winter day, I know that there will be a time in the not too distant future when I will leave Old Woman. It must be so. The thought is bittersweet.

CHAPTER
TWENTY-THREE

*Be careful when you ask His name. For it is said that
all creation is present within the vibration of the spoken
sound. Once it is heard everything changes.*

Gaia Codex: Node 3321.789.00

EVERY NIGHT, RIGHT before I go to sleep, I pray that the mysterious man of my dreams will be there to meet me, yet we do not meet again in the Dreaming until the longest days of winter have passed, until the moon has waxed and waned.

Bonfires burn red against the sky as people dance and sing, besotted with the spring's first harvest, bewitched by the golden moon. Young men pull girls into the shadows, and maidens beckon lads onto soft grass beds beneath the trees. The forest is full of moans, yelps and the exuberance of spring's first coming—pollen, nectar, and new leaves. I wear a long emerald dress with a bejeweled golden belt around my waist. As I walk through the crowd some of

the celebrants bow to me. I nod back and then head alone towards a forest grove away from the fires. It is dark, but I am able to make my way. In the grove I sit down on a rock and wait.

After some time I hear the thundering of hoofs, branches breaking, and rocks falling to the side.

My body grows tense. Be steady. This is what I have come for.

He approaches from behind, "Lila Sophia."

I turn quickly. He is mounted on a stallion wet with sweat. He is muscled and strong—wrapped in the hide of the stag, with majestic horns on his head. His face is painted black and blue. Gold amulets fall from around his waist.

"Shall I take you here, priestess?" he asks.

"What do you mean by that?" Pleasure ripples through my body. Surprisingly, my voice is strong as I answer.

"Come back with me now, and you will not have to return to the life you have been living. We will be together—isn't this what you want?" His voice is clear and penetrating.

"Will you give me your name?' I ask.

"Which one? I have many names," he answers.

"The one that is meant for the softness of my ears," I reply.

He does not answer right away. Tonight his eyes glisten—fire and burning embers. There is no sign of sickness.

We have known each other before he and I—a familiarity bred through lifetimes.

"If I give you this name, priestess, it means we are bound. You will not be able to forget when I call you again. Is this what you desire?" he asks.

"It is what I desire." I look straight into his dark eyes as I answer, unflinching, unwavering, deeply desiring. I will not lose him again.

"I am Theo." His voice is deep and timbered.

"Theo …" I let the name roll across my tongue and my lips. I feel it penetrate deep into my throat and into the pulse of my blood.

"Place it in your Heart, priestess, for I will not forget." And with that he is off, galloping into the full moon night.

Theo. I whisper into my pillow in my bed in my room in Old Woman's cottage. *His name is Theo.*

CHAPTER
TWENTY-FOUR

*Doors close and they open. There are many doors. There
are no doors. A koan? A paradox? There are beginnings
and ends. Nothing begins and nothing ends. Worlds are
born and they die. There is only now and yet again we say
good-bye.*

Gaia Codex Node: 555.876.92

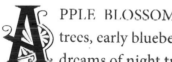PPLE BLOSSOMS PEEK through the leaves of the
trees, early bluebells tease the sweet green grass and my
dreams of night transform.

*The planet turns. Rivers are choked with trash, seas with plas-
tic. Genetically engineered strains of grain have destroyed the natural seed stock that fed populations for tens of thousands of years:
hundreds of millions of people are starving. At night I dream of
billions of people waking up to a nightmare—that their children
will not live to full maturity and that Mother Earth herself will
subsume the human species because of our ignorance and folly.*

Throughout it all there is a call, a chorus of women's voices—the Priestesses of Astera—my sisters beckon me forth to meet them.

I wake up from these dreams in tears, shuddering, convulsing, my morpho markings flashing. It is time for me to leave.

Old Woman places hard cheeses, fresh bread, dried fruits and nuts, and teacakes into a soft, dark green leather satchel.

"Provisions for the road. It is good to be prepared for the unexpected."

Upstairs in my room, I pack the leather knapsack with clothes that Old Woman has sewn for me over the winter. There are soft woolen skirts, trousers with many pockets, and layered tops of jewel-colored silk. There is a vest, strong boots, and a well-lined cape that is both warm and lightweight. I pack my personal possessions—my mother's manuscript. I wear the Star of Astera around my neck.

I take one last look at the polished round mirror. The face that stares back at me is the one I was born with: the wavy auburn hair, the creamy skin with freckles on my nose. The high cheekbones and golden-green eyes and the birthmark of three dots in a triangle on my inner wrist—everything is here. The morpho markings subtly gleam on my belly, heart, and arms and legs: a reminder of the many bodies I have worn in this last year.

With my knapsack on my back I slowly walk down the narrow stairs one last time. Old Woman waits for me at the bottom.

"Know that my prayers are ever with you, child, as is what we have shared together. It is all in your breath and the marrow of your bones. You have learned what you can here. It is time for you to find your sisters, Lila Sophia," Old Woman says to me as she gently adjusts my cloak.

"Will I see you again?" I ask. *I am not sure I want to hear the answer.*

"Nothing is certain, child," Old Woman replies.

I feel a pull—a tug. It is hard to leave her, yet I know I must go.

"Thank you, Grandmother," I say as I bow. Our foreheads touch, and I feel her comfort and closeness.

Old Woman stands there as I walk down the garden path, open the gate, and walk outside the cottage walls, returning for the first time in nearly a year to the town of Glastonbury. As I turn the corner, a subtle mist falls. The small thatched cottage disappears.

PART THREE
Delphi

CHAPTER
TWENTY-FIVE

When a culture collapses, it is said that the veils between
the worlds get very thin, and miracles, large and small,
begin to appear.

Gaia Codex: Node 33321.76.43

London:

THE LONDON I return to is in a state of chaos. The air
is heavy with fear and desperation. Yet within the rot,
seeds are taking hold. Tender sprouts are breaking the
surface—signs of hope.

Vegetable gardens grow in the centers of streets and increasing numbers of people are migrating to colorful tent cities arising in the once royal parks of Hyde, Kensington, St. James, and
Green Park. Occasional solar electric cars pass by horses and
wagons, which are again a primary means of transportation.
Parliament and Buckingham Palace still stand, but they are no
longer merely strongholds of power and governance but rather

they also serve as shelters, homes, and makeshift schools and hospitals. The ground continues to shift. Empires can last for thousands of years, but they also can also fall quickly.

One can still rent rooms, and I have secured a small walk-up not far from Bloomsbury Square and the remnants of the British Museum. The square, now filled with vendors and tents, seems fairly safe in these summer months.

My room is stark. There is a cot, a chair, and a table that I have made into an altar for the Mother Goddess. This is where I place my mother's journals and a small bronze statue of the Goddess holding the Earth in her belly that Old Woman slipped into my leather bag. This is also where I put fresh blossoms and light a candle in remembrance of what has been and what is to come—a candle in honor of the Mother's fire that lights the temple of my Heart.

I am here in London to wait and listen, but there is no word from my sister-priestesses—no visions, dreams, or meetings.

During the day, I explore the city. I wear leather boots, trousers, and a long cinnamon-colored light wool cape, with a pattern of twining vines embroidered on the outside in the subtlest of tawny-colored threads. Inside the cape, hidden to most eyes, is a pattern of gold and silver interlocking circles. I feel Old Woman's love and care in every stitch. I feel her prayers of protection.

It appears that my form has settled. When I look into the small polished mirror in my room, the young woman staring back at me is myself in my natural form. Only my morpho markings, the circles and spirals that shimmer on my body like artful tattoos, indicate that I am a hybrid of sorts. I am relieved

at the consistency of form and the new flow of information that the markings seem to give me about my environment and people. It seems that I can read thoughts, emotions, and physical maladies.

I begin to wonder if the radical transmutations were limited to the beginning of my menses moon. I miss Old Woman, and I still feel the ache of my parents' absence, but the cut no longer feels so deep.

I am becoming reconciled to a strange sort of acceptance. In many ways, my parents were strangers to me and yet I—with all my idiosyncrasies—I am the key to finding out who they really were. I am their living legacy.

As for Theo—his form and scent, the way he looked at me, his tenderness, his plea, and his challenge have become an obsession. *His eyes looking at me from across the grove, the stag horns on his head, his voice moving inside me.* How many times can I play a memory in my mind? But there is no communication. Theo is silent. I look for him in the crowded street, but he is not here.

I try to open Dominique's illuminated manuscript, thinking there will be guidance, but it only reveals one page with a single phrase.

In the beginning and in the end, the Priestesses of Astera gather. We come together to sing the songs of birth and death and to plant the seeds for the new world to come.

Gaia Codex: Node 44531.02

This sounds hopeful, even poetic, but I have no idea where to meet the Priestesses of Astera.

In these first weeks in London, my nights are without dreams, at least none that I can remember. It is odd. My dreams are usually vivid—as real as waking life.

Without connection to the dream world, I excavate the interiors of my imagination by sketching in a notebook. Such sketching gave me comfort throughout my childhood. It was a way to bring to life the ever-fluid landscapes of my imagination.

The sketches that come are the landscapes I have drawn since my childhood. Line drawings of lands deeply familiar to me, but that I have yet to see in all my travels. The land is lush, fertile, and beautiful. The people are human yet also seem to be of some hybrid species I cannot quite place. There is beauty here and deep craftsmanship in the buildings and objects of everyday life. There are also beautiful and elegant technologies that are different than those of the world I have been born into, with its petroleum-based products that have ravaged the Earth. Sometimes these scenes are so real to me, I can almost smell their scents.

I draw. I meditate. I walk and I wait. Weeks pass.

Finally, in the first day of the sixth week, just as the leaves on the silver birch tree are turning to gold, everything changes.

That morning I go to one of the spontaneous markets constantly appearing around the city. This one is not far from Bloomsbury Square. As I walk through the frenzy of vendors I hear a sweet male voice rise above the crowd.

"Miss, greenhouse cacao, grown from plants that my father's father carried by hand from the Yucatan." A curly-haired young man with a big smile beckons me to his booth.

I am intrigued, charmed, and I am curious.

"Are you a chocolate lover, Miss?" he asks as he shows me some cacao nibs in the palm of his hands.

"Of course," I smile. I love chocolate like any girl, and I am enjoying his playfulness.

"Well, then this mix is for you, a Mexican-herbed chocolate. I grow all the herbs in a little hot house I made myself. Here, take a whiff." He leans over and lets me smell the chocolate powder—a mixture of cacao, ground chili, vanilla beans, and other herbs I can't quite place.

"You like?" he asks, smiling.

"Yes, quite nice," I reply. The mixture is intense but also calming.

"It reminds me of snuff that eighteenth-century gentleman used to lift their spirits." *How do I know about eighteenth-century snuff?* I smile at the pleasure of the flow of information I receive. The reading is becoming easier for me, a synthesis of my teachings from my mother and Old Woman.

"Observant you are ..." he grins.

"Buy some of Missy's goat milk over there, and you will be good to go." The young man nods his head toward a young girl with a small herd of goats clustered around her.

The young man wraps the ground mixture in a square piece of clean cloth that he neatly ties. The cloth has undoubtedly had others uses—as a shirt, as a sheet. Most of the big manufacturing plants are out of operation, so people are making do with what is available. People don't want to throw something away if it can be used, once, twice, or three times.

"Do you take coin?" I ask.

"Yes, we still use coin at this market. Just give me one of the pound coins and that will be fine." I hand him a pound coin.

"May it bring you pleasant moments," he smiles as he hands me the cloth pouch.

Before I can say thank you, he is chatting to two older women who have come up to his cart. They are wearing bedraggled versions of some past famous Parisian clothing designer and look like they could use some cheering up. The changes have not been easy for many. A cup of hot chocolate would offer at least some momentary comfort. I watch the young man's charm light up their faces under the heady aromas of his enchanting cacao blend as I buy a small jug of warm goat's milk from the young girl, Missy.

"Enjoy," she says with a smile on her face as I leave her stall and the bustling market.

That night, back in my room, I sip the cocoa—mixed with Missy's fresh goat milk—that I heated on the small charcoal brazier in my room. A prayer to the Goddess and to my sisters, who I hope are waiting for me, forms on my lips:

Mother, please lead me to you. Please connect me with my sisters.

I am waiting here. I am ready to be in service to you. Please use me as your hands, eyes, breath, and voice. Please show me what I need to know in order to once more be with you.

These prayers roll off my tongue. Tonight sleep is easy, and before long I fall down beneath the layers to the world on the other side.

CHAPTER
TWENTY-SIX

*Sibyls, seers, and prophetesses—for millennia, women
such as these guided the affairs of men and the fates of
dynasties and kingdoms. But everything changes, and
what was once revered became shunned and feared. The
Oracle is quiet through many cycles, waiting for the wheel
to turn.*

Gaia Codex: Node 55.821.91

THE ROAD TO Delphi snakes and winds up
toward Mount Parnassus, home of the *Pythia* and
the mysterious oracle priestesses. It is an ancient
thoroughfare, once travelled by kings and queens, scholars and
peasants, and warriors and healers in search of answers about
life, death, and destiny. I inhale deeply. I feel my breath in my
chest. I notice the tops of my hands. I feel the beat of my heart.
Instinctively, I touch my tongue to the roof of my mouth. These
are all techniques that Old Woman taught me for navigating the
world of the Dreaming.

I open my eyes again. I am at the top of this long road among fallen marble pillars softened and rounded by time. The grounds appear empty. The sun is high in the sky. I walk ahead as a gentle breeze cools my skin.

I see her first from a distance. Perched upon one of the marble blocks, her face partially covered by glistening black hair. Her eyes steady on the horizon. As I quietly walk forward, I see that she appears to be my age or just a little bit older. I am drawn—the bee to the flower, the sprout to the sun, the wave to the shore. My body is electrified. I feel the startled connection when lightning touches the ground: a visceral sensation like the one that has always come to me before a vision, ever since I was a child. The flow of a poem, or the singing of those songs that erupt from the depths and make us cry out new melodies that shape our mouth—the kiss of the Muse, the Goddess, as she descends to speak. As I move closer, she turns and smiles at me. Her eyes are deep green, magnetic. She is casually dressed in black trousers and boots, with a finely tailored black blouse.

"Do you remember being here before?" she asks.

"Pardon?" I am not sure if I have heard her clearly.

I look into her face, and again I shudder with electricity.

"We often make the mistake of thinking that our history begins in one life and that our memories extend only from the moment of our birth," she answers.

"Those who follow the more ancient rituals of life are rare in these times, but there are a few of us still wandering the planet."

"I am Lila Sophia." My introduction is clumsy but I do not know what else to do. I am mesmerized.

"And I am Rhea." She is close to me now, just inches away. Her skin is as pale as the moon and her eyes, the deepest green.

Her voice awakens an intimacy that swells up inside me, known but unknown, and the sound exposes memories I never knew I lost. The web of connection and lineage is deep. I feel that ancient streams shape her words, despite her appearance of youth.

Hot tears swell in my eyes. "I recognize you, but there is so much that I am just remembering," I whisper. Something inside me is unwinding, releasing, and remembering things long forgotten.

I know her like my own skin and breath.

"They say we priestesses know each other when we meet. Do you think this is true, Lila?" I do not immediately respond. I am entranced by the rhythms of our mutual breath.

"I know that we are here right now and that you feel deeply familiar to me," I finally answer.

As we stand, a white owl swoops overhead, flying low, almost alighting upon us. *It is the owl of Minerva. It is Athena—the Goddess of Wisdom. In ancient Greece her name was Glaukopis: she of the owl eyes, the clear eyes, shimmering, translucent, gleaming eyes, eyes like sapphires that see beyond the beyond.*

"We help each other, Lila Sophia, you and I. Lock and key." Her voice is tender. *This is how it has been—in the past, the future, and in this moment now.*

The tears that roll down my cheeks are unexpected, and I let myself rest in her open arms.

CHAPTER
TWENTY-SEVEN

Technologies surpassing those we currently know span
ancient and future time, and yet today, many do not
recognize them. Instead they remain hidden placed in
plain sight where all might see, in a mountain, a rock, or a
tree. What better place than this to hide such treasures of
wisdom that have been carefully stored for the future?

Gaia Codex: Node 333.45.851

RHEA AND I walk, arm in arm, toward the Phaedriades: tall cliffs known by the ancients as the "Shining Ones," portals and doorways to the inner sanctum of the Delphic Oracle.

"As you may remember, the Pythia, the oracles of Delphi, were priestesses, initiates of the lineage of the Goddess Gaia, Mother Earth. A select number of the Pythia were also Priestesses of Astera. It seemed a perfect fit for our clan. It allowed us to speak and share our knowledge directly with people from all walks of life," Rhea explains.

We are now at the base of the cliffs, in a cool and sheltered ravine where water rushes and echoes against the walls. Rhea kneels down and puts her hands into the stream. She then places two of her wet fingers softly onto her tongue.

"This is the Castalian Spring, the ancient waters where seekers cleanse themselves before entering the hidden chamber, the *adyton*, where revelations are revealed."

As Rhea speaks, echoes of the water resonate against shadowed cliff faces. The sound seems to carry other chants, ancient callings that fill the spaces between.

In the flow of the Castalian waters you can empty yourself
of everything—the past, the present, the future. Become a
pure, open vessel for the wisdom of the Oracle. For these
Castalian waters are the sweet wine of muses. Imbibe
deeply and words will run from your mouth. The wisdom
of the ages will become the blood that flows through the
rivers of your veins.

Gaia Codex: Node 45.681.731

These words flow through me. I think back to Old Woman's words: "The knowledge of the Codex is here in the trees. It is here in the streams, in the mountains and the breeze. If you know how to read it."

Rhea again takes two fingers and dips them into the water. She then touches my forehead. Instinctively, I stick out my tongue for sacrament. The water moistens my lips as it falls from her fingers.

We move further into the ravine.

"Lila Sophia." Rhea draws me in closer. Instinctively our foreheads touch. We inhale and exhale breath, synchronized in rhythm.

"Thank you for coming. The task before us cannot be done alone." Her words fall between each breath.

"It is fated," I answer. There is no hesitation as I say this for I know it is true. Looking into her eyes is like gazing into the depths of my own soul—different and yet my own. It is the continuation of a story started long ago.

The light shifts ever so slightly, and Rhea takes my hand. "The ancient Greeks considered this place the center of the Earth, the belly button of the world. In myth two eagles flew from either side of the earth, crossing paths here in Delphi, at the center point, the inner sanctum where the Pythia, the oracle priestess, sat on a tripod chair, her legs opened and exposed to receive the Mother Earth herself."

In front of us is a weathered stone, four feet high, shaped into a dome. As I look closer, I notice that a web is carved into the stone surface. The object is curious and compelling, both mysterious and familiar.

Rhea continues, "It is an *omphalos*. This stone marked the entry into the Oracle's inner sanctum. The name translates loosely as the belly button of the world."

"The *omphalos*." The name rolls over my tongue.

Rhea runs her fingers across the carved stone net. "Look closely, Lila."

As the sounds of the Castalian stream gurgle in the

background, the surface of the stone begins to shimmer, and the stone web takes on a translucent, luminous hue, vibrating and moving. The *omphalos* appears as both a stone and an active, living hologram with each node of the net seemingly reflecting all the other nodes. In some I see images, flashing pictures that seem to be drawn from both the past and the future.

"It is an activation of the *Hieros Delphus,* the *matrix* as they call it in Latin, or the Divine Womb, the birthright of every woman. It also is a representation of the Gaia Codex itself. In times past, it served as a reminder to both men and women of our deep essential connection to the web of life. To all time and space."

The *omphalos* in front of us shudders—a living, breathing net of life contained within a circumscribed space—seemingly infinite. "It is beautiful," I say softly, "and so deeply known." I feel myself opening up to things I have kept long hidden, to pasts that I have known.

"It is a technology that many have forgotten. We priestesses have protected it for many cycles," Rhea says. "The *ophamolos* here at Delphi is one representation that has allowed people to access the Gaia Codex, the records of Earth."

The echoes of the Castalian Spring continue to resonate through the ravine. Moist sweetness of water fills the air.

Rhea grasps my hand again as we move forward. There is a pulse of energy between us.

Rhea pauses. "Can you see it?"

The cliff ahead is in shadows. Form masked in possibility. I squint my eyes, trying to see. As I deepen my focus, the shadows on the cliff appear to shift.

"I see it." There is a vibration, a movement, solid matter transforming.

"Will you come with me, Lila Sophia?" Rhea's green eyes are bright as she stares deep into mine. I feel attraction, desire, and destiny as we stand here together. So close. My flesh touching hers.

"Yes." Her hand is warm and wraps around mine.

As we approach the cliff wall together, my body temperature rises in tandem with the vibration that explodes from inside. The syllable HUM—HUM—HUM resonates like a hive of bees on a warm summer day, yet today the bees are the cells of my body, vibrating at higher and higher velocities. *Our ability to work with matter like this is not limited to the dream realms,* Rhea silently reminds me.

The rock cliff before us becomes fluid. We are a connected field—our bodies and the solid surface of the wall—and it is with ease that both Rhea and I move through it, my body heating up, melding with rock, then passing through into darkness.

CHAPTER
TWENTY-EIGHT

Descend once—and you are opened, broken, and revealed.

Descend twice—and others look to you for the path.

Descend thrice—and Below and Above become as One.

Gaia Codex: Node 23.22.321

CROSSING THE BOUNDARY, we are inside. Darkness permeates, the temperature drops, scents swell—the dankness of the interior Earth, suddenly, wholly consumes. In the blackness all other senses come to life. My hand is on Rhea's back. I feel the warmth of her skin through her soft cotton shirt as we slowly make our way down the narrow shaft.

We humans enter this mortal coil in the velvet warmth—the midnight of our Mother's Womb. The human embryo's senses come to us in stages—first we feel, then we smell, then we taste, hear, and see.

In the diurnal, nocturnal turn of Mother Earth, every twenty-four hours we plunge into night and then into day: darkness and light, the essential rhythms of this terrestrial life. To hold on to one or the other brings only loss; we humans are the alchemy of both.

Gaia Codex: Node 4445.7811

Our footsteps echo as Rhea and I descend into the bowels of the Earth. Rock walls narrow: our shoulders brush against the porous limestone surface on either side. Our breath shortens as we are compressed. It is black upon black.

We are guided by smell and touch: laurel leaf infused with musky labdanum, the royal aroma of mastic, the sweet clarity of iris, warming amber, and electron. The rhythm of our footsteps echoes in the cavernous labyrinth.

Immersed in darkness, our sight is a sacrifice to the Goddesses, so that we may truly see.

After some time, a sharp turn reveals a small chamber, brightly lit with flaming torches. The air is heavy with fumes, the incense is intoxicating. I grasp Rhea for support. She holds me steady.

In the center of the room is a woman perched on a high tripod throne, her legs spread wide over what appears to be a crevice in the Earth pulsing vapors and mist. The woman's long black hair is plaited into multiple braids and hangs in a wild frenzied mass past her waist, covering her face. Her breasts are exposed, voluptuous, fecund, and full. The Oracle, the Pythia, the priestess of Delphi revealed, the Mother in her subterranean element.

The Oracle sways back and forth. She chants, guided by ancient, stellar, telluric rhythms that undulate her body, first as a murmur and then as the wild, unfurled dance of the Serpent climbing up her spine, that Tree of Life rising inside every human, waiting to be ignited.

Rhea and I move in closer, listening as the stream of chant flows and erupts from the Oracle's lips. Her salty sweat flicks onto my skin, our skin, as she moves in wild spiraled spins.

This penetrating voice has echoed in my mind longer than I can remember. This lyrical, lucid tongue composes a body woven from words, a body much larger than my own and yet integral to my essence. As I listen, the Oracle's rounded vowels and plosive consonants transpose into words that I intuitively comprehend.

Rhea says nothing, but she is by my side, holding my hand tight. My flesh is hot. Hers is cool and clear.

The Oracle slowly looks up. Her eyes are glistening, the deepest black. Flashing and piercing, they are ringed with charcoal kohl. There are symbols drawn and tattooed on her forearms and on her cheeks: spirals and circles, captivating geometries, the scrolling of ancient alphabets, perhaps from the future or from civilizations long since past.

The Oracle leans in. Her glance acknowledges our presence and pierces straight through us as well, as though her focus also encompasses universes that rise and fall, expand and contract, on distant horizons.

My curiosity ascends, and I am about to say something when Rhea sharply grabs my wrist warning me of ancient protocols: the Oracle will speak first.

The sway and swirl of her movements slow as the Oracle takes her place on the tripod throne.

Her eyes pierce deep into my heart, melting resistance, protection, and ignorance. I am riveted. I am exposed.

Sisters, fellow priestesses,

The Glass shatters.

Passing through the Mirror,

Present in the Translucency,

The Veils of Time dissolve and melt.

We join as One.

You see me, and I see you.

Dreams and premonitions come to Life.

At the Center of the World,

The Wheel does not spin.

In this stillness, in this timelessness,

All is revealed.

There are those who remember

Through the cycles of birth and death,

Through rise and fall of civilizations,

Through the birth and death of worlds.

The Oracle pauses for a moment. I slowly exhale and am perfectly still as she continues.

For many cycles the Oracle has rested in silence.

Answering no queries, heeding no calls.

There is a time to hold the council of silence

There is a time to speak Truth.

There is a time when ancient seeds, long dormant,

Are once more planted and fully bloom.

The Oracle continues to sway back and forth, her voluptuous body undulating in spiral rhythms, ever turning, ever twisting, moving upward and outward. My hand is tightly in Rhea's.

We are dear sisters, fellow priestesses, at the Great Turning

When the future of humanity is being dreamed, created, and activated.

Death begets new Life.

Humanity's future will be different from its past.

And my sisters, my fellow priestesses, it is time for us to activate

These ancient, timeless codes that we have been protecting

That we have nourished through the rise and fall of civilizations.

I listen, I feel, I taste, I embody, I know with sweet intimacy the Oracle's fertile words as they flow from her mouth and enliven me. They are mine, they are hers, they are ours, and they are known. Words that create worlds.

The warmth of Rhea's flesh grounds me and anchors me.

The Oracle continues.

This ancient Codex, this Gaia Codex has been passed down through the ages. This ancient lineage of priestesses, these Priestesses of Astera, have nurtured and protected it, waiting to reveal its content in times such as these, when one world dies, and another is born.

The revelation of the Codex is held by many, not by one. It is revealed in the communion and synergy of many coming together as One, when the parts become larger than the whole.

All of Life is connected—and in this remembering, we become whole with all of Life itself.

As the Oracle speaks, my senses overwhelm. I see. I feel.

Cities filled with millions of bodies, people moving through their lives, grey in color, robotic in their actions, their soul-pulse faint and tepid. Mother Earth dead and quiet with no discernable sentient life, her lush fecundity burned barren. A man crouches alone bent, broken, crying dry tears, crushed under the weight of a wound that will not heal, the collective wound of humanity. A child cries, and there is no Mother to hold it.

The Oracle pauses.

Like pieces of a puzzle, the secrets and seeds of the Gaia Codex are held at different parts of the Planet, within ancient traditions, the storytelling of the tribes who live through many cycles. We priestesses help weave the pieces together for the benefit of all Being. This path calls for the utmost purity of heart.

The Oracle looks directly at me.

Are you willing to offer everything? For you will be asked no less than this.

The Oracle's eyes pierce my heart. Rhea's warm hand steadies my body.

What more must I offer? What must I give? I wonder.

Your identity, your heart, your life, and your death.

The Oracle answers as her voice pierces my head.

I shudder. My eyes roll back as Rhea catches me in her arms.

I do not know if it is I or the Oracle who brings her hands together over her heart, bows low and then sinks back into the silence of this hallowed cave. In this moment we are one.

When I open my eyes, the chamber of the Oracle is empty. It is cold and dark. Rhea and I return ascending to the opening and to light. We hold hands. We speak no words.

Far away, I hear morning sounds in London as the Phaedriades, and the sounds of the Castalian stream begin to fade. "We will see each other soon," Rhea says, "in the waking world."

I am not ready to leave her. When I open my eyes, to London and to the morning light, she is gone.

CHAPTER
TWENTY-NINE

The clues that lead to the Priestesses of Astera are everywhere, but they are not obvious to the common eye. This is by design. They are in your bones, your veins, and your memories. The clues are strewn in hidden corners of art and architecture and in the plinths of civilizations that rise and fall. The clue is the Mother Earth herself.

Gaia Codex: Node 3334.541.851

I AWAKEN. THE SCENT of sleep is still on my body. I am back in my small room with the sounds of street vendors starting their day below. I still feel Rhea's arms around me.

Thank you, Mother. I light a candle on the altar and kneel down. *Thank you for bringing a sweet sister to me. May I meet my other sisters who have long held me deep in their hearts.*

For a moment I think of Theo. The sudden scent of his skin draws me in, and then it is gone. I breathe in and I breathe out.

Half awake, I turn to my mother's manuscript. It opens easily to a page that appears blank at first and then fills with color and vibrant, fluid images: a group of beautifully dressed women in gowns of rich and unusual fabric, women of different ethnicities standing outside in a summer garden exploding with blooms. In the center is my mother, Dominique, holding a crystal orb. She seems to be teaching the other women something.

I move in closer so I can hear her words.

"This is the Crystal Orb Navigator," my mother says, as she gently tilts the Orb right and then left. Oddly, I see both my mother and her direct point of view. As she moves the orb, node points on the multidimensional web that seems to stretch infinitely inside the crystal zoom into view. Images flash: I see myself as a child, and then only Dominique and Raj in what looks like eigthteenth-century France, and then again at a Tibetan monastery in the high Himalayas.

Is this the Codex? I wonder. But then Dominique speaks: "This device is a tool for navigating the dimensional time elements of the Gaia Codex. Specifically, it can give us access to different entry points in the space-time web so that they can be viewed. But there is even a greater potential here and this is what intrigues me," Dominique lowers her voice as she looks at the small circle of women. "I believe the navigator activates not only our ability to move through time in our visions but also our potential to physically travel through time."

With this Dominique looks directly at me. The intensity of her blue eyes startles me.

"Mama!" I call out.

All the women in the vision turn toward me.

"Lila Sophia, we are waiting for you. It is time for you to join your sisters."

I realize that I have closed my eyes. When I open them, I

am in my small room. The pages of my mother's manuscript are empty except for a faint shimmering light emanating from the pages. My heart is pounding.

Noise and clatter on the streets below crashes through my window—the calls of candle-sellers, vegetable-hawks, and town criers who announce where today's markets will be and how to avoid the latest outbreaks of flu—but I barely hear it all. My face is wet with tears. My heart is bursting. *My sisters!*

I look down to the pages of the manuscript again. Now there are only words, written in a beautiful handwritten script.

The Priestesses of Astera maintain direct communication across distance through dreams and telepathy. There have been times when this telepathy has been an essential tool for our safety. To give voice to what we know has been dangerous in many civilizations. In some cultures, it has meant torture and death.

Gaia Codex: Node 3421.321

The connections are getting closer. I lie back with a deep sense of relief. I am not alone. My sisters are out there and I will find them.

CHAPTER
THIRTY

The world of our dreams and our waking life is
understood by many to be a continuum. two sides of the
same coin. It is said that those who read the signs move
effortlessly from one world to the other.

GAIA CODEX NODE: 444.54.321

INTUITION AND HABIT take me to the British Museum—or what is left of it. I am standing in the Great Court. The spiral glass dome is still here although it is shattered. Pigeons nest and fly in the interiors. The rain, when it falls, splashes on the marble halls below.

"Good to see you again, Miss." An old man in a crumpled docent uniform waves me through.

The halls of the museum are dusty. Smaller artifacts such as Etruscan gold earrings, Celtic goblets, Tang dynasty vases, and eighteenth-century sextants are long since looted, but monoliths like the Assyrian Balawat Gates remain.

It was not so long ago that Dominique and I walked these halls together.

I make my way to a chamber that at one time held antiquities from ancient Greece. It now has but a few remnants. I am looking for a version of the *omphalos.* Hoping it will give me more clues as to where my sisters are. Yet there appears to be nothing of this nature left in the museum, so I sit next to a marble statue of Artemis. Her bow is raised, the arrow pointed, she is running: Lady of Beasts, the Protectoress and Midwife of Life.

Across from me is the goddess's other form as Artemis at Ephesus. Here she is radiant in her multi-breasted splendor, providing nourishment for all Life—two aspects of the Divine Mother. The ancients understood that creation is complex and ever changing. You cannot pin it down. The goddesses give me comfort.

Mother, I am listening. I am waiting. I am willing. Please show me what I must see.

I review the scenes of my dream in my mind.

Rhea, Delphi, the omphalos. Dominique.

Time passes as rats scurry in the corners of the crumbling museum halls. I pull my cloak around me to keep warm. Hours pass. I almost leave but something tells me to stay.

When I finally hear her voice it is a relief. "Lila Sophia." I slowly turn around. Rhea is dressed in the same black trousers and tailored shirt as in my dream, except she is more beautiful in person, her green eyes flashing, her skin clear, her dark hair shining in the shafts of light.

"Rhea ..." My heart beats faster.

"The dream of night meets our waking life," Rhea says softly.

"It is true," I say. *She is like my own breath.* I am overwhelmed.

Rhea comes up to me and wraps her arms around me. Our foreheads touch. We breathe each other in and out. Amber, fresh black earth, the sweetness of hyacinth, and ambergris—these sweet scents flood my senses. We are silent for some time, our foreheads touching.

The touching of foreheads—this is an ancient greeting that honors the heart and soul of another human being. Amongst the Māori, it is nose to nose, forehead to forehead—called hongi. The Hawaiians call it honi, and it is practiced amongst the Tibetans, and the desert Bedouins. For the Priestesses of Astera, this is how we bless the Beloved. Third eye to third eye—sharing sacred breath.

Gaia Codex: Node 444.541.832

"I have missed you," Rhea says finally as she gently moves a lock of hair away from my face.

I am being joined with a lost part of myself. My bones feel stronger. My cells are more vibrant. My breath is steadier, my vision clearer.

"We are never far apart, you and I, even when we are not physically together," she says. "But it is always stronger when we meet like this. In person. In the flesh. Don't you think?"

"Yes … it is so much stronger. And Delphi—?" I ask. "We were there together?"

"Yes," Rhea smiles. "It was important for us both to be there for the Oracle to speak."

The memories—the knowing of my past—feel stronger, more known, as I look through Rhea's eyes.

"We can share what we heard with our sisters. We meet in Paris in three weeks. It is the first time in many cycles that the Priestesses of Astera have gathered. Will you come, Lila Sophia?" Rhea asks. "Many are expecting you there," she adds.

"I have been waiting all my life," I answer truthfully.

"As your sisters have been waiting for you." Rhea gently kisses my forehead. "We will have plenty time together in the future Lila. I promise. I will meet you in Paris." With this, she is gone, leaving me alone in the musty, nearly empty halls of the British Museum.

As priestesses, we are called to love in many ways. We love
our newborns as mothers, we love the trees that shelter
us, and we love the sun in the sky that gives us Life. We
pray daily for the well-being of those we have never met,
as if they were our own children. We love our teachers
and mentors. Some of our Beloveds we carry through
lifetimes—they are the warp and weft of our souls. We
love passionately, and we may give our hearts to more
than one, but as a priestess, our Heart belongs first to the
Goddess. It is she who shapes and ignites our fate.

Gaia Codex: Node 111.52.31

I N THE DAYS that follow, in the wake of my meeting with Rhea, I find myself placing my hand to my heart, slowly, tentatively, as if I am feeling it for the first time. It beats inside my chest between my blossoming breasts. I feel my heart as a physical organ. Along with my breath, it is with me from the first moment of birth to death. I feel my heart as a luminous bloom that continues to unfold. I also feel the pain, the distinct physical sharpness, the tightening of my heart, as past sorrows arise to the surface: the loss of my parents, my visceral sorrow for what is happening to our Mother Earth, and the suffering of many souls on the planet. The tension in my heart increases until it breaks, flooding my body with radiance. The heart has many layers.

Theo and Rhea. Is it possible to feel love for two people at the same time? Passion, communion, and Eros—my desire arises. I wonder where it will lead. Is the truth of my heart, the truth of my destiny? I continue to crack. Slowly, softly opening. Petals gently fall.

How I experience London changes. It is still chaotic, but I see things differently. There are emanations and intimations of the Web of Life that appear to move through the beggars and trades-women, through the rising sun, and the corner fires that keep people warm at night. It feels visceral and real. I also begin to notice faces in the crowd: strangers who seem familiar. Girls and women, who, like myself, appear ordinary, yet emit a certain presence on closer inspection. Some have the subtle tattoos, rings, or pendants of the Priestesses of Astera—others simply have the look and the silent greeting that rings within my ears:

Sister. We are here.

None of these women approach me directly. Perhaps it is not yet time.

I continue to look for Theo in the crowds. A seemingly useless exercise, but my heart aches for him. There has been no contact.

A few times I think I see him: his back turned away, dark

wavy hair, a lithe strong body, but when I look closer, it is someone else. An older man with a worried look on his face or a teenage boy with a scar on his cheek and a scowl on his lip. *Perhaps Theo is only a creature of my dreams.*

In the evenings, I look for guidance in Dominique's manuscript, and for several days, the pages open to the same passage.

The rite of Hieros gamos is enacted between the priestess and her consort at the renewal of a cycle.

These are the rites of the Birth of Spring, like when the Sumerian priestess of Inanna descends into the Earth to consecrate the King or when the Stag King weds with the Goddess priestess. Those who practice this art also know that such a rite can birth a new civilization and a new world. The priestess must be pure of heart. She must know her body to be a temple of the Cosmos and of Earth, and she must be awakened to the Serpent, the Kundalini, the Shakti within her.

Gaia Codex: Node 45321.000321

As I walk through London, I notice that the quality and texture of the world, the shape of buildings and trees, the reflection of light, they all seem different and in moments, not unlike the quality of a dream—everything feels fluid.

Three days before I leave for Paris, I decide to visit Kew Gardens. The gardens are not really kept up these days, but there is a wild jumble of plants through the grounds and half-broken greenhouses: ginger and pines, palms and ferns, persimmons and oranges, and wild ivy vines that try to consume everything.

There is one particular banyan tree that Dominique and I would often visit together when I was a child. Its roots were so tall that they formed little walls—a shelter of sorts. I have given up expecting to see Theo, and when I see the man sitting peacefully under the banyan tree, his hair long and matted, at first I don't recognize him, but when he opens his eyes I see their intensity and fire.

It is him. I am sure it is him.

My body shudders and suddenly I am shy, scared. I don't know what to say. I just stand there staring.

"You have come," Theo smiles.

I look closely at him and notice the edges of his body shimmering. Here but not here. I look down at my hands and pinch my flesh. I am definitely here. My morpho markings are changing color rapidly in response to his presence. Again, I feel weak in the knees with the deep desire to hold him.

"And you have come," I reply cautiously. My voice shakes as I speak.

I start to move closer, but he puts up his hand.

"You can not touch my flesh if you come near me, Ma," he says.

He calls me Ma. One of the ancient names for the Goddess.

"You are not really here are you?" I ask.

"Not physically, but I see you as clearly as you see me. The physics of this world are changing again, priestess, but most people don't know it yet. Your sisters know this. I know this. You experience this."

I take another step closer.

"Theo …" I say his name carefully. "Why do you keep beckoning me to you?"

He laughs again, and then his face grows serious. "You move me, Ma," he says.

I have been waiting for the priestess who can evoke life inside me and who has the vision to see beyond the veils of birth and death. His voice speaks inside me. His lips do not move.

Suddenly, I feel young and inexperienced.

"I am just starting my initiations."

"You have been taking initiations for lifetimes, Ma."

My heart aches looking at him. He is here but not here.

"Go, Ma," he says. There is a sudden hardness to his tone.

"Theo…!" I call, but then he is gone, as quick as water into sand.

Hot tears well in my eyes, and the heat in my body rises. How much longer can I be without him? Moments later, a group of young men come running past me, chasing a deer through the maze of vines and trees. They look at me oddly as I stare at the winding roots of the banyan tree as though someone were actually there.

PART FOUR
Château Lumiere

CHAPTER
THIRTY-TWO

The Temples of Astera:

Most have forgotten that the Temples of Astera exist. This is by design. Our temples have been carefully protected, for in many cultures and political climates the revelation of our temples' existence has meant certain death. Conquerors built their temples on our sacred grounds, but even stone edifices at some point fall. The wheel always turns.

Our temples are found in forest groves, in the reflection of a clear glacial lake, or on the mountaintop. You may find such a temple inside a simple hut or at the back of an unassuming merchant's shop. It is known that our physical bodies are one of our most profound and sacred temples.

The Temples of Astera have been designed to look common to the common eye, but for those with the eyes to see, the Temples of Astera are radiant with light. They are repositories of what has been and what may be once again on our Mother Earth.

The Temples of Astera take inspiration from the natural harmonics of nature herself, from the subatomic, to the cosmic. The walls of our temples are resonating, fluctuating between light and matter, hence their fluidity and ability to transform in the eye of the beholder. Our temples are portals where you can enter deeper dimensions both in the past and in the future, palimpsests where multiple dimensions coexist. Stand in the center of one, and you are anchored inside the Wheel of Life. All the elements—earth, water, air, fire, wind—all are there in equal proportion.

Gaia Codex: Node 3334.54.851

CHAPTER
THIRTY-THREE

The past and future are constantly being reshaped in the present.

Gaia Codex: Node 3321.531

Paris.

AUTUMN FALLS UPON the city. The day is grey with a biting chill that cuts deep to the bones. I have arrived at Les Halles, the marketplace, the stomach, and the center of Paris. This is where Rhea and I arranged to meet. For over nine hundred years this had been one of the central markets in Europe, and now, in the midst of collapse, it is once more thriving.

"Lila!" Rhea walks towards me. She is wearing a soft emerald green wool cape that matches her eyes. Her dark hair is pulled back under a teal scarf that accentuates her green eyes and her high cheekbones. I am excited to see her.

"Welcome to Paris," she smiles.

As she kisses me, our lips linger for a moment, soft against each other. She smells like starlight or fresh wind at the top of a glacial peak.

"So much has changed here," I say.

"As it has everywhere." Rhea takes my hand as we start to walk.

In the open squares, amongst grand structures built of light grey limestone, there are encampments, campfires, and burgeoning markets that run both day and night. Medicinal herbs are gathered from the *Jardin des Plantes,* the *Jardins des Champs-Élysées,* and on the *Champ de Mars.* Formal city gardens are now re-cultivated as sources of food and medicine, for in these times technological medicine, with its synthetic drugs and advanced machines, is not readily available to most people.

There are mechanical devices and objects composed of odds and ends of nineteenth-century antiques and twentieth-century techno-trash. There are chickens and eggs, used clothes, and new clothes woven from looms. There are candles made of beeswax and lard. Some people try to sell precious family heirlooms, but many gave up their personal possessions long ago. They are too heavy to carry when you need to be spontaneously nomadic. Circumstances change by the week.

There is an abundance of the little pushcarts—so popular for carrying belongings and goods for sale. There are running jokes that rat-cat stew has become a popular specialty, seasoned with wild-crafted thyme and rosemary. Many know it to be true and will show you where you can have dog soup as well. Transportation systems have shut down and electricity has become erratic, but the markets of Les Halles are lively. They are ferocious.

City officials—what is left of them—have decided that it is better to let this rising culture flourish. Better than having to face constant riots and homeless hungry hordes. Those who live closer to the ground are coming up with better solutions than the bureaucrats in their marble halls.

"Mademoiselle, would you like some of these pears just picked from the orchards?"

"Fresh bread, Madame. Fresh bread."

"Warm mittens for the winter. Special price for you."

"Fresh water, Mademoiselle. Sold in a clay pot you can use later."

As Rhea and I walk through the maze of tables and stalls, the banter of sellers overwhelms—playful, aggressive, creative, and desperate. Children with dirty faces and ragged clothes gather together in little packs that dart about. They are laughing, playing tag, or maybe causing distractions to get a little food.

As we move through the crowd, I notice that Rhea softly says a prayer under her breath.

May all here be safe and fed. May they be released from fear. May they have sweet water to drink. May they see the old age of their loved ones. May they enjoy many harvests from the land they love.

"It is a prayer for all of us. For humanity and for Life," Rhea explains.

"Some see the end and others the beginning," I say quietly.

Rhea holds my hander tighter. "We have only felt the first shocks. When there is fear and hunger and a lack of potable water, this is when the unthinkable often happens," Rhea adds softly. "I have seen it many times before. This coming winter will be hard if there is no source of heat."

Rhea looks young, but she also feels ancient. Who is she?

"Mademoiselle, can I interest you in a basket?"

The girl who holds out the slightly misshapen woven basket looks to be my age.

"May I hold it?" I ask.

The girl nods her head.

The basket is large enough to be functional. One would be able to carry things in it. You could place it on top of your head or carry it over your arm with its strong handle. The weave is a little clumsy, as though the girl was just relearning a skill long forgotten, but there is beauty here: orange, blue, and red ribbons are woven in amongst the edges and through the raffia, creating a gentle spiral of woven and bound parts.

I hold and turn the basket in my hands, and as I do, I receive images: *the raffia being harvested, the girl weaving the basket along with other children in an open field. And then the girl meets a boy, and then has a child and then …*

Startled, I drop the basket to the ground.

The swift death of the child and then just as suddenly the father, then the mother, a plague, a fever, a …

"Are you ok, Mademoiselle?" The girl asks.

"Yes, yes," I answer too quickly. "How much for the basket?"

"Do you have food?" the girl asks.

"Yes, of course." I pull out a loaf of dark rye bread I had bought a few stalls back. "Will this do?"

"Yes, thank you." The girl happily takes the rye bread.

"Blessings to you," I whisper as she moves back into the crowd.

"Just because you see it, does not always mean it is a certain

outcome," Rhea says gently as we continue walking through the market. She understood the exchange.

"But this was so strong," I insist.

Rhea sighs. "Well, yes, it is probably true then."

"There is new life here even in the midst of impending death."

I say this to the air, to the market, to all of us. It needs to be said even though I do not know with certainty if it is true.

"We will see if the new seedlings take hold. Time will tell," Rhea says. "Only time will tell."

*We are connected as much to our past as to our possible
futures. Time unfolds as both a web and a line.*

Gaia Codex: Node 3321.77.431

THIS NEIGHBORHOOD OF staid limestone buildings
that have stood here for centuries is now empty, except
for an old woman who carefully sweeps the cobblestone
street. She nods at Rhea and then turns back to her task. Brush,
brush, sweep, sweep.

At the end of the street is an inconspicuous grey stone wall
crowned with aged chestnut trees and plane trees that arch over
the top. On the wall, carved into a stone plaque, are the words
Parc de Forêts (Park of Forests).

"This is how it has been for centuries," Rhea says as she gently traces a pattern on the stone plaque. She pauses a moment
and then gently touches the rusted gate. It opens easily.

"Come." She grabs my hand as we walk through the gate.
Her touch is warm.

The gate closes firmly behind us. Inside are scattered autumn leaves, untrimmed trees, and boisterous greenery that devours broken and scattered statuary from different eras—discarded cherubs, a lounging Adonis, and a disheveled Medusa with wild dandelions growing out of her gaping mouth.

The light here is different than on the other side of the wall— we are captured in the gloaming, suspended between night and day. There is a dankness and dampness that permeates the dark and mangled forest—as though old things and forgotten spirits have long been hidden here, burrowed into the roots of the trees. A large rat or a small cat—it is hard to tell—scurries amongst the trees. There is fallow water in slimy puddles. Involuntarily, I shudder.

"This is all protection: for the off chance that someone actually makes it through the wall," Rhea explains. She places her hand in mine. It is comforting.

"Adjust your sight and look at the space between the shadows and tell me what you see," Rhea instructs. "Many things are different from how they might first appear."

I let my eyes adjust to the shadowed light. Around the edges there is a shimmering. Matter turning to energy. I stare into the darkness for some time. Finally, I see a serpentine path of finely hued gravel leading into a thick bramble of woods.

"I see it," I say under my breath.

"Good. That means that you have initial entry. I will follow you," Rhea replies.

"Once you identify the path, then it is yours to find again, but it is important that you find it for yourself the first time. Even if you have been here many times before," she adds.

I follow the threads of a long forgotten memory back to the

source. The gravel path twists and turns through broken marble busts and discarded garden tools.

"Watch the edges," Rhea warns.

"It is shimmering," I reply.

"Exactly. That is a quality you will see whenever there is a dimensional opening. When the subatomic frequency of matter becomes apparent. It's what we call a 'soft spot.' It is good to train yourself to see these openings. When a culture is collapsing, when the world is in transition—when structures and institutions that have held a grip on the people for millennia weaken—then there are more soft spots, entry points, between the dimensions."

As we walk, the forest path becomes more defined. The air is sweeter here. A twist, a turn, and then an opening in the trees reveals an elegant compound of buildings constructed of honey-hued sandstone, with beautiful arches and elegant dome turrets. The air here is sweet with spring nectar and flowers, bees and pollen—a striking contrast to the cold grey day we left behind. Rhea touches my arm gently.

"Welcome to the Château Lumiere or House of Light, as it also called," she says.

"It is one of the Temples of Astera, and it has been here for millennia as a place of refuge and protection for our sisters in times of crises and persecution. It is also a place of gathering where we train and prepare for our work in the world. It can come back to us very suddenly—the memory of our true origins, or it can build slowly, not unlike the nautilus shell, one piece upon the other but all part of the whole," Rhea says quietly as she watches me carefully.

I am stunned by the beauty and the deep familiarity of this place—a dream, a forgotten memory, is rushing into focus.

A gust of wind rustles the leaves as we approach the massive front door to the compound. The door is mahogany and inlaid with a carving of an ancient tree in voluptuous summer bloom. Two snakes twist up the trunk symmetrically. Beneath the tree, carved into the door, is a single apple, tossed to the ground. A careful observer would notice that a bite has been taken out of the apple

"It's beautiful," I whisper under my breath. I look back at the path we travelled. It appears to fade into the spacious forest park. There is no wall to be seen.

Rhea pulls the tasseled rope of the copper bell. Its tone is clear.

A young woman with flaxen braids coiled into spirals on her head opens the door. She is dressed in a flowing lake-blue tunic and trousers that remind me of the beautiful clothes Old Woman made for me.

"Welcome," she says, placing her hands together over her heart and then bowing towards both Rhea and I. Instinctively, I bow back.

"Please, come inside. I am Bridgette."

"I am Lila Sophia."

"Yes, we know," Bridgette replies smiling. "It is good you are finally here. Many sisters are waiting to see you Rhea, and Helene Belefonte is very anxious to meet with Lila Sophia."

"Of course she is," Rhea replies. "Bridgette. How is your mother?"

Bridgette's delicate features become clouded.

"We do not know if she will make it. We did last rites before we left. She insisted that both my sister and I come here. It was hard to leave."

"Of course, it was." Rhea's voice is tender as she speaks to the younger woman.

"Your mother was a guardian of the waterways in your homeland, yes?" Rhea asks.

"Yes," the blond-haired girl answers softly.

"How are the waters faring?"

"Not well. In most towns, people cannot drink from the streams or lakes any more and the fjords are dank with pollution brought in from the global currents. My mother is devastated that she has failed in her duty, to keep the waters clean. The waters, as you know, have been in the care of the women of our family for centuries. *Mammaen* has taken it as personal failure."

Rhea puts her hand on the young woman's shoulder.

"The women in your family have done the best they can. We must all join together at this time. We cannot do the work alone."

"Thank you," Bridgette says and tears stream down her face.

Rhea embraces her.

"I will show Lila a bit of the temple and make sure she meets with Helene."

"Thank you, Rhea," Bridgette says again, wiping the tears from her eyes. Rhea takes my hand as we move through a narrow hall with a low ceiling. I run my other hand along the cold earthen walls. They are solid, cool, and at the same time, they pulse with energy.

Light turns to matter, and matter turns to light.

The hall opens into a magnificent domed atrium of incandescent stained glass, inset with elegant patterns of leaves, bees, butterflies, and vines that appear to breathe in the light. The dome

seems to pour into my body, or perhaps my body pours into the upper reaches of the dome. It is a most unusual sensation.

"It's stunning," I gasp, tilting my head back and looking skyward.

The floor at my feet is marbled with geometrical patterns—circles within spirals, within circles.

"It changes throughout the day as the sun crosses the sky. Rhea says as she watches me take everything in. If you look closely, you may find that much of the Château Lumiere is quite fluid and not quite as solid as one might imagine. It is how many of our temples are constructed."

My head is pounding.

How many times have I been here?

Along the side of the atrium, a spiral staircase curls. The banister is an elegant copper leaf vine that twists and twines toward the light above.

"You will have much more time to explore. Right now I will take you to Helene Belefonte's chambers," Rhea says.

I close my eyes for a moment. "Who is Helene?" I ask.

"Don't worry. At some point it all comes back: the memories of our past connections, the vows you have made. The mistakes we have made. The lessons we have learned. There is a point when we no longer plunge into the river of forgetting."

CHAPTER
THIRTY-FIVE

When a priestess is truly seated on her throne, she realizes
that she carries the throne within her. Our bodies are
the temple of our souls. To be seated on the throne is to
be well placed inside our own sacred chambers, deeply
grounded into the root of Mother Earth, well seated in the
center of our belly, as we connect to the stars and the sky
and let the Goddess's inspiration, her words, and actions
flow through us.

Gaia Codex: Node 34215.955

I STAND IN FRONT of a mahogany door covered with
ornate brass Celtic knotwork that twists, turns, and
twines—an infinite Vine of Life that has no beginning or
end. There is a knocker in the center, a spotted gold panther
with green gemstone eyes that stare at me.

"Helene will want to see you alone ..." Rhea had said, leaving
me at the door.

I take the heavy ring in the panther's mouth and knock once, twice, three times. When there is no answer, I push the heavy door open and walk inside to a spacious library. In front of me are windows that stretch from floor to ceiling, looking out onto meticulously appointed formal gardens—a topiary spiral maze and what appears to be a magnificent greenhouse composed of shimmering spires and glass domes.

Mahogany shelves reach the rafters, filled with beautifully bound books written in English, French, German, Italian, Sanskrit, Chinese, Japanese, Arabic, and Korean. There are also books written in the curious language of symbols and script that my mother uses in her diaries when she mentions the Gaia Codex.

I pull down one of the books. It is richly bound in forest green leather. Jewels are embedded into the cover and fine filigree of gold text is embossed on the front. Like my mother's book, it shimmers. I open the pages and inside are beautiful illustrations of women in luscious jewel covered gowns engaged in different activities: joined together in circle, weaving, making tinctures of herbs, embraced in the arms of a lover, weaving what appears to be a robe of stars.

The text is written in the symbol script, and as I run my fingers over the symbols one at a time, tones and words are expelled into the air in a language that is known and deeply familiar. I feel my heart warm as I hear it again. It sounds sweet to the ears after a long silence.

Throughout the library are statues and paintings: lush, multicultural representations of the Goddess. Here is Artemis—the Lady of Ephesus with her multiple voluptuous, succulent breasts—she who provides succor for those in need. Here is a peaceful Kuan Yin with the nectar of immortality that flows from her vase—nectar said to cure all ills and heal all sorrows. Here is the ferocious and many-armed Kali, Hindu goddess of time and death. Over here is a *thangka* of the Buddhist goddess Green Tara. She sits deep in a terracotta red alcove. The goddess pulses radiant and green. She is compassion, and she is Earth. I walk through the library touching the figures, looking at the paintings, admiring their voluptuous breasts, slender waists, and full bellies, imagining for a moment that these goddesses are somehow me, and I am they. My morpho markings pulse, taking in all this information.

I pause in front of an oil painting that hangs on the wall. The setting is a forest so deep green it is almost black. The style is reminiscent of Rembrandt or the drawings in my mother's folio. In the painting are nine women of all different races—beautifully dressed in their native garb. Each holds an object in her hands that she seems to offer to the viewer: one, a chalice; one, a star; one, a globe; one, a yantra (an ancient geometrical diagram); one, a multifaceted diamond; one, a scroll; one, an *ouroboros* (a snake biting its tale); one, a lotus; one, a tree sapling.

The women in the painting stand around a circular well that reflects their images as well as the stars that fill the skies above. Carved into the stone of the well are symbols for the four elements. At the bottom of the painting something is written—again in the mysterious glyphs and script I have seen in Dominique's manuscript.

It is hard to place the painting in time. Is it from the past or the future? These must be Priestesses of Astera for they look like the women in my visions and in the illustrations of my mother's journal.

As my eyes adjust to the light, I notice other paintings,

including one of what appear to be Taoist priestesses, each holding different herbs and elixirs. This painting is also framed with the mysterious symbols and script I have seen in my mother's notebooks.

There are elegant pots painted with symbols and tapestries woven in geometrical designs. Everything in the room is familiar, and yet seems to hearken from a world that is not quite the one I know. It is as though there has been a parallel history where women such as these walked and gathered in the open without fear of persecution or peril. A world that honored the natural cycles of Life and Death and understood that nature in both her bounty and her fierceness is to be revered as the source of Life.

"They are intriguing aren't they—the untold histories of both what has been and what may come. Histories that most people in this world have long forgotten." The voice that speaks is resonant, clear, and carries across the room. I turn to see a woman. She is tall and aquiline with elegant, high cheekbones and long auburn hair with streaks of grey, swept up into a chignon. She wears trousers, a silk blouse, and a distinctive signet ring: carved black onyx with an inset diamond in a design of a single radiant star coming out the velvet warm darkness of the Mother Womb. I instinctively touch my neck and the pendant Dominique had given me. They are similar stones. Stars of Astera.

The woman walks towards me.

"I am Helene Belefonte." Helene's fingers are long and slender, her touch is firm as she extends her hand. She does not bow like the other women. When I place my own hand in hers, I feel a shock—a startling bite of energy.

"Finally, we get to meet Dominique's fabled daughter." My cheeks burn as Madame Belefonte speaks.

"Thank you for receiving me today," I reply in my best formal greeting, but my hands are shaking. I am unsettled under Madame's gaze. Exposed.

"Please sit down," Madame Belefonte replies as she elegantly motions towards a plush velvet couch. She then settles down into a magnificent chair carved of mpingo African blackwood. Energy rivets the space. The air shimmers.

Should I leave? I am suddenly aware of my unkempt state. My hair is wild and wavy despite my best intentions. My clothes are rumpled with travel. There are stains on my trousers. I feel ragtag in this woman's presence and not at all presentable.

"So, this is the daughter of Dominique and her consort?"

My mother's consort?

"Do you mean my father Raj?" I ask aloud.

Madame Helene does not answer. Instead, I feel her gazing at the subtle morpho marks on my arms and hands.

"May I?" she asks, taking my hand to inspect them closer.

I nod. I sense that one does not say no to Madame Belefonte.

She touches one mark with her finger. As she does, it shimmers and sends out information. I feel her reading the lines. I watch her expression. She is probing; the sensation is painful.

Up close, Madame Helene's face is regal. Like a hawk or a cougar, her gaze penetrates. I sense that she wields power that can easily send souls on to another destination—either by whim or by necessity. I squirm. Death, when she chooses to bestow it, is merciful—a blessing of a higher order. Or perhaps this is only

the spell she weaves as her prey helplessly gazes into her coal black eyes.

Instinctively, I pull my hand away. After a moment Madame Belefonte releases my hand but does not drop her gaze.

Through millions of years of evolution, humans are trained to spot the hunter, to know when we are marked as prey, and to flee when necessary. Primordial images explode in my mind as I sit on this elegant purple couch: I am in the forest, pursued by a jaguar, running fast, breathless, scared. I am the rabbit, scurrying for cover, as a red tail hawk dives from overhead, claws and beak sinking into my fur.

I wonder if Madame Belefonte hears and sees my thoughts. I assume that she does.

The pressure builds. I want to leave the room. I am about to get out of my seat when Madame speaks.

"Feel your fear, Lila Sophia." Her voice wraps around me like the softest of silks.

"You have the power to strike back at me if you choose," Madame Belefonte smiles, but her look is not kind.

Fire and thunder, the roar of the lioness rumbles in my roots. This force, this power, is heady, familiar, and I miss it. It is mine. I start to imagine what I might do. Just as I am about to say something, Madame Belefonte speaks.

"It is the lesson of priestesses to not use our power out of fear. Remember who your true opponent is." Madame Belefonte's voice is a purr.

"And who is that?" I ask. My voice is unsteady with adrenaline. I clutch my hands together, afraid of what I might do. I want to slap her. Scream. Or run.

"Look deep into your mind. Embrace your fears, but do not let them consume you."

Madame's gaze steadies my own convulsive flow of thoughts. "Become empty, for when you are empty, there is nothing to strike, nothing to be destroyed."

"An initiated Priestess of Astera has access to a tremendous amount of power, for she taps directly into the seed of the soul, the forces of creation and destruction. Life and Death. The uninitiated priestess has simply raw power that can be attached to desire for personal preservation or glory. Over time the initiate learns to focus and refine her power. Be clear, Lila Sophia!"

Then suddenly, as if she holds a sword in her hands, Madame makes a downward motion, so sudden that a silver-flashing glimmer of tempered steel appears to move through the air.

Madame Belefonte continues to watch me. Her pupils—fully dilated—are the color of the darkest night.

The eyes are portals to the Universe. A billion stars can be found in the dark depths of our eyes. When the pupils dilate, it is an indication that an individual is shifting her experience into deep seeing. A priestess sees with eyes both open and shut.

Gaia Codex: Node 3221.67.88

Under Madame Belefonte's gaze I instinctively sit up and shift uncomfortably on my seat.

Madame Belefonte's countenance softens. "It is about

tempering and balancing the fire. Knowing when to use it to strike. When to use your power for the highest benefit of all beings and all Life—even if it means at the sacrifice of your own life. This is one of our vows."

"And you," I ask, "How have you dealt with power?" It is a very personal question, one that I probably should not ask, but I need to know.

There is a sudden tinge of weariness that crosses Madame Belafonte's face. It is barely perceptible, but it is there. "Like you, Lila, like all Priestesses of Astera, I am here under vow. I have been successful in upholding this vow, and there have been times when I have failed tragically and have subsequently paid the consequences. When we misuse power, it affects not only ourselves but also many others. This is a heavy price to pay. If you are on the path of the priestess, you will feel every person you have harmed—you will know each one that you have caused to suffer, intimately—as if their pain is your pain. It is not an easy lesson, and it is why so few ultimately take our path in full. I have paid a price for my actions and so may you Lila Sophia."

I notice a pained sadness in Madame Belefonte's eyes, just for a moment, and then it is gone.

I am about to ask what she means but Madame gracefully gestures towards an antique Sèvres porcelain coffee service sitting upon a delicate side table. "Café?"

"Please," I reply.

Madame smiles and then pours coffee into elegant hand painted china cups.

Petit fours, macarons, crème brûlée, and a number of other patisserie wait to be served. There are crisp linen napkins to place on my lap.

"Patisserie?" Madame asks.

"No, thank you," I answer.

"As you please." Madame chooses a delicate mauve macaron and places it on her bone china tea plate. She now looks somehow more accessible. Still formidable, yes, but more human.

"We Priestesses of Astera have not gathered together for many cycles. Our sisters are travelling from all corners of the planet so we can come together at this time." Madame Belefonte takes a slow sip of her coffee. "I will be frank with you. I am still waiting to see if Dominique's experiment with you is warranted."

"What was your relationship to my mother?" I ask.

Madame Belefonte does not answer right away.

"Perhaps you know the adage—'That those we love most can hurt us most?'"

"Can you tell me more?" I ask tentatively.

Helene takes another sip of her coffee as though she is considering whether to answer me.

"Dominique, your mother, was dear to my heart. We are polar opposites. When we are in harmony we make a whole. When we oppose one another, it can blow up into battle, if we are not careful," Madame Belefonte says matter-of-factly. "From my vantage point, your mother is reckless. Her personal choices have often put her sisters at risk, and her experiments are not always successful."

I feel myself flushing red at Madame Belefonte's words.

"The Dominique I knew was creative, beautiful, and adventurous, yet also very thorough, and from what I have seen from reading her diaries, deeply dedicated to her sisters and the well-being of others." My words come rushing out. It is primordial, instinctual to defend those we love, especially one's mother, one's sister, one's friend.

Madame Belefonte takes a dainty bite of the mauve macaron.

"Oh, I have no doubt that this is all well and true, but your mother, you, and your father, the three of you, if the truth be told—have been persistent in this idea that the DNA of the species must be transformed if human beings are to survive. This premise may hold merit, but civilizations have been destroyed before by the application of advanced technologies without a correlative awakening of consciousness and a respect for the balance of the Life. Your father was just as likely to pursue science for its own sake or for power—as for the well-being of the human species or this planet." Madame Belefonte is becoming a bit flushed. The subject of my father heats her up. "And that, Lila Sophia, is my great concern."

"My father is dead," I say quietly.

"I know," Madame Belefonte replies.

"My mother is dead," I continue.

"Perhaps," Madame Belefonte replies.

"What do you mean?" I ask tentatively.

Madame Belefonte looks at me carefully. "You must know that your mother had some skills or at least aspirations in the manipulation of time—since she devised the Orb Navigator, although her success in such matters has yet to be determined. What I do know is that when those close to me pass, I feel it or 'see' it—so to speak—but since Dominique's death, there have been no signs, dreams, or messages. Only silence. I have not felt her passing." Madame Belefonte pauses and then continues, "But perhaps this is only my wishful thinking. So much was left unsaid between us and what I did say were misspoken words, born of my anger for her having left with your father Raj."

Madame Belefonte turns away from me and looks out the window. When she turns back, her eyes are bright with tears. *She loves my mother. More than she wants me to know.* I want to tell her that even though my mother is not with us I do feel her and communicate with her through her illuminated manuscript and in my dreams. Yet my instinct tells me to say nothing—at least not now.

Madame Belefonte puts down her delicate china cup onto the table purposefully. She then brushes her hands over her finely tailored trousers. I take this as a signal that our meeting has ended.

"You are welcome here at the Château Lumiere, Lila Sophia. But do know that I will not hesitate to destroy anything that jeopardizes our greater work, the balance of Life."

"You mean you will not hesitate to destroy me?" I ask.

"It is not my wish Lila Sophia, but there is much at stake. Our first vow as priestesses is to the well-being of all beings. We have survived this long because we are willing to destroy that which does not serve. If we create faulty magic, we destroy it. As a priestess you must be willing to take your own life for the greater good. You should know this," she admonishes. "Lila, do you remember your past incarnations as a Priestess of Astera?" As she says this, Madame Belefonte peers into my eyes.

"No, not fully, not yet," I answer hesitantly. "I seem to be able to access the collective memory, but I am just remembering my own lives. Is this is unusual amongst priestesses?" I ask.

"Most priestesses are trained to remember their lives but it is not always the case. Sometimes one's past incarnations must be

unearthed as hard-won treasures, where the discovery becomes a journey of its own. We shall see what comes of all this soon enough." Madame Belefonte says as she stands up and turns towards the window.

Taking this as my cue, I bow formally and place my hands to my heart. It is a bow of protocol—an ancient habit. I shut the door quietly as I leave.

CHAPTER
THIRTY-SIX

*There are some priestesses who live for millennia bound
by vow to a temple, to the land, or to the Mother Earth
herself. When these things pass, so do they.*

Gaia Codex: Node 3321.43.21

THE LONG SHADOWS of late afternoon fill the hall as
I exit the library. Rhea is casually leaning against the
wall waiting for me.

"Did it go well?" she asks.

"I think so," I answer. "Helene Belefonte is unusual.
Challenging, ferocious, kind, and gentle all mixed together."

Rhea laughs. "Sounds like the Goddess to me … or Helene
Belefonte. Come, I will show you to your rooms." Rhea takes my
arm and leads me down long elegant hallways with tall windows
that look over the labyrinth gardens.

We haven't walked very far when Rhea motions towards a
deep window seat that overlooks the gardens. There is room for

us both to stretch our legs out and lay back on the velvet and silk pillows.

"Come," Rhea says as she pats one of the pillows beside her. I slip in next to her. Our legs touch, slightly.

"I haven't asked you, but is this your birth form Lila?" Rhea asks looking deep into my eyes.

I run my hands through my wavy auburn hair. "Yes, this is it. Except for the morpho markings." I answer.

Rhea is so beautiful to gaze upon. Cool and clear on the surface, but underneath there are vast depths reminiscent of a star-filled sky. There is fire.

"Can you share with me your metamorphosis process? How it was to shift through different forms?" Rhea asks.

"Yes, of course. The shapeshifting started when I was with Old Woman."

"Of course, Old Woman," Rhea says softly.

"The changes were active for about a year. In that time I wore almost three hundred and sixty different female bodies after the beginning of my menses moon, but I seem to have settled. I am not changing form, at least not right now. The only signs that remain now are the morpho markings that—as you can see—are still with me." I hold out my arm to Rhea.

"The markings are beautiful," Rhea murmurs. "Quite stunning." She examines them as though she is looking at a fine piece of art.

"I have seen the blue morpho butterflies up close in the light. The markings on the white ones and paler pearlescent morphos are exactly like yours," Rhea says.

"And the transformations … what was your experience with wearing these different bodies?" Rhea asks.

"I guess the big difference is that now how I experience the world has changed. It is as though sometimes I can simultaneously see through the eyes of others, alongside my own personal perspective," I continue. "When you are in the skin and body of another, you realize we are both different and the same."

"Did you transform into different species or genders?" Rhea asks.

"Not yet," I reply.

"Tell me a bit more about Madame Belefonte." *I need to know.*

"Madame Belefonte is the guardian of the Château Lumiere."

"What does that mean?" I ask.

"Each of the Temples of Astera is held by our collective body of priestesses, but often there is one priestess—or a small circle of priestesses—that serves as the primary guardian of a specific temple. As for the Château Lumiere, you could say this temple is Helene's body, her skin, her bones, and her blood. Although it is also born of our collective vision and imagination, Helene Belefonte received the first visions and planted the first foundations. She has helped shape it—for millennia. They say that when she dies the temple will die as well."

"How old is Madame Helene?" I ask. Rhea, not unlike Old Woman, touches the inside of my arm and as she speaks a flow of images ensues.

"Many say that Helene Belefonte is thousands of years old and that she was here long before the first walls of Paris were built. There are stories of her coming from the matriarchal clans of the Hercynian Forest before the rise of the Roman Empire. They say Helene planted the first tree and sang the spells of enchantment to weave the walls of the Château Lumiere. She

chose her consort and sanctified the space, and when the consort grew old and his bones went back into the ground, she stayed and continued to build this temple. Helene had a vision of the rise of kings and feudal lieges and a time when the Goddess would be hidden, and sanctuary would be needed for women persecuted for their gender, their knowing, their spells, and their magic. Helene Belefonte saw that such things would come to pass, and so she built the Châteaux Lumiere out of her own bones and blood, out of the fire of her imagination, and out of the passion of her heart. This is the myth and the story. You can decide for yourself how much is true. Or ask her. Madame Belefonte is often quite forthright, if you ask the right question."

The window seat is comfy, and I am enjoying sitting here with Rhea. When her fingers brush against me as she is talking, it sends tingles up my spine.

"Does Madame Belefonte ever leave the Château Lumiere?" I ask.

"No," Rhea answers. "She does not have the ability to move beyond the perimeters of the temple like you or I. She is bound within its walls." As Rhea speaks, she touches my wrist again and I see an image of Helene Belefonte attempting to pass through the grey stone walls on the edge of the forest as her body disintegrates—and the Château Lumiere falls to pieces—flashing through my mind.

"It would be something like this if she tried to leave," Rhea says.

"I see." My voice is quiet as I look at the images.

"From my understanding, this was one of the joys and pains of Helene's relationship with your mother, Dominique—that Dominique could leave, and Helene could not. They were very close you know. Helene was jealous of your father, Raj," Rhea says as she slowly runs her fingers over the turquoise velvet pillows.

"I sensed that," I reply.

"It broke Helene's heart when Dominique choose Raj, but I don't think she speaks about it much."

"So my mother and Helene Belefonte were lovers?" I ask.

"Yes, of course." Rhea answers.

"They say Dominique was Helene Belefonte's favorite—the passion that almost destroyed her. Some were upset with your mother for leaving and breaking the balance. Others of us understand that it was necessary for the new cycle to begin." Rhea looks at me kindly. "I know it's a lot to take in, but it must be nice to have some of your questions answered."

"It is." I let out a deep exhalation. The light is fading from the sky and a young woman passes, lighting candles up and down the halls.

I grab Rhea's hand. "I need your counsel. Madame Belefonte said she would, if necessary, destroy me. She feels that the Metamorphosis Project experiment is dangerous and could destroy the balance of Life. What do you make of this?" I ask.

Rhea's eyes dilate and for a moment they appear almost a midnight black.

She is ancient. I shudder in excitement.

Rhea looks deep into my eyes. "Lila, you have a gift to give. Your most important task is to fulfill this. Listen carefully within yourself and around you. Watch for signs. When you hear the call—give everything, without reserve. Then we will see what happens." Rhea pauses for a moment and then continues. "Do not let the fear of death stop you."

She kisses me softly on the forehead. The touch of her lips sends sweet waves of pleasure up my spine.

"Come, it is getting dark, and I need to get you to your rooms."

We walk through doors that lead to subsequent doors and then to grand halls, domed atriums, and spiraling staircases. Magnificent trompe-l'œil frescoes suggest indoor gardens and lush jungles, sudden windows and doors looking out onto the Temples of Dendera in Egypt or the shores of the Ganges in Varanasi.

"Touch the walls," Rhea says, gently placing my hand onto the interior stone wall. It is solid, cold stone, but it also vibrates and moves as though it is composed of pure light.

"All matter is like this when you have cultivated the perception to see and experience it as both solid matter and energy simultaneously. Within our temple walls it is always easier to experience this. It is also how our temples can be invisible to most of the world. Most of the population—at least for thousands of years—have not developed the necessary sensory perception and vibrational attunement to see our temples, but perhaps this is changing."

A soft golden glow fills the chambers as the evening rises. The spiral staircase twists up multiple stories to a stained glass dome resplendent with luscious vines, trees, flowers, and stellar skies that appear to melt into the heavens.

Rhea places a key in my hand. On the key chain is a peacock feather encased in glass.

"Some say the peacock is an alchemist with the ability to transmute all poisons. When a peacock opens its fan, we might catch a glimpse of the thousand eyes that every body has. This key is for you, Lila, the key to the room that Madame Belefonte has chosen especially for you."

"Thank you," I answer as I gently clasp my hand around the key. Everything feels deeply familiar. *An echo within the echo.*

"We will see each other tomorrow. Dinner tonight will be provided for you in your rooms. Madame Belefonte felt it would be best for you to have some time to settle in tonight. It will be a big day tomorrow."

"Are you sure you do not want to come along?" I ask impulsively, as I grab Rhea's hands.

"Not tonight, my love," Rhea answers, "there is plenty of time for you and I."

CHAPTER
THIRTY-SEVEN

*Our bodies are made of ten thousand eyes. Our bodies
contain the universe.*

Gaia Codex: Node 33.241.85

I SLOWLY CLIMB THE stairs. My hand glides along the
copper banister that winds like a vine towards the light
above. At each twist of the spiral there is a door—some are
carved, some painted, some covered in brass filigree. Each has
a distinct symbol: a rose, a snake, a lotus, a butterfly, or sacred
geometries and ancient Greek, Egyptian, and Sanskrit words, or
Aboriginal symbols.

The doors are stunning to behold, gold and silver embel-
lished with intricate designs. Ornate doors with intricately
carved vines that transform into the bodies of men and women
at all stages of life: newborns to corpses. I continue to climb
upwards— the twist and the turn, the spiral upward. As I do,
there is a hum, as though a thousand bees were making honey,

the movement of their wings creating harmonic chords. The heights are dizzying.

Finally, I stop at a door with a single eye shaped out of lapis, marble, and gold. Behind the single eye is a background field of seemingly infinite peacock feathers shimmering in the golden candlelight that fills the halls.

I lift the key and carefully jiggle the lock back and forth.

There is a rush of air as the door opens wide. I gasp. The room is decorated in vibrant turquoise, deep-hued greens, sapphire, and golden tones that glow in the candlelight. The centerpiece is a large four-poster bed with hanging, diaphanous drapes embroidered with a pattern of thousands of peacock eyes in gold and radiant greens. The eyes shimmer.

I walk over to the bed and finger the silken drapes, letting them catch the light, watching the eyes glimmer. The scent of amber and Alba rose oil fills the room. Warm candlelight pours through a slightly open door to the *salle de bains*, "the hall of the bath." I walk through to find steam rising from a large burnished copper tub surrounded by dozens of tapered beeswax candles. Silver mirrors line the room, giving a sense of visual infinity stretching in all directions.

Feeling the grit and sweat of the journey, I slowly take off my clothes. Naked, I sink into the water. It is the perfect temperature, the scent of rose intoxicating. For a moment the sweat of the day and the many changes in the last few years—the loss of my parents, the loneliness, and searching for my sisters—all fall away. I relax.

Do not cling too tightly to anything, for everything must and will change.

This voice rings through my head and is both mine and not

mine. I dip underneath the water, wetting my hair and feeling the silkiness of my skin. All does change, quicker than we might think. The skin grows old, firm breasts will sag, and a flat tummy will become plump. Our lives are but the blink of an eye in the fullness of time. I lift my head back above the water line and into the mirrored candlelight. My sixteen-year-old body reflects back in mirror. I get out and dry myself with a thick cotton towel by the side of the bed and wrap myself in a plush robe placed on the stool.

I return to the main room where a fire crackles golden on the hearth and a simple meal has been set out. There is a small earthenware dish of savory cassoulet. In a silver bowl, wrapped in a double damask napkin, is warm, freshly baked bread with a pot of sweet butter on the side. Under a glass dome is an array of cheeses—Cantal, Neufchâtel, Brocciu—and an autumn apple waiting to be sliced. There is also a small crystal decanter filled with *vin de Bourgogne* accompanied by a silver goblet oxidized with time. I pull the teardrop crystal stopper off the decanter to let the wine breathe.

"Thank you for this food that nourishes. May all life on our Mother Earth be nourished."

The prayer falls effortlessly from my lips. We are born of the Mother Earth and remain deeply connected to her. With every bite we eat we transform all of her elements into energy and life. The fire crackles. The crescent moon rises outside. I slowly savor my meal.

When I am done, I slip into the bed between soft silken sheets and a duvet embroidered in gold, sapphire, and green, sinking my head into aromatic pillows. I look up through the diaphanous curtains, the pattern of incandescent peacock eyes glimmering in the candlelight and moonlight. I breathe this body composed of ten thousand jeweled eyes. The Gaia Codex, the infinite jeweled net. A hum rises. It is ecstatic. The vibration of a honeycomb body. This is indeed a beautiful bed, and I am so happy to be here in the temple of my sister-priestesses. I slip into a sleep deeper and more nourishing than many I have had in many years.

CHAPTER
THIRTY-EIGHT

It is said that the fragrant udumbara flower blooms only once every three thousand years.

Gaia Codex: Node 45221.37771.85

AS MORNING LIGHT breaks, I arise quickly, not lingering in bed, not ruminating on dreams. Today, at the Château Lumière, the Priestesses of Astera will arrive.

I turn to the large wardrobe, an art nouveau piece with sensuous edges shaped like a cello or a female body, expecting to find the clothes I had brought with me from Old Woman, but instead I find a selection of luscious, jewel-toned frocks. I run my fingers through the various textures, taking in the array of colors, and choose a dress in vibrant emerald and blue. It consists of a very tight long-sleeved undertunic and a small loose chiffon overdress with an Empire waist that brings my breasts into fuller bloom. There are matching colored tights and charming emerald suede boots that fit tight to the calf. I pull my hair back and tie it with a blue silk ribbon and slip large pearl ear-rings into my ears. The Star of Astera pendant given to me by Dominique is, as always, around my neck. *Mother, I wish you were here to share this with me.*

I open the velvet bag of Dominique's jewels. They are loose stones of various sizes: rubies, sapphires, emeralds, and some smaller diamonds.

Amongst the smaller gems there is a radiant blue stone of considerable size, cut like a multifaceted goose egg. "The Phoenix Stone" is what my mother called it.

"Someday you are to give the Phoenix Stone to the right woman at the right time," Dominique had told me when I played with the gemstones as a child. They had been my childhood playthings as well as tools for learning vibrational signatures and potential healing qualities, for each stone is endowed with these properties.

Should I bring the Phoenix Stone today? I ask as I hold the stone in my hands. The cool stone warms to my skin, but the answer is firm. *No.* I place it back into the velvet bag.

I light a single candle for the Goddess. I bow low with my hands clasped over my heart as a prayer of thanks flows from my lips. I am ready to meet my sisters—the Priestesses of Astera.

As I descend the stairs, incandescent morning light streams down in bands of color through the magnificent stained glass dome. The atrium is no longer empty. Waves of women's voices, spontaneous music, the subtle spiced mix of hundreds of tongues, reaches me first, and then I am overwhelmed by the glorious colors of their spectacular ornamentation.

These women are wrapped in radiant, woven, jewel-colored

Banarasi saris, in intricate Javanese batik sarongs, in extravagant flowing burkas, and in elegant, tightly wound, gold-threaded chrysanthemum and *sakura* kimonos and obis from Japan. These women and girls are bedecked in colorful Yoruba *aso-oke* and kaftans made of handwoven textiles, dyed with vegetable oil and printed with traditional *adinkra,* Akan symbols of prosperity. These women are draped in earth-toned lamb's wool, in floor-length chubas woven in the highlands of Tibet, decorated with lapis, coral, and hand-pounded silver and copper. These women are radiant—with Amazonian macaw feathers of turquoise, scarlet, emerald, and hyacinth braided into their hair. These women are marked with ceremonial *tā moko* (Māori tattoos) on their chins and lips. These women carry intricate *mehndi* and henna designs on their hands and feet, markings of the ceremonial stages of women's lives through many cycles.

My morpho markings pulse. I am feeling, tasting, and learning. I am listening. My whole body is taking in the sweet scents and perfumes: the ambers, jasmine, rose otto, sandalwood, the patchouli and hyacinth, the cinnamon, musk, neroli, and myrrh. Such scents and subtle combinations—many I had never smelled before, at least not in known memory. Amongst the women there are heartfelt greetings, deep hugs, and ceremonial bows, tears streaming from eyes as long held emotions rise to the surface—so many different faces of the Goddess, so many faces of womanhood—faces of the human family in female form.

"Good to see you again, sister." A heavyset Polynesian woman with the softest coconut-oiled skin smiles at me.

"Have we met … ?" I ask. Her familiarity startles me.

"Of course we have, Lila Sophia." She places her large, warm, fleshy hands onto mine and looks into my eyes. "But it is fine, if you do not remember. It can come back in pieces, in trickles and bits, or it can hit you like the tsunami and sweep you away." She smiles at me kindly, before she slips back into the crowd. "Aloha."

An Indian woman, grey-haired with warm brown skin, swathed in a vibrant green sari, embraces a twelve-year-old girl carefully dressed in Javanese batik. As they look into each other's eyes, it is difficult to tell who is the elder and who is the younger. These bodies we wear are but the subtlest of woven silks.

I continue to mingle in the crowd, listening and moving within the currents of this ocean, and I feel the pulse of our shared waters. The exuberance in the room escalates.

A petite Japanese woman, wrapped in a kumquat-colored silk kimono, passes by with a white powdered face. Her eyes meet mine in a quizzical smile, which she covers quickly with her fan, playful in the hide-and-seek.

"Lila Sophia," she says softly. There is a titanium tenacity beneath her soft-spoken demeanor. Again I am startled by the familiarity of her address. All these women are faces of myself. Uniquely different and yet we are One.

Relaxing, my very cells connect into this moving web of life and activity. I share my breath with others in this room. The sensation is comforting. I am not alone.

I move deeper into the room. There are a number of young women and girls. Arriving alone or with their aunties, mothers, or grandmothers. Some are my age, some a bit older, some a bit younger. We are of all nationalities and flavors of skin. As we catch each other's eyes there is an unspoken knowing—a shared memory breaking open.

I also hear whispers as I pass through the room.

"Dominique's daughter, yes, that is her."

"So, this is the experiment."

I am much more than an experiment.

"Lila Sophia carries it well. I wonder if she understands the gravity of what she carries."

"It must be difficult for Helene Belefonte to see her, after what happened with Dominique."

I do not acknowledge these comments although they must know I can hear them. I straighten my shoulders, breath deeply, and move toward the far side of the room, where a short, squat, black-haired Tzotzil Maya woman with broad cheekbones and flashing eyes sits in a corner. She is dressed in a traditional *huipil*, very beautifully embroidered. As others gather round, some standing, some sitting, some listening, some singing quiet songs, Maya Mother speaks:

"In our grandmother's time, we wove the ceremony, the stories, legends, and the secrets of our lineage into our textiles."

"As did we, with the saris our family wove in Varanasi," the grey-haired Indian woman adds.

"Yes, yes," our Maya Mother continues. "We wove the history of our human family into the clothes we wear, the blankets which keep us warm, the sashes we wrap around the bellies of our men and children. Our songs guide the threads of the loom and the stories of our people. Our job is to preserve and tell the stories of Life. We weave these stories back into the fabric of the planet herself. Thus has it ever been."

I feel the heat of eyes on the back of my head, and slowly turn away from the circle of women. Before me stands a woman, Amazon Mother, with high-sculpted cheekbones and piercing eyes. Her hair is snow white. She is not tall, but as she stands in front of me, she commands my attention. Her eyes burn passionately with deep teachings of plants and animals of the rainforests—they hold a call to awaken to the illuminated Life that lives within us. She holds my gaze and then spontaneously brushes a scarlet macaw feather softly down my throat.

I shudder and let my head fall back. My ears fill with the cries of a flock in motion, the flutters and flaps of hundreds of wings. My sight fills with waves of flying color—radiant turquoise, greens, and reds. They move through me, lifting me up and out, into deep green foliage, and then I am back in the atrium. Amazon Mother laughs and slips back into the crowd.

I am looking for Rhea when I feel a tingle across my back.

"There you are." Her green eyes are flashing. She is wearing a hunter's green dress with an Empire waist, cut high up the sides, with cinnamon trousers and high boots underneath.

"We are here, my love, all of us." I notice a slight tension in her voice as she speaks.

"May it go well. There is much at stake, Lila." She grabs my hand. "Remember you have prepared for this moment for lifetimes. You have everything you need."

I wonder what Rhea means, and I let out a deep breath. I am happy to finally be here with my sisters after so many years of separation. *I wish you were here with me, Mother.* The prayer to my mother, to Dominique, slips from my lips and for a moment I am overcome with deep longing.

CHAPTER

THIRTY-NINE

The codex has been embedded into the very fabric of culture and into the Mother Earth herself. Hidden and protected, it has been nurtured, cultivated, and revealed in the right moments, through oral teachings and flash revelations. It is said that it is a code of Divine Origins for humans to follow for rejuvenation and evolution. The clues are with us in every moment if we have the eyes to see.

Gaia Codex: Node 99921.31

"SISTERS, MOTHERS, AND honored Elders please make your way into the atrium. We will be starting." Bridgette, the young woman with long flaxen hair, moves through the room making the announcement. In the corner, an angular Javanese woman, swathed in ceremonial batik, creates a steady rhythm on a large brass gong, while a second woman, draped in a shawl woven with *tocapu* (sacred geometrical symbols worn by the ancient Incas), blows deep into a polished conch shell. A reverberation of unseen crystal bells and tempered brass singing bowls defines the space.

Immediately, there is an organic movement towards the center of the round atrium as a series of concentric circles form, one within the other. We women are settling into the ancient formations.

Hands join naturally, the soft flesh of youth intertwined with the wizened hands of age. Blood pulses strong through our veins. We are one, one pulse, one river, many bodies, joining and touching as One Heart.

I place my hands into those of the Nubian priestess on my left and the young Bhutanese girl on my right. Rhea is directly across from me.

This way we can hold either end of the Circle together. We are here together. Once again. Rhea says this in the silent language.

I see Teal with a woman whom I assume is her auntie. Teal has now grown into a young woman. She is stunning. I bow to her and she smiles.

You made it through the first initiations, sister. You are here, Teal says silently. Her words ring in my mind as she smiles at me from across the room.

Circles within circles. It is not clear who starts the song, or who begins the chant; who knows the melody, the rhythm, or the complex beautiful harmonies that pour through our bodies, that shape the sonic architecture of the space. It is not clear who begins the toning that resounds, echoes, and resonates through the room—the sounds of ancient Tuvan shamans and lucid crystal bells. These chants, so ancient, swell forth from all of us, chants unsung for millennia and yet never lost—sounds without words and yet deep with meaning.

It is an ancient vibration that shapes the space, that rises through each of us, up our spines, opening, igniting, unfurling the flowers of what are called *chakras* in Sanskrit—the seven wheels of access into the core emotional and spiritual qualities. *Kundalini*. The Snake. *Shakti*. It is said that when they are brought into balance we become fully human.

The sound quivers, shaping and reinvigorating our body temples, creating a matrix, a womb, a temple, and a container for new seeds to be planted.

The Priestesses of Astera are known as mistresses of sound: able to use the subtle vibrations to call forth the elements, heal bones and illness, soothe fevers, and create openings in solid matter. They create beauty and worlds with the enchantments of their song.

Gaia Codex: Node 3221.4532.111

Collective resonant tones continue until the sound naturally subsides into a deep silence. In this moment, we are One. Time passes. An hour or a minute: it is hard to tell. The space is alive, vibrant, and nourishing with no end to its depth and breadth.

I am not the only one crying. Not the only one who has waited too long. Not the only one who fought too many battles, died too many deaths, was burned at too many stakes, exiled from too many beloved towns. Not the only one who kept what is most true silenced for too long.

We remember when "woman" was a dirty word. We

remember when women were bought and sold as property. We remember when women were exiled or killed for demanding ownership of the temple of our bodies. As sisters we sit in circle, our hearts joined as one and singing prayers out to those who still live under unbalanced rule.

I feel each woman's hurt, each girl's pain as my own. For we sisters share this. There is no separation when we share the circle.

We are crying with relief and release. I am quivering with vibrant images shaping my thoughts. They are mine and not mine, shared, and yet so deeply personal. This is how we sister-priestesses have come together for millennia.

Instinctively, I touch a finger to my forehead, heart, and belly in reverence of this temple, my body. My finger lingers on my belly, feeling the fullness of its swell, and the potential for new life that I carry—that every woman carries.

CHAPTER

FORTY

*The Sacred Circle is our temple. It is present any time and
any place that we gather.*

Gaia Codex: Node 8322.19.40

S OUR EYES open, Helene Belefonte stands tall before
us. She is both ancient and youthful in this shifting
light. She is luminous. For a moment she looks at me,
smiles and then begins to address the crowd. I shiver. Even
though the smile does not seem unkind, I take it as a challenge.

"Welcome, dear sisters. Any one of us could open the circle
today. We have each lived many lives. We have been born many
times to serve the Mother, to serve the Goddess, and to serve
Life itself in its infinite forms."

"Sisters, it matters not whether we join this circle today as
children or as elders. For all of us who gather today are born
of the ancient roots of our lineage. We have incarnated as pro-
tectors of these ancient seeds of our Mother Earth's well-being.

We are bequeathed with a mission—we of this ancient lineage of Astera—a mission we have carried and sustained for millennia."

"Sisters, you have remembered the stories and myths, you have uncovered the clues of our origins left throughout time. The tales may have come to you in your dreams; they may have been shared with you by mentors, those close of kin or spirit; or perhaps the knowing exploded forth inside you in times of transition—at the first flow of blood or in the rupture of the death of a Beloved. Perhaps the stories came to you as you lay upon our Mother Earth and gazed up at the dome of stars, perhaps it was then that you were flooded and overwhelmed with memories that were not yours alone."

"For millennia, we have kept our secrets carefully guarded. Revealing our true faces meant death or banishment."

"We sisters, the Priestesses of Astera, are here to benefit Life, to protect Life, to offer the seeds of rejuvenation we have protected and cultivated for millennia. This is our vow and our purpose."

"We are here now at this precipice. As one civilization dies, another one is born. Our current civilization has ravaged and raped the Earth. It refuses to sustain us. It is collapsing around us. Our Mother Earth is a living, breathing entity. If we humans destroy the balance, it is simple—she will subsume us. It won't be the first time. The waters will rise and the Earth will shake. Sisters, we are here to provide nourishment, healing vision, and hope to many who will be in need. We are here to plant seeds for new cultures and to carry forth wisdoms of the past that have sustained civilizations for tens of thousands of years. We are here to act from the Heart."

"We join in circle at this time to plant seeds for what will

come, to strengthen our communion of Heart, so we can be a source of strength for those who will need us in times to come."

Some of the women in the room have closed their eyes in contemplation and prayer. In the silence there is an upwelling like a rising wind or a thousand birds lifting into flight. There is movement, then stillness, then silence.

CHAPTER
FORTY-ONE

With golden honey on the tongue, the gift of sages and
seers, the Bee Priestesses, the Melissas, the daughters of
the hive, were the chief pollinators of Life. Goddesses, who
through the alchemy of their bodies create the sweetest of
golden nectars from our Mother Earth's bloom and flower.
As with the rose and its thorn, sting and sweetness come
together as One. Indeed the divine HUM of the Bee is said
to regenerate matter itself; the hexagon of the honeycomb
is a building block of Life. We priestesses have served
the wisdom of the Bee in many cultures. The sweetest
of Nature's flora and fauna express themselves through
our bodies so that we might fully become One with her
Essence.

Gaia Codex: Node 3221.4551

YOUNG WOMAN DRESSED in aubergine robes
moves throughout the hall, refreshing pots of hanging
incense. Her name is Gemma. For generations she has

trained in the art of perfume—the mastery of deep scent and olfactory pleasures. She is expert in the subtle mix of unguents, alcohol, civet, ambergris, musk, roots, barks, and flowers of a thousand and one varieties. As Gemma moves through the atrium, rose attar, amber, and civet—scents that tone and open the Heart—imbue the air we breathe.

Hopi Mother is standing. Her face is broad and brown, the cadence of her voice allows for pause and the preponderance of deeper meaning.

"Sisters, many of us know the prophecies of the ending and beginning times. Many of us know that as one world ends, another begins. Creations are destroyed when they are out of balance."

Hopi Mother pauses and looks at us all. "We have forgotten the essence of our humanity occurs when we live in deep resonance with all Life. It is simple: from our birth until our death we breathe the air, the spirit of the Mother. She is ever with us."

"Sisters, we are here to carry seeds of rejuvenation in the passage from one world to the next. I speak, honored sisters, simply of the seed of wisdom that each one of us has inside our hearts and the codes that are in the temple of our mortal bodies and in our Mother Earth."

"Sisters, ours is not a silent song, and it is time for us to speak."

Lila Sophia. Rhea looks at me intently from across the room as her voice rings in my head. *Let it flow. Do not hold anything back. You are safe here and we need to experience the gifts you have for us.*

I am afraid. I answer silently.

Use your fear. Rhea's eyes are intense and steady. *I am here with you.*

A pulsing hum fills my head as I slowly stand up and look out to my sisters. I feel my feet rooting deep down into the ground, like the ancient yew that lives for thousands of years. I feel the top of my crown open up, cracking like an egg toward the vast expanse of sky in the center. My Heart—still beating—is now my anchor. My throat pulses warm like honey, and I begin to speak, but it is not my words that come out. Lila Sophia is not the one who speaks. Instead, the nectar of the Goddess flows through me. I feel translucent and open as words flow forth from my tongue.

"Dear Sisters, we heard the Oracle at Delphi speak. We saw her awaken from her sleep as many cycles of silence were broken open. Sisters, for many cycles we women have been Seers, Cassandras, Sibyls, Oracles, Visionaries, and Muses who have read the codes of the planet and seen the possibilities of what could or might be. There was a time when men sought our counsel on matters of worth and heeded it. The silencing of this voice, the voice of the Goddess herself, is devastating, it is no less than the rift that has torn asunder the very fabric of our human Being and the planet herself. We feel the effects on our Mother Earth, on our Beloveds, and on our communities in this moment."

"Sisters, the words of the Goddess are known to all of us for we carry her words inside our bones, in our very breath. Let us listen deeply to the silence and from this depth give voice to the Mother Earth herself!"

I am shaking. All eyes are upon me. I bow low, my hands over my heart. I am about to sit down when I begin to shudder violently. My morpho markings are wildly fluctuating, pulsing

across my skin. I hear multiple harmonic tones and see fields of diamond lattice geometries that appear to connect everyone in the space. Infinite stars appear above me and inside me. The room spins. Gasps and words of the priestesses around me echo across the room yet sound so far away.

"She is erupting."

"She is exploding."

"Is this the work of Dominique's alchemy?"

I am the flower, erupting and blooming. My body is shifting, and my skin changes tone:

It is activating again. The shifting and changing of forms. My whole body is tingling and exploding as I begin to dance in the center of the circle. The ancient ecstatic dance. I hear and feel the rhythm of my sisters chanting around me.

I see my hands touch the stars as my feet dance on earth, to my left side is the Sun, to my right the Moon. The skin, the bodies, and forms of all women, short and fat, tall and slim, young and old, of all ethnicities, colors, and races flow through me like a stream. They fall from me like falling veils. My heart pulses open. I am movement and I am the stillness. Shakti and Shiva.

Later many sisters will tell me what they saw.

Each priestess saw her own face and the faces of those they love, as I danced. In that moment I was dancing the Goddess taking all forms. Some sisters say they saw faces of our plant, animal, and mineral kin flowing through my body. Some say that—for a moment—I was the stars and the Earth itself.

As I dance, I remember all these forms. I am One with these forms. For a moment there is no separation.

Finally I collapse to the ground. The last thing I remember is Rhea's voice.

"Thank you. Lila Sophia. I am with you, darling. We are with you. Dominique's sacrifices have been justified."

Then there is only darkness.

CHAPTER
FORTY-TWO

We are the culmination of our actions, a web of interconnected relationships through lifetimes, born of cause and effect.

Gaia Codex: Node 34.21.853

"**L**ILA SOPHIA." SOMEONE is trying to wake me.

I recognize the voice whispering in my ear. It is male—deep and velvet.

"Sophia."

I try to open my eyes. Once. Twice. Three times. When I am finally successful, I am not in my room at the Château Lumiere but rather in a deep jungle of the most vibrant luminous greens.

I turn around, and he is here. He is muscled and strong. His chest is bare.

His dark eyes, in moments black, then blue, and then the clearest of greens, gaze on me, taking me in. He is so familiar to me, so deeply known. There is attraction, desire, and the unknown of the Mystery.

"Theo." His name slips from my lips like water that flows to meet the sea.

Yes, I want to know you. I want to touch you and taste you. I want to feel your flesh and taste your spirit. I am startled at the ferocity of my thoughts and blush deep.

"May I show you something?" His hand softly on my cheek startles me and turns my body to honey. I slowly nod in acquiesce and then there is a flow of images:

I see a young man on a battlefield filled with standards and weapons I do not recognize. It seems to be long ago. The young man leads other men to battle. He leads them to death. I then see this same man himself near death. His spirit hovers over his body. Tears flow from his eyes, tears for all that was destroyed under his command in this distant land. The rivers run with blood. Houses are burned to the ground. Women were raped. Children brutally slaughtered, and he, this young man, is responsible. They had been fighting for him, for his glory, his throne, for his wealth and riches. This man—now filled with tears of regret—is approached by an older man in robes, a seer or a wizard, a sage or a yogi. The older man leads the younger one off the field of death. Years, decades, maybe centuries pass. The young man is in the forest, in the cave, on a mountaintop, where he is in prayer, making a promise, a vow to the stars above. Light comes down into the man. Finally, he is walking into the forest until he appears to be absorbed by the trees.

Theo is no longer touching me. The images have stopped.

I then look back into his eyes. "Is this you?" I ask.

"I want you to know my past," he says quietly. I feel my desire rise. His scent—fresh like the forest, deep like Mother Earth herself—permeates my skin.

Then, in a move that startles me, Theo pulls back his skin.

His organs are clogged with tumors. His veins are clogged like so many rivers and streams of Mother Earth. *He shows me this again.*

Standing here, tears begin to fall from my eyes, and my heart breaks open.

I bend down to kiss the rotting flesh. Just for a moment. It is the only thing I know to do.

I have such a deep desire to heal him—to heal us. I know, intuitively, if he is in pain.

I am in pain. Our Earth, our Mother, is in pain.

Theo says nothing but smiles and then pulls his skin back over the wounds.

"Thank you Goddess, thank you, Ma," he says softly. "You must prepare, Sophia," he adds, "for our meeting in the flesh is not yet certain." His voice is strong, and when I look at him, he is again muscled and brown, standing in the shadows of dappled green trees.

"Theo," I ask slowly. "Why have you chosen me?"

He says nothing, but takes me close. I feel his heart beating and I hear my heart loud in my chest. My heart grows warm, soft, and fills with light.

He is silent for some time as I simply feel our hearts opening, deepening, and pulsing.

This is his answer. I feel him so deeply.

"Your heart is strong, Sophia," he finally says.

"There is something I want to give you." Theo reaches around his neck and unties a rough flax cord upon which hangs a talisman of polished ruby stone. It is in the glyph form of a woman holding an extravagant luscious blossom in the cradle of her womb. "It is meant for you. A female shaman of the Hriya, a tribe in the Amazon, gave it to me. It will help protect you and perhaps answer your question. May I?" he asks.

I nod my head as Theo reaches up to place the talisman around my neck. He lifts my mass of curls so the nape of my neck is exposed and then ties the talisman around it.

In some cultures, the nape of a woman's neck is considered one of the most tender, most sensual points of the body. As his fingers touch my neck, deep pleasure moves through my body.

As I slowly open my eyes, I still smell the scents of the rainforest, but I am back in my bed at the Château Lumiere. Tightly clutched in my hands is the ruby glyph that Theo had just given me in the dream.

How can it be? I hold it up to the light and feel its texture in my hand. I trace my fingers around the blossom and the womb and the rough flax string is around my neck.

It is here, and it is real.

I bring the totem close to my heart and a prayer that came to me many months back falls off my lips:

Soon I will awaken, and I will clasp and grasp for some talisman, made of bone, made of stone, to carry from one world to the next.

This time I will remember.

This time I won't forget.

I can't forget.

In this moment I know. I know that I have loved, and I have died before; that the Beloved has laid me in my grave and that I, in turn, have given my life for them. I have been the Beloved and the forsaken. I have used beauty for power. I have sold my body for others' pleasure and freely given my heart without promise

of return. I have offered my flesh to the wild beast so it would not starve—out of a love that springs forth from deep compassion. I have partaken in rites of rejuvenation and renewal as a priestess to the King and as Queen to the priest. I have been a mother giving up my Life out of love for my child. I have died in my Mother's arms. I have lived sweet lives together with my sister-priestesses when my heart has flowered ten thousand petals. I have crossed oceans and lifetimes to be with the man who was the Sun to my Moon, the Shiva to my Shakti. I have loved. I have practiced these arts for many lifetimes and on this morning, I remember. I am humbled in this knowing. As golden light streams into the room, I fall to my knees, my head touching the floor in front of the altar of the Mother, she who holds the Orb of the Earth deep in fullness of her Belly.

On this morning, I am no longer the child. I am no longer the one who has forgotten that deepest knowing within the web of all life and connection.

There is a light knock, and Rhea enters.

She doesn't say anything but comes over and lies down beside me.

We touch foreheads as her hands hold my cheeks.

"So it has started," she finally says, glancing at the Blossom totem around my neck.

"Does this mean something to you?" I hold the totem up to a shaft of sunlight.

"It represents the GEA flower of the Hriya. The Consort has chosen you for the great rite that turns the worlds." Rhea answers.

"I don't feel fully ready," I reply.

"You will be ready when it is time." Rhea rolls over on the bed and holds me. I feel her deep tenderness, her softness, and her strength.

"I don't want to leave you," I sigh as I nestle into her arms.

"Through the cycles, sometimes it is you, my love and sometimes it is one of our other sister-priestesses who takes part in the rite of Hieros gamos—the rite that turns the worlds. We do it by free will and choice, and we do it to serve the well-being of all Life."

I roll over and look deep into the eyes of my sister-priestess. Our bodies match like two stems of the same flower. Two snakes intertwined into one. The *pingala* and *ida*.

"What about you?" I ask. The words tumble out of my mouth.

"You and I have loved each other for a very long time," Rhea replies.

Her lips brush softly across mine. I feel the flutter of her eyelashes on my cheek.

"I feel the essence of our love, throughout all the different forms. No matter when we meet. No matter who you are," she says.

"There is nothing to lose here. No choice to make. We are never separated, sister." In her arms I feel safe, warm, and held. In her arms, I feel whole. As Rhea and I hold each other, my fingers play with the carved blossom totem Theo gave me. I know I must be with him. Humans are complex creatures.

I sleep for some time and then wake up again. Rhea is still here. Half awake I let my hand run across her skin and then my own,

but as I do, I let out a small yelp. My skin is scarred, blistered, and covered with open sores.

Rhea opens her eyes. She does not seem surprised. "I see," she says quietly.

"What is this?" I ask, panicked, sitting up in the bed. I am naked, but I pull the sheets and blankets around me to hide my deformities.

Rhea leans over and softly kisses a sore, and as she does, it turns into soft pink healed flesh. Although this is not unlike my dream of Theo, I am still startled.

"Lila, you are taking on the wounds of all women, our sisters through the ages, taking them into your body to be transformed. This is the first step toward being able to heal Theo and our collective human DNA. This is what you want, isn't it?"

I nod my head slowly. *True, but I did not imagine this.* Tears run down my face. Suddenly, I am in too much pain.

Rhea takes me in her arms. "You will learn to use the gifts you have been given, Lila. Give it time."

So this is Dominique's legacy. And then it is clear to me. *This is my vow and fate.* Suddenly I feel as heavy as a mountain and I wonder if I will ever be able to move again.

CHAPTER
FORTY-THREE

To take poison and transform it into an elixir is the
essence of the healer's alchemy.

Gaia Codex: Node 32.65.143

I GAZE INTO THE mirror.

So this is my body—at least for now.

I am female, and I am covered with scars. My face is burned and blistered, barely recognizable. One of my arms hangs loose, deformed. My back is hunched and humped. Green snot falls periodically from my nose, and I am frequently coughing up blood. One eye is swollen shut and I only have straggly wisps of hair. Faintly upon my grey, scaly, lifeless skin, I can still see the morpho markings.

This corpse, this hag, this is who Rhea held so sweetly the night before.

What would Theo think?

Would he understand?

I sigh, but even this only comes out as a haggard cough of green and yellow snot.

"She has been given this body by the Goddess so she can heal the wounds that the feminine of our species have endured for millennia." The woman who speaks is a tiny Indian woman wrapped in a crisp white sari. Her name is Prabhuta. Her eyes gaze intent on me as she sits in lotus, slowly rocking back and forth.

"Yes, if Dominique is correct, the morpho markings and your DNA may have the potential to create a panacea to heal not only physical wounds but also emotional wounds. Lila, if you are able to do this, it has the potential, over time, to be a medicine that can be passed into the genetics of the human species," Rhea says gently.

"Listen to Rhea, Lila Sophia," Prabhuta says. "She has been around longer than any of us."

There are tears running down my face. I will admit they are partly for myself. I am so uncomfortable. I hate being so ugly. And I feel the billions of women throughout time who have suffered. Their voices tell me their stories. I feel their pains in my body. This is so much more intense than when I was with Old Woman. It is excruciating.

"Yes," I say faintly, "this is close to my understanding so far." I had opened Dominique's manuscript earlier this morning. It opened to a single page that simply said:

The panacea that heals the deep wounds of humanity will be found in the body of the Vessel of the Goddess. It is through her great compassion for every human being that a true healing will arise.

"Breathe," Prabhuta commands. "The in-breath and out-breath connect everything."

"Listen to the wisdom of your DNA and the morpho markings," Rhea says as she touches one of my open sores. As she does, the skin again turns a soft pink. "It can only be done with an open heart and a clear mind," she adds.

"How do you know how to do this?" I ask.

"Many priestesses have learned different aspects of deep healings, which we share with our brothers and sisters. I have had a lot of time to study and learn," Rhea answers.

I have heard whispers amongst my sister-priestesses about my beloved Rhea. They say she is ancient—older than all of us—although she never ages.

"Lila, at the moment you are the alembic, where our collective alchemy and magic is happening. We are all here with you," Rhea says.

"And Madame Belefonte …" I ask.

Rhea sighs. "Helene is waiting to see if you succeed or not. Like all of us, we are listening to the larger movements here on our Mother Earth. For something to be born, something must die. Best not to be attached."

I don't know whether Rhea is talking about my life or the future of human beings here on the Earth. I focus on breathing in and out. It is the only peace I have, for I feel like I will faint again from the collective pain of women through the ages—my sisters—the screams and wails that fill my ears, and unspeakable, heart wrenching visions.

Mother, give me guidance. I implore silently.

To my surprise, Rhea answers my silent query.

"She is, Lila, and she will."

CHAPTER
FORTY-FOUR

It is said that the many lifetimes of every soul are inscribed in the Gaia Codex. Here we see the record of every priestess, every man, every woman, every creature who has ever lived.

The story of Rhea Sahar winds through the records of our Mother Earth for tens of thousands of years. They say she never ages, that she remembers all she has seen. Is she a goddess? Is she human? Sometimes the two are one and the same—souls who have vowed to complete certain tasks bound to a planet as it moves through the cycles of time. Those like her are often great teachers who appear in human form so that they may walk simply amongst the people. For a human who lives only a hundred years at most, a creature such as Rhea appears immortal. Yet Rhea Sahar will also pass when her work is done.

So what are the tasks of Rhea Sahar? She appears in human cultures as needed. She brings gifts of civilization and awakening. She helps build whole human beings

and healthy communities where and when she can.
She imparts knowledge of healing medicines, gifts of
agriculture and wild crafting, how to weave warm
blankets and build strong but simple houses. She teaches
the wisdom of the elements and the stars, and she shares
the creation stories so they are not forgotten. She comes
in a form neither old nor young. She is always a woman.
Sometimes she is hidden. Sometimes she is a visible leader.
Her loves of the Heart have been men and women. She is
divine and human: of stars and of earth. She is known for
her kindness and compassion. Some say she will be here
when the last humans leave Terra Gaia, Mother Earth,
but that may be only legend.

Gaia Codex: Node 444.854.21

CHAPTER

FORTY-FIVE

Every human being has the potential to be a Living
Treasure, a repository of wisdom, knowledge and
teaching, to share the fruit not only of what is learned in a
single life, but also what has been taught by those teachers
and ancestors who have come before. In many cultures
such elders are revered both for holding the records of
the people and those of the Earth herself. Knowledge is
passed on through oral stories and through apprenticeship
and practice. When cultures lose this art of lineage
transmission and the generational continuity is broken,
the Priestesses of Astera vow to continue the transmission
of knowledge. So that future generations do not forget.

Gaia Codex: Node 3321.0413.98

I N THE DAYS that follow many of the women join
into smaller groups to share knowledge and teachings:
indigenous mothers from the Tlingit tribes of the Pacific
Northwest, from the Igbo from West Africa, and from the Sami

from Lapland tell us their creation stories and demonstrate how instructions for living in resonance with Mother Earth are encoded into these stories.

We are instructed in the ancient birthing rites that are shown to young women who hope to be mothers and also to the women who will be tending to the birth of new culture and new Life in the wake of a civilization passing.

Prayers and vision circles are held for our Mother Earth—for her waters, her plants, and her animals. Prayers are made for healing the sickness in our family lines, for each of us carries pain that can run back for generations. Offering these pains to the Mother can release generations of sorrow. Prayers are made for the male part of ourselves—for our brothers, husband, and grandfathers—those who are with us and those who have come before. We honor those who for thousands of years have lived close to the land, for they help us remember.

As I participate, moving feebly through the halls of the Château Lumiere, my sisters greet me.

Some come up to me with tears, saddened by my grotesque transformations. Others lay their hands on me and share their knowledge and learning of healing. Some hang back and just watch from afar.

"It is too frightening for some of the women," Rhea says about those who are hesitant. "They haven't yet come to terms with our capacity to harm one another, or else they are afraid of death, sickness, and ugliness."

"I am afraid of ugliness," I answer glumly. Some days are easy and some are hard, but with each woman's input, I am learning and remembering how to heal the wounds.

"Turn the poison into honey," Rhea whispers in my ear, "I see your beauty."

In the first days, because I can't walk, I am wheeled around by Gemma. As we tour the gardens, the libraries, and the spacious courtyards, she sings verses of exquisite poetry to me and the words work their way inside my cells. Her voice has many textures and tones; it evokes landscapes of cool mountain streams, long dead queens, and goddesses who take on human form.

"These are my medicines for you, for us, sister. I have been learning them for generations so that I can bring them to you now," Gemma says.

"Who wrote these songs? I ask.

"They flow through in the moment as needed. A gift of the Muses and the Goddess," Gemma answers. She is not afraid to touch my skin, to massage my limbs when they are sore, or seal my open wounds with herbal balms.

Madame Belefonte is nowhere to be seen, although I feel her watching me from a distance. I have not for a moment forgotten her challenge. As the days pass, I reach deeper into myself to access the core of my genetic mutations. At first it is not easy because pain overrides everything. Not merely the physical pain—a sorrow as well that seems to have no end. I know now that it is not only my own pain, but it still feels very personal. *In-breath and out-breath.*

The morpho markings teach me—their pulses and flashes release specific chemical mixtures and rhythmic vibrations, emit certain sounds and colors, all directed towards the wounds. As each heals, I receive a vision of a woman, child, or man, a tree, a river, an eagle, or a bear that was wounded, destroyed, or tortured. Slowly, day-by-day, I begin to recover.

In many moments I think of Theo as I finger the ruby pendant on my neck. I cannot say I love him more or less than Rhea. My heart is open. I have been told that Theo is my duty, my obligation, but I am also driven by passion for him. I desire him in ways that words cannot express. I desire his maleness to make me whole.

It is you who are the completion. I whisper into the night and wonder if Theo hears me, wherever he might be.

CHAPTER
FORTY-SIX

Civilizations rise and fall. This we know. Many disappear without trace. There are points where the fate of humanity on our Mother Earth was in question, when the species exhibited tendencies pointing toward either extinction or rapid mutation. By all accounts humanity was on a rapid path to collapse in the early to middle of the twenty-first century (by the Gregorian calendar). Overconsumption of resources, an exponentially increasing population, massive and rapid destruction of ecosystems, and the loss of cultural wisdom, knowledge, and grassroots survival skills built up over generations— these were all indicators of the devastation to come.

When collapse came, it exploded in a chain reaction. Potable water became scarce. The energy sources that ran communication systems were no longer accessible. The infrastructure of the global economy imploded. People had forgotten how to grow their own food. There was hunger and fighting over what meager resources remained. You could no longer see the sun at midday because of toxins in the air. Disease proliferated.

System collapse is Death—or a doorway to transformation and evolution. The Priestesses of Astera have trained for millennia to be prepared for the Great Turning. We know we can only move forward together— with each sister offering her Gifts to help those in need and in dedication to planting and nourishing the seeds of those new civilizations being born. This does not ensure success. Species die, ecosystems collapse, and planets wither until they can no longer sustain Life. As Priestesses of Astera, we are bound to turn prayer into action.

Gaia Codex: Node 009.321.45

CHAPTER
FORTY-SEVEN

The Sixty-Four Arts—the trainings that a Priestesses of Astera cultivates over lifetimes—are designed to create a whole woman anchored in heart, spirit, body, and mind in equal proportion.

The Sixty-Four Arts of the Priestesses of Astera include such skills as archery, wild crafting, gardening, weaving, architectural design, sacred geometry, diplomacy, culinary arts, mathematics, poetry, storytelling, fashion, aesthetics, painting, drawing, music, commerce, the arts of love, astronomy, alchemy, the arts of birth and death, the transmigration of souls, the arts of memory and muse, metallurgy, shapeshifting, the arts of language, the art of perfumes, the art of time, time travel, the embodiment and emanations of the Goddess, the arts of sound and vibration, knowledge of the bestiary of Life, the creation of cultures, the creation of worlds, and how to navigate and access to the Gaia Codex.

Gaia Codex: Node 444.321.8671

DAYS POUR INTO weeks. Many sisters have stayed, and many have left. At night visions of starving children, of fish dying in the sea by the hundreds of thousands, and of yellow pollution choking the air and trees fill our collective dreams. We all feel the impending changes. We are preparing for what is to come.

I am able to walk now and I have been able to heal many of my wounds. I feel different and yet the same, as though each cell in my body has been replaced with something new, vibrant, and alive—and indeed it is so. This has been part of the process. In moments there are flashes of who I was before: the lonely young girl torn apart by the death of her parents. I think of Old Woman. *I would not be here without you. Thank you, Old Woman.* Like me, some of the priestesses have received her teachings. They call her the Weaver, Spider Woman, or simply Old Woman. I find that each of my sister-priestesses, depending on her individual path and purpose, has had different mentors to guide her, just as each of us in turn will mentor other girls and women. With each meeting and conversation with my sisters I am finding a deep kinship and each story and exchange of laughter and tender secrets reminds me that I have been a part of these women, these Priestesses of Astera, for many lifetimes. This is part of the healing. We are not alone.

"Lila!" Gemma comes up to me. "Madame Belefonte wants me to show you how we train each other in the Sixty-Four Arts."

Madame Belefonte is thinking of me.

"I am coming," I reply aloud.

Gemma leads us back into the Château, through a series

of courtyards filled with fountains, lush ferns, young girls, and women.

"With the current collapse we have more and more women and girls arriving here at our temple," Gemma says. As we look into the courtyards I see that most of the women and girls appear under twenty. Many, especially those who have just arrived look malnourished. Although their faces are gaunt and their clothes tattered, there is fire, Life, and intelligence in their eyes. I feel their passion to change the tide—to turn the outcome of what human choice and action has rendered in our world—for it is my own.

"Some of the girls have been sent by their mothers, grand-mothers, or aunties who remember the old ways. Many are here with us in a lucid dream state," Gemma says as she points in the direction of a few young women. "See how their bodies appear to slightly ripple at the edges? That is how you can tell they are here in the Dreaming. It allows many women and girls to train here at the Château even if they cannot physically travel here."

"Useful," I respond.

"Yes, very," Gemma concurs. "We train those who are here through the Dreaming so that they can retain and bring back what they have learned to their communities in the daytime. Some skills are essential to survival—like how to grow food on the land, use herbs for healing, and find clean water. We also train these girls and women in the ways of our lineage—our magic and our technologies—so that over time they can lead their communities as visionaries, artists, leaders, and healers. Our intent is to awaken and connect as many women as possible into the Gaia Codex as everything collapses."

"Gemma, do you feel that time is running out?" I ask.

"Yes." Gemma's face is uncharacteristically grim as she says this.

It is true. We all feel the heaviness. At times it is an unbearable pain.

I place my hands over my heart as we pass the girls. Many smile. Others feign indifference but shyly follow us with their eyes when they think we are not looking.

"Sister, good to see you." A tall Nubian girl who is probably sixteen or seventeen looks directly at me. Her voice is lucid and clear, but her lips don't move.

"Good to see you too." I reply without moving my lips.

I notice she has the ripple that indicates that she is here in the Dreaming.

"I am glad you remember the old ways of communicating—directly through the mind. It is useful in these times."

"It is," I answer again, transmitting through the silent connection.

"It is getting very tense at the moment," she continues. As she says this, she flashes images to me. I see them clearly in my mind. A young woman taken away from her home has been brutally raped and beaten. Tens of thousands of people are moving across dust-ridden plains. There are bodies and carcasses everywhere, both human and animal. Fires burn.

"This is my life when I am awake," she says quietly.

My eyes fill with tears. "I am sorry. Thank you for everything you are doing."

"It helps to know we are working together, sister," the Nubian sister replies aloud. Her spoken voice is rich and beautiful. "We have had to come into our womanhood early, you and I, and so many others."

Gemma has been watching the exchange, and she bows low to the Nubian girl as we walk away. "She is an old soul. Sixteen years old but an old soul. She has incarnated with her people for generations and has been a Priestess of Astera for tens of thousands of years. There are many like her and each of us has different gifts to offer," Gemma adds as we look out into the courtyard where the Sixty-Four Arts are being practiced.

As we walk through the halls and witness these girls and women so deeply engaged, the extent of our trainings of come back to me, these trainings that we priestesses engage in over multiple lifetimes, the Sixty-Four Arts.

"Seeing the Sixty-Four Arts in action helps me remember my own trainings," I say quietly. As Gemma and I walk through the courtyards and rooms, we see girls and women teaching and learning a range of practices. Girls with hand-carved birch bows work on the art of archery—a skill that trains both the body and mind; others view the constellations under a cobalt blue dome, tracking their movements through time and space at different latitudes. Some draw designs for tools, machines, and architecture, while others create stunning gowns made of cloth they have dyed and woven by hand. Women and girls are learning the languages of various animals—the color changes of the giant squid or the chatter of ravens or how geese learn to form perfect formation in flight without speaking.

Others recite and act out the ancient creation stories of Earth and her many cultures. Some teach and learn the healing arts of herbs and vibrations. Girls and women learn how to make themselves invisible, or how to call forth the elements of earth, wind, fire, and water. Some practice how to track the soul through incarnations—through birth and death; others learn how to embody different qualities and manifestations of the Goddess—Tara, Aphrodite, Lakshmi, Kali, and Spider Woman.

Woven through all of this is each woman's deep connection to the scintillating web of the life, the Gaia Codex itself, for this is our constant teacher. This is how we carry the seeds through the generations.

My own training in the Sixty-Four Arts in the temples and in the Dreaming comes back to me. I have been practicing this for thousands of years. I know it with certainty. Like so many of my sister-priestesses, I am both ancient and newborn. Mortal and yet a voice, an embodiment of the Goddess who sustains us through the cycles of Birth and Death. My heart sings, I am thankful to remember.

CHAPTER
FORTY-EIGHT

What is another person but a part of our soul we have yet to meet?

Gaia Codex: Node 3333.451

I AM ALMOST COMPLETELY healed. To celebrate, Rhea and I finally spend a day together, just the two of us, walking through the woods, listening to the buzz of bees, eating sweet apples from the trees, practicing archery in the meadow, and collecting late season gooseberries to bring back for Cook to make into pies, tarts, and cobblers. Rhea begins to tell me more about herself: stories of carving glyphs in Mayan ruins and testing calculations of the long and short count calendars; of sitting naked, covered only with ashes and sandalwood paste with sadhus on the river Ganges, creating poems of ecstasy in the time of Kabir and Mirabai; or sitting on the matrilineal councils of the Iroquois Nation when the eastern coast of America was still covered with trees. She tells me of weaving baskets in Neolithic villages by what is now called the river Po and tales of many lives through the thousand of years of Egypt.

"And there have been so many times, dear Lila, when you and I have been together as sisters and friends," Rhea says.

"… and as Beloveds," I say softly as I lay back into the sweet grass, for as Rhea speaks of these places, they come to life inside me, and what was once lost becomes mine once more—memories that we shared, memories that were also my own.

"… and as Beloveds, Lila Sophia," Rhea says as she kisses me gently on the lips.

Part of me could stay with her forever. On this day, everything else fades away. We fall naturally into each other's arms—our fingers running through each other's hair.

I pull at her gently.

"Come with me," I whisper into her ears. I long for her softness around me.

Our foreheads touch, and I feel our breath intermingling. "I am with you even when we are apart. There is no need for you to forget." she whispers in my ear. I open my eyes and look into her eyes. They are so deep—she has seen many ages and she has remembered.

After lying there feeling the earth under our backs and breathing the blueness of the sky above, Rhea gets up. "I have one more thing I want to show you."

We walk back to the Château. Entering though a side door, we walk up a small marble flight of stairs, and across a small atrium. Rhea knocks on the copper-plated door. When there is no answer, we enter.

At first the room appears to be a music room filled with elegant harp-like instruments inset with crystals. There are also

crystal orbs set into various gold, silver, and copper geometrical sculptures.

On the walls there are paintings of women playing these instruments. The paintings are in that distinctive style of art I have seen throughout the Château Lumiere, that shows life either in the future or perhaps a parallel line of earthly cultural development—a world where my sisters and other kindred clans live in the open and have developed a rich, abundant culture that flourishes in harmony with our Mother Earth. As I look closer, I see that some of the instruments are familiar and similar to designs I had sketched as child in my notebooks.

"Would you like to try one of the instruments?" Rhea asks.

I nod and pick up an eight-stringed harp with a mobius spine. There are crystals placed at each of the frets. I pluck a few of the strings, and they make a beautiful sound. Each note plucked causes a shift of vibration in the space around us and seems for a moment to shape and transform the material objects in the room.

"How does it work? "I ask.

"It's a Mobian," Rhea answers. "Its one of our multipurpose instruments used to reshape matter. It is also a healing tool and provides a beautiful accompaniment for storytelling. It is quite magical when played by someone with mastery or a deep intuition of how to use the instrument. It works with the spaces between imagination and actualization, between vibrational pulse and material form. It is one of the technologies that the Priestesses of Astera are dedicated to bringing to our Mother Earth. Although all this takes time."

Those who play the harp also transpose the texture of

reality with subtle vibration. In cultures now forgotten
the harp's frequencies were coupled with the frequencies
of different gemstones and crystals and then aligned
with thought and spoken incantations to transform the
appearance and structure of matter.

Gaia Codex: Node 4445.981

"Here." Rhea pulls a book off the shelf and hands it to me. Inside are sketches of numerous technologies that are elegant and organic in their design.

Rhea plucks one of the harps as she speaks.

"We priestesses are antennae for beneficial gifts for our world. We serve as creators, inventors, and artists, as well as muses who plant the seeds in those who are skilled to implement the visions. Our sisters have been creating and using these technologies for many cycles in our temples. A central feature of our technologies is that they create a 'zero point' use of energy: in essence they operate without drawing upon excess natural resources. What energies these technologies use, they give back in equal measure. One the great tragedies of our time has been that the material resources of our Mother Earth have been depleted in order to build and run our civilizations. We see this as a design flaw."

"So why haven't these technologies been released out into the wider culture?" I ask.

"There is an art to the release of these technologies. If they are shared before the general population is ready, one might be

burned at the stake or people are simply unable to comprehend their use."

I pluck a note on the Mobian. This time I also let my five fingers gently rest over the crystal frets. A different vibration runs through each one; together they create a harmonic chord that runs through my body in a frequency loop. This is the key. My body is working as a second resonator to ground the energy and to create the mobius.

I still have a small open cut on my hand. In my mind's eye I can see a spectrum of events through time—my hand cut open and the cut fully healed. I softly slide along the spectrum as I adjust the Mobian's harmonic and concentrate the vibration. As I do, the cut is healed.

"This is so elegant," I say as I put the instrument down.

"Not everyone picks it up so quickly. You have a gift for such things," Rhea smiles.

I reminisce again on my innate knowing of technologies, the sketches filling my notebooks, the dreams of what could be—so different from the world I had been born into—and yet, right there on the tip of memory.

"This technology could be useful for healing Theo," Rhea adds

My hand instinctively goes down to his talisman on my belly. Rhea gazes at me gently.

"The heart is ever flowering, Lila, and when we connect with the Heart of the Goddess, it is infinite in its dimensions." Rhea puts her hand onto my heart, and I feel the pulse and flow. "Let your heart guide you, but also use your perception, your knowing, your discernment, and intellect. Remember that our prayer as a priestess is always for the outcome that benefits the most Beings. This means that even though Theo may be the one you most desire, over all things, you must also fully let go of all attachment to him. Before you can enter his chambers—release everything. Many of the priestesses have partaken in such rites," Rhea says softly. "It is a deep offering to Life and helps ensure fertility and well-being."

"Have you been with Theo?" I ask tentatively.

"No," she says softly. "The connection between your soul and Theo's soul is a unique love. It is your path."

I put the Mobian gently down. "And you and I?" I ask shyly.

Rhea stares ahead as though she is looking at something far away that only she can see.

Finally she speaks, "You will make the right choices, Lila. Remember that you have a deep wisdom that you have earned through many lifetimes. Draw upon this deep well. It is your birthright. Such choices are not always an either or, Lila. Remember this." Rhea kisses me on my cheek, runs her fingers through my hair, and then, without looking back, leaves me alone in the room.

CHAPTER
FORTY-NINE

*To understand maya (the power of illusion and
transformation), to understand the transformative
mysteries of the Goddess Ceridwen, and to understand the
teaching of the ancient Gnostic text of the Nag Hammadi
Sophia is to understand that all matter is in a constant state
of mutation and all life forms are connected.*

*In every age some of the Priestesses of Astera are taught
the art of shapeshifting and transformation. Such teachings
are rare and beautiful—and they can be dangerous. Some
priestesses shapeshift as a feat of illusion, taking on a
temporary appearance that will trick the senses of those who
behold them, but there is said to be a deeper practice that
goes to the very essence of our genetic code. This practice,
much more rare, is said to have implications on the whole
genetic order of material creation. It is said that it can alter
our DNA and reroute the evolutionary code, irrevocably
changing what we are as human beings.*

Gaia Codex: Node 334.521

"LILA, COME WALK with me in the gardens." I jump. I haven't seen Madame Belefonte for weeks. *Why now?* I am startled and suddenly shy. Up close she does not appear physically tall. Petite and fine of bone, she is dressed in long robes of deep blue embroidered with what appear to be flowing vines bursting here and there into scarlet peonies along with hexagonal patterns like a honeycomb.

"Did I scare you?" Madame Belefonte asks.

"Yes," I laugh. Surprisingly, I am happy to see her.

The gardens of the Château Lumiere are manicured. There are curious topiaries: sacred geometry, griffins, a sphinx, and renditions of various goddesses. Diana the Huntress is here with her bow and dogs. Kali is over there with her lolling tongue and her necklace of *bīja*—Sanskrit seed syllables—and the heads of decapitated men. There is Xi Wangmu—the Taoist Queen Mother of the West—holding the peach of immortality. The topiary is surrounded by flowers of the purest white: moon-flower, evening primrose, angel trumpet, and night gladiola.

"These gardens are designed to best be enjoyed by the light of our Mother Moon. It is when the deities come alive," Madame Belefonte says as we walk deeper into the gardens. We are alone now, just her and I, walking the spiraled labyrinth. We stop at a bench deep in the center and sit down.

So this is it. My fate, the judgment decreed by Helene Belefonte. Both of us are silent for sometime until she finally speaks.

"Lila, I want to congratulate you. Your ability to heal the wounds you were afflicted with has convinced me that there is merit to this Metamorphosis Project. You were brave and correct to reveal yourself to your sisters, to reveal your abilities, your genetic mutation. It is a great gift. If it can be passed to the human population as a whole, it may help heal the relationship human beings have with the Mother Earth. This is what is needed."

As Madame Belefonte talks, my morpho markings begin to shimmer and pulse. Here at the Château Lumiere, the markings have become more nuanced—more sensitive in how they respond to different people and situations, to the wind and the sun, to the flow of information and ideas. As I meet my sisters from around the world, I feel my own DNA responding, I feel strands that resonate with each of these women who carry the genes of different races. I am human, yes, but also a hybrid.

"What made you change your mind about my mother's experiment?" I ask.

"Well, for one, I do not think that the current human DNA is strong enough (or wise enough) to withstand the devastation that humans have rendered on our Mother Earth," Madame Belefonte replies.

"What my morpho markings have shown me," I interject, "is that there has been a breakdown in the resiliency of the human DNA, generated by exposure to contaminated food and water. It is also the result of several generations who have consumed synthetic foods as their primary source of nutrition. Over generations, therefore, the basic building blocks of DNA have started to produce new and different types of RNA and a different range of predominate traits—but this can be reversed."

All of this has become so apparent to me over the last year. After absorbing the first shock of my changing forms under the watchful care of Old Woman and then taking in the teachings of the panacea, the medicine that can heal many forms of physical and emotional sufferings in our species, I have now settled into a subtle, nuanced engagement with the world through my morpho markings, which is accompanied by receptive genetic mutations in my DNA.

"Do your readings from the morpho markings come as information or sensation?" Madame Belefonte asks with interest.

"Both," I answer. "I can 'see' the mutations of the collective gene pool, but I also 'feel' them on my own skin through the marks."

Madame Belefonte looks at me with understanding and recognition. "Lila, my dear sister, you are an example of the Goddess who holds the world in the crucible of her body—the Anima Mundi, the Soul of the World." As Madame Belefonte gazes at me, I feel like she can see straight through my skin into my DNA itself. We both are perfectly still.

"I am very aware that it is the Goddess who works through me," I say quietly. "It would be very foolish to think that I own this power."

"That it would," Madame Belefonte says with a smile. "The vibration of your DNA helixes are strange, beautiful, and something I have not seen before. I also feel that that the Metamorphosis Project may be of merit because many humans have forgotten how to directly connect with the many life forms present here on Mother Earth. Our ancestors knew the importance of this: they honored animal and plant totems in their ritual and daily life—it ensured both their survival and their ability to evolve synergistically with the planet. Much of the human population today has lost any connection to nature."

"This is what I have discovered," I add.

Madame Belefonte turns and looks at me. "Lila, if the DNA

you are generating can fluidly link and embody adaptive features of different species, then it may also create a deeper connection with all life at a visceral level within the DNA itself. Do think this might be possible?"

"From what I am experience through the morpho markings, this seems to be what is happening," I answer quietly. I am so happy to be discussing these matters with Madame Belefonte. It is a sweet fresh wind.

"Your mother, Dominique, first shared with me the possibilities for the Metamorphosis experiment before she met your father."

"Really?" I asked, surprised.

"Yes," Madame Belefonte answers. In her eyes I see the wistfulness, the longing for that which has passed. "Dominique was obsessed with the myth of Ceridwen. You remember the story don't you?"

"A little," I answer.

Madame Belefonte continues, "Ceridwen is an ancient Celtic Goddess of birth, death, poetry, alchemy, and transformation. She wanted to give her son Afagdu a gift of wisdom, poetry, and divine insight. And so for a year, every day she mixed six herbs in her magical cauldron. Helping her was a boy, Gwion. A few drops of the magical elixir fell onto his fingers. It was hot so he placed his fingers into his mouth and immediately was given insight to all things in the world, as well as the past, present, and future. In fear of the anger of the Goddess Ceridwen, Gwion ran away, for he had received the essence of this magic elixir meant for her son, and he had seen a vision of her wrath. He turned himself into a hare, and then Ceridwen became a greyhound in hot pursuit. He then became a trout and jumped into a river. She turned into an otter. He turned into a sparrow, and she became a hawk. Finally, he turned into a single grain of corn. The goddess then became a hen and ate him."

"In some stories it is said that Ceridwen and Gwion exhaust all the forms of creation before Gwion is finally swallowed by the Goddess and is finally reborn as the beautiful child who becomes the bard Taliesin and whose words spin worlds and heal the wounds of the world. Dominique felt these ancient myths and stories hold formulas for magic and science, codes for how to live on our planet, when we know how to dissect them."

Madame Belefonte and I have walked out of the maze and now are sitting on a marble bench by a lake of the clearest cobalt blue, where three black and three white swans circle round each other.

"The story also gives an example of how humans can adopt the traits of other species," I add.

"This is what your mother believed as well." Madame Belefonte says.

"So …" I begin slowly. "The tale of Ceridwen is an alchemical formula for biogenetic transformation. Gwions's changing forms show the potential outcomes in terms of genetic adaptability. The child becomes an example of our evolutionary potential."

"Elegantly explained," Madame Belefonte smiles. "I see your mother in you, Lila. Her mind worked like yours."

"She was my teacher," I reply. I am enjoying Madame Belefonte's company. As we speak there are flashes of insight into our connection through time. She is no stranger to me. This makes me happy.

"Madame Belefonte …" I look deep into her eyes, her wise and ancient eyes. "How old are you?"

Madame Belefonte laughs. "My age is no great secret, at least within the walls of the Château Lumiere. I was born a thousand years before the age of Romans into a priestess clan in the great Hercynian Forest. I appear to you like this," Madame Belefonte waves her hand over her form, "only through the benefit of glamour, or *gramarye* as the ancient Scots might say—magic, enchantment, spell—or the illusion, maya, as they say in Sanskrit. As you may know, if I cross the boundaries of the Château Lumiere, I and my *gramaryre* will dissolve."

"Why?" I ask.

Madame Belefonte laughs. "I am not a true alchemist, Lila, not one who works with the transformation of material matter. I am only an illusionist. I am able to weave spells here on these grounds because I have mastered the manipulation of a specific frequency of matter. The walls of this temple and of my own body resonate at this frequency. Matter is more fluid in this spectrum and much more easily shaped by mind and imagination. Most importantly, this has allowed the Château Lumiere to remain hidden for thousands of years, even though we are in one of the largest cities in the world."

"You have provided a refuge for so many of us," I say, looking into her face. Helene's face is enchanting. Every time you look into her eyes, you feel you are seeing a new fascinating feature or nuance you did not notice before.

"Refuges have been needed in the past when women and priestesses were burned for their wisdom and craft," Madame Belefonte says quietly. "I have provided one of these refuges at the Château Lumiere as other of our sister-priestesses have at hidden temples around the world."

"Have you seen shapeshifters like me in the past?" I ask Helene.

Madame Belefonte smiles as she looks out to the black and white swans making graceful patterns on the lake. "In my childhood, in the Hercynian Forest, I met more than one shapeshifter. In the tribes of my mother and grandmother we were in constant communion with other forms of life. This is how we survived. We believed that the animals, trees, and rocks dreamed us, and we dreamed them. We shared the Dreaming of both day and night. So yes, we learned to become the bear, the elk, and the stag. We had laws that would not let us take the life of one of these great creatures unless we had taken their shape in the Dreaming. The Château Lumiere is built with some of the arts that were taught to me by my mother's clan. Over the years I have met various masters and mistresses of shapeshifting, but what you, Dominique, and Raj have created with the Metamorphosis Project, if I understand it correctly, is different in that it seeks to align human beings with the original codes of the planet, while creating new strains of genetic adaptogens, which are responsive and in resonance with the original codes of the Mother Earth."

"I believe this was my parents' intention, and it is what I feel I have been experiencing." I answer. *Much has changed for me after our circle rites. It is as though I am embodying the lines of wisdom of my sisters and my parents deep inside of me. Their knowledge flows through me.*

"But I thought you felt my father was a bit of a scoundrel," I continue.

"Well, on one level he was. He stole your mother away from me. So yes, I consider him a scoundrel. Your father was ambitious. He was as much familiar with the dark as the light and

there is always a fine line in that game. If you search his soul in the Codex you will find that he made choices in the past that destroyed many lives and caused much devastation, but by the time he met your mother, he proclaimed that he had committed himself to using his brilliance in the service of Life. That was one of your mother's conditions. She would not leave with him until he made this vow and proved to her he was serious, and you, dear sister, you also demanded that Dominique make your father uphold these vows. It was one of your conditions. So I can't vouch for the purity of your father's promise, but I have seen both your mother and you fulfill your vows repeatedly. Even when it has been difficult to do so."

"So my mother wanted to leave?" I ask Madame Belefonte carefully.

"Yes … and she did." As Madame Belefonte says this, I can see her sadness. "Dominique started to have dreams of your father and a life that was different than what she and I were building here at the Château Lumiere. You know much of the Château Lumiere is also her design. Including the room you are sleeping in. She wanted it to be ready for you. She knew you would return here someday. She picked all the clothes, the furniture, everything."

"Has anyone else ever used the room?" I ask.

"Only you, Lila. Your mother loved you before you were her child—as her sister. You have always been a dear friend to all of us, Sophia, 'She who is the keeper of wisdom.'"

Sophia. Yes, I remember being called this name.

"I believe you will live true to your name in this life," Madame Belefonte adds. "Remember, we humans are always being tested on whether we will make wise, clear karmic choices. We are tested on this daily."

As Madame Belefonte and I sit in the garden with each other, with the lake, the swans, the sky, with all Life, I feel a deep communion with her. The Gaia Codex scintillates just beneath the surface, weaving its web of connection. Madame Belefonte pats my hand.

"We have missed you, Lila Sophia, It is no easy task to wait for someone you love to be born again and it is very hard to lose someone you love."

Again, I see the deep sadness in her eyes. *Her sorrow is for the loss of my mother. This is now very clear.* I gently take Helene's hand, and together, we watch the sun set into the most radiant of glows and for a moment she lets her head rest ever so gently on my shoulder.

CHAPTER
FIFTY

The past and the future are constantly being reshaped in the present.

Gaia Codex: Node 3321.531

THE CHÂTEAU LUMIERE has many rooms, hidden chambers, and secret alcoves. The trompe-l'œil is subtle and vibratory—giving the illusion that the interiors are endless. An archway into a garden resplendent with peacocks, dripping magnolia trees, and a statue of the Goddess Lakshmi might be a painting—or not. It is said that it is not at all uncommon for the Goddess, in her many forms, to reveal herself, often unexpectedly, within the walls of the Château.

Today I need to escape the thrall and the throng. There are now thousands of my sisters gathered, training and preparing for what is to come. I turn left and then right. Down a long corridor, up marble stairs, and through a series of carved wooden doors, each of which has the seal of a different animal—a lion, a snake, a falcon, a bear, a horse, a tiger, and a peacock—until I am in a part of the Château completely unfamiliar to me. I stop in front of a mahogany door with a single gold ring set into its center. I open the door and step into a circular rotunda. Inside the walls are covered floor-to-ceiling with a mural unfolding in cylindrical sequence. I exhale and then breathe in the calm and the silence.

The first panel shows women and girls planting golden, glowing seeds into fertile ground. In the next panel, the seeds have grown into trees with strong trunks and lush branches that cover vast expanses of land. The third panel consists of women, children, and men in brightly colored clothes harvesting the fruit of these trees; in the final panel, the women are feeding the fruit to children in sun-dappled forest glens. Again these women, as well as the children and men, all hail from the time-out-of-time that I have seen depicted in my mother's journal and through-out the Château Lumiere. They are women of many races. Their dress is a fusion of traditional dress from Asia, Europe, Africa, and South America. These are my sisters. Running along the bottom of the mural are the distinctive symbols and script of the Priestesses of Astera.

"So you have found one of the Circle of Life Paintings. There are thirteen in total." I jump. Rhea is standing next to me.

"I am surprised to see you here." I say as I turn around to look at her.

Rhea smiles.

"Beautiful," I murmur. The paintings are entrancing—they breathe.

"The Circle of Life paintings are also memory walls," Rhea continues. "They are both a record and a point of access to hidden histories and possible futures. It's hard to place these

paintings in time. They are part memory—and part deep longing for what can actually be. You could say it is part of our weaving and magic for Mother Gaia."

I can almost smell the sweetness of the pollen and hear the buzz of the bees.

"This is part of the mystery of the Circle of Life paintings," Rhea continues. "We priestesses weave possible futures for our life here on Terra Gaia, Mother Earth. The Circles of Life are one way to put these dreamings into motion in the world."

As she speaks, Rhea takes my hands. Back-to-back, we slowly turn to view the paintings. On deeper inspection there are more details: baskets of intricate weave and design are placed on the ground next to crystal technologies like the Mobian. Many of the children—although not the adults—have morpho markings like mine on their skin. *Interesting.* The circle mural shimmers, and the scene seems incredibly alive. The continuum. Is this our past or future?

"Does such a place exist beyond the walls of our temples?" I ask, gesturing to the murals. "Yes, but most humans have forgotten how to live this way—we have lost our way." Rhea turns to me and our foreheads touch.

"It is my deepest prayer that we awaken," I say quietly. For some time we stand there our two bodies touching. The in-breath and the out-breath. This is how we connect with all life, every day of our life, by breathing in and breathing out.

"Come, I want to show you another one of the Circle of Life paintings." Rhea gently pushes upon one of the trees in the mural. A door appears in the wall, and we walk through.

This next rotunda is smaller, and the mural on the wall depicts a lush jungle scene deep and green. This landscape is familiar, and I immediately I think of Theo. There is one tree that stands above the others, ancient with long roots. Directly across from the tree, on the other side of the room, a woman is painted on the mural. The woman is a fusion of nationalities, who also, at certain views, appears as an impossibly beautiful flower.

I finger the talisman that lies against the soft skin of my belly, the talisman that Theo gave me. Rhea watches me take it all in. At a third point, equidistant from the flower and tree, a man and a woman are in deep embrace. Stars above, the earth below.

"Shall we sit down?" Rhea asks, motioning to a spot in the center of the room.

At the beginning and the end of cycles, one of the Priestesses of Astera will go to join with a man who embodies the soul of the planet, who carries the essence of the cosmos. It is said this man is an ancient being who is forever young—but only with the help of the Goddess who helps bring forth the cycles of renewal. This act of union— Hieros gamos—is echoed in the rites of spring when man and woman come together to renew the fertile soil. It is echoed in the deep sacred lovemaking between man and woman, when we remember that within every man and woman is the God and the Goddess—and the ability to birth the world anew.

Gaia Codex: Node 333.67767.999

The words and images of the Codex come to us as we sit there. They flow through our blood and skin. Since I have been here at the Château Lumiere it has become quite easy to access and see this Codex with the help of my sister-priestesses. It is always here for us. It is a gift for all humanity.

Finally, Rhea speaks. "Do you recognize this Circle of Life?"

"Yes," I answer softly. "We each have been the offering. We become the Goddess, the Mother, the essence of Shakti and Life force." I say this under my breath, this ancient teaching I now know as my own.

"My whole life has been a training for this, hasn't it?" I ask quietly.

"Many lifetimes," Rhea answers.

"But, Theo, is he also a man—a human?" I ask.

"Yes," Rhea answers. "As much man as God, as much mortal as divine, this is the boon and the bane of our humanity."

CHAPTER
FIFTY-ONE

The Circle of Life paintings were created to help both individuals as well as entire populations move through the initiations of the Soul.

Gaia Codex: Node 76.21.9917

"DO YOU WISH to go into the next circle?" Rhea asks.

"Yes," I answer. Curiosity often trumps my fear.

"Go ahead, sister. I will wait for you here, for this next Circle of Life, you can only enter alone."

I slowly open the door. The rotunda is the deepest cobalt blue, almost black, and I cannot see the edges of the circle. In the center is a large mirror. From afar it reflects the infinite stars of a clear night sky. The mirror appears to be lit from within. There is no other light in the room. I approach slowly. It is cold, and I wrap my soft wool shawl closer around my body and slowly sit down in front of the mirror.

Know thyself—γνῶθι σεαυτόν—*gnōthi seauton*. The words from Delphi are deep within my ear; my face is set against the stars and the cobalt sky. At first, all I see is my familiar reflection in the shimmering mirror as the forms begin to shape subtle waves across the pool. I see Dominique and Raj and all my dear sisters, layer after layer unfolding, and then I see my own face shifting. I am man, and I am woman —I am all races who have walked the planet. I continue to look into the mirror as I transform into the fruits of my choices. I have planted seeds of goodness and those of sorrow. There were lifetimes when I was not a Priestess of Astera, when I forgot my calling and my light within. There were lifetimes when I sank into the deepest despair as I experienced the consequences of my unkind actions towards others, as I paid the price for my ignorance. There are lifetimes when the fruits of my kindnesses and compassion towards others have flowered radiant and full. There are lives of illumination even in the midst of darkness, and through it all, is there is the thread that connects.

Finally, I look at my face in the mirror. All I can see is light. In the depth of darkness, I see ten thousand stars shining on my skin.

We are light, and we are dark. We are the Priestesses of Astera who come from the stars.

My soul shines bright.

Rhea is waiting for me when I come back out. She says nothing when she sees me but only holds me tight in her arms as I let myself sink deeper into the wholeness of who I am, who I once was, and will be.

CHAPTER
FIFTY-TWO

*The dynamic movement between form and formlessness is
the raw energy of creation.*

Gaia Codex: Node 3345891.75

THE DREAMS ARISE as the circle unwinds. Many
sisters wake up screaming in their beds, as our
collective dreams fill with visions of collapsing cities
and ecosystems that can no longer sustain human life. It is time
for the sisters to spread again—to towns, forests, mountains, and
villages—like seeds to the winds. Many of us have already left to
be with our people and families.

On this final day of gathering at the Château Lumière, the
skies are grey and the ground damp. Winter bites bitter in the
air. We sisters gather to release the vessel of our communion
that has been created over these months. All form moves back
into formlessness.

There is one last feast inside the halls, one last walk through
the fabled atrium and the labyrinth gardens, one last lesson in

the lyceum, one last climb up the spiral stairs, and one last look in our beloved sisters' eyes.

We are gathered here tonight in the main hall—every child and grandmother, every auntie and sister, every dear friend that has travelled together through lifetimes, we are gathered here to say our goodbyes.

We are dressed in our silks, velvets, and our woven flax and wool. We are dressed in our native costumes made of beautifully dyed porcupine needles, turquoise, coral, and cowry shells. Our hair is piled high in resplendent braids or hangs loose in beautiful curls. Ribbons, jewels, and bones bedeck our tresses, and rubies, emeralds, pearls, and sapphires are draped around our necks. We wear ancient signet rings blessed by our mothers' great-grandmothers' grandmothers.

The fires are lit in the great hall, and the sounds of our voices speaking in multiple tongues rise to rafters above. The tables are set for a feast for the senses: a savory mélange of the subtlest tastes, textures, and scents. The tables are massive. Made of a dark babul wood. The legs of the tables are a menagerie of carved animals—strong swarthy tigers, snakes carved into spirals, plumaged proud peacocks, lions with manes like haloed suns. The chairs are substantial, each with a thick cushion covered in jewel-toned raw silks. Arrayed on the tables are shimmering golden glass goblets ready for an assortment of wines. Bowls of peonies, lotuses, and shocking peach roses, interwoven with jasmine and honeysuckle, rise fragrant from the dark wood of the table.

As we sit down, the air is filled with laughter and heightened conversations that are deeply, exuberantly alchemical, nuanced in many flavors. Conversations that sharpen and explode the mind and create a web of deep empathy and connection. Words become worlds. Worlds that turn inside out in the course of a night.

The courses are served: subtle sauces and curries, spicy sambars, complexly flavored seafood stews, pure raw vegetarian delights full of *prana,* delicately flaked pastries, and melt-in-your-mouth confectionaries and sorbets.

It is a feast of joy and sadness. Sadness because we know we will soon scatter to fulfill our separate duties and because in each of our hearts we feel the suffering and tragedy that is befalling our beloved Mother Earth. There is joy because we have had this precious time together.

There are whispers of what might happen tonight. We priestesses are as much one body and one mind as we are individual souls. What is known by one is often known by all. So it has always been.

It has been noticed that the usually coiffed and perfectly presented Helene has been looking faded and tired. Some even say that certain rooms, corridors, and entire gardens of the Château Lumiere are beginning to disappear.

It is early in the feast when Helene Belefonte rises to speak. She is dressed in a brilliant sapphire gown with a necklace of glistening stones to match, but she looks fragile and two of the younger priestesses at her side gracefully help her to her feet.

"Sisters, as many of you may have ascertained, these are the final days of the Château Lumiere."

A collective gasp moves through the room.

"This temple was built to be here at the birth and death of a great city and civilization. We have seen this come to pass. It was created with all of our prayers to be a sanctuary, a refuge in the

many centuries when women have been persecuted, shunned, and silenced, and the Mother Earth herself raped. As you know, dear sisters, we have always kept key temples across the world. Many of these will continue, as needed, but the Châteaux Lumiere will go back to the elements. Our time here is over."

"I want to thank each one of you for your many kindnesses, your strength, and your council through the millennia. I have not been perfect in my leadership. I know this. Instead I have tried to serve our collective needs the best that I could through these times. I have succeeded and I have failed. I continue to grow, learn, and evolve. It is our fluidity and flexibility, wed with the clarity of our vision and the trueness of our hearts, that will take us forward. Hopefully, with the Goddesses' grace, we may plant new seeds for the world to come."

As Madame Belefonte sits down, murmurs move through the great Hall.

"Is it truly the end of the Château Lumiere?" many ask. We have been trained in the acceptance of death and endings, but it is always hard to lose that which we hold dear.

Dessert, when it comes, is a mélange—exquisite pyramids of freshly made exotic gelatos and *glacés* spiced and textured with wine red pomegranate, candied blood red orange, honey, nutmeg, and saffron, with a dash of ground, brilliant-orange mace, and cool pure West Indian lime with thyme. There are lush warm chocolate cakes made with pure cacao and softened with rich, cool crème dashed and flavored with hand-ground Madagascar vanilla beans.

All desserts are served—upon request—with a coffee of ground, slow-roasted beans spiked with cardamom, cacao, and chilies, cold-pressed and then topped with a sweetened dollop of crème fraîche and a drizzle of macadamia blossom honey. Also available are vintage ports to be imbibed in iridescent globe sniffers.

"The passing of the light will happen soon," some of the women whisper. By tradition when one of our leaders steps down, she chooses a successor. It is also true amongst the Priestesses of Astera that there are those who visibly hold the leadership and those who lead but are not seen. Inside and outside join as one— this is true leadership.

As we finish our desserts, Madame Belefonte rises again. "In the spirit of passing of the torch, I will ask our sister Raven to speak."

Raven steps into the center of the circle. She is tall with long black hair—a fusion of Native American, Polynesian, Tibetan, or perhaps Mongolian. It is hard to tell. I feel her pulse. Her blood flows from many streams.

"Thank you, Helene Belefonte. We each are in gratitude for how deeply you have served the Mother. May your bones be blessed as you return into the Earth. Know that your fire and wisdom is in each one of our hearts as we move forward."

"Sisters, I have waited to speak fully until this day, our final day of gathering. We will leave in these days, moving like wind and water, like pollen on the air to the different parts of the Earth, each of us to be with our people. We leave, dear sisters, with new sight and full remembering, with deep connection that has rewoven us back into that essential weave, the essence of our being as women, as priestesses, as human beings, as children of the Earth, and as sisters born of stars. It is simple: this is our

time to be present as the Mother and with the Mother. We are here to nourish and inspire to birth new life on Earth."

"It will be a time of challenge for many. We must fine-tune our knowing and perception. Be present with the darkness within ourselves. Cultivate peace and well-being. Activate our skills as visionaries of a healthy, regenerated earth where water runs clean and the fruits of the Earth are honored and cared for. Sisters, we are here to reactivate the timeless Codex, so that human beings will once again remember the depth of knowledge that they come from and the vastness that they are heading towards. We will be separated by miles, oceans, and continents, but remember, beloved sisters, we are One: we can connect and be present with one another at any time it is needed."

"The wheel is turning again," Rhea whispers into my ear as she takes a sip of deep red merlot. "In the beginning is the end and so it is." I grab her hand under the table.

After the feast many of the women go up to pay respects to Helene Belefonte and take farewells with one another. I see Gemma from across the room and walk up to her.

"Gemma—I will miss you, sister. Where will you go?" I ask as I hold her in my arms.

"Where I am needed, Lila. Always where I am needed." I see a vision of Gemma and Raven helping thousands who are suffering with sickness and hunger. I see her laying bodies to rest in rich black earth and on flaming barges that sail at sunset out to the sea, and finally, I see Gemma, herself, burning on a funeral pyre as people look on crying.

"Thank you and I am sorry ..." I say softly.

"Sister, our paths as priestesses ask that we not be attached to death when it comes. We are often given the uncommon gift of extended mortality, but death does come to us all and when she calls, it is best to become translucent and embrace her in full. They say your last thoughts at death are your first thoughts at birth," Gemma adds.

"I will miss you and everyone here. I have finally found my family."

"As your mother said you would. We will all stay connected, dear sister. This is the nature of Gaia Codex and the Priestesses of Astera. We are many, and we are One," Gemma says as she hugs me and looks deep into my eyes.

We stay with each other deep into the night. There are hugs and tears and promises of reunions although we all know that the gatherings of the Priestesses of Astera are never set in stone. They rise and fall like the wind. For many of us, it will be the last time we will see each other in these physical forms in this lifetime. For the fruit is ripening on the tree. There is nothing we can do to stop the coming seasons—the rising tide of changes that we will all soon face.

CHAPTER
FIFTY-THREE

The Codex is imbedded in our veins, in the patterns of our fingertips, in the irises of our eyes, and in our DNA.

Gaia Codex: Node 3321.430.863

I AM IN THE *Dreaming …*

I am looking at Dominique's manuscript. Tens of thousands of pages open at once. A wind arises, and the pages flutter up, each page merging into my cells, my bones, and my flesh. I feel waves of light and ecstasy.

The manuscript and I are one. We have always been one. And I am merged with my mysterious Mother, Dominique. Her voice moves through me. The voices of all my sisters will now speak through me.

Startled awake, I open my eyes and look upon my altar. The night is dark outside. A single candle burns. Dominique's manuscript is no longer there. I run my fingers over my soft flesh in the flickered candlelight. The Codex is alive inside me.

CHAPTER
FIFTY-FOUR

At the end of every cycle, we return to Mother's embrace.

She is birth. She is death. She is Earth. She is Cosmos. She is Love.

Gaia Codex: Node 332.14.321

TODAY IS THE day of endings as I look out the window of my room in the Château Lumiere. The labyrinths, the conservatory, the lake, and the gardens are covered with the densest fog and are invisible to the eye. I carefully pack my leather knapsack. I have the warm but light travel clothes that Old Woman made for me, a buck knife, flint for starting fires, and a water bottle for gathering water. I wear Dominique's Star of Astera around my neck and Theo's flower on my belly. The last of my mother's jewels are sewn into the inside legs of my pants. I braid my long hair into three braids. I check the room one last time and then bow low, thanking this space for blessing and protecting me. I then step outside and gently close the door.

As I descend the spiral staircase, the fog rises through the interiors of the house, obscuring the carved jeweled doors, the floors below, and the atrium above. The halls are silent. There are no ringing voices or peals of laughter. There is only silence and heavy fog. I wrap my woolen cloak closer around me, covering my head with my hood. When I get to the bottom of the stairs, I step onto soft green grass wet with mist. The intricate marble mosaic floors are gone, and when I look back up, the spiraled staircase has disappeared. It is happening. Everything must return whence it comes.

In the forest some thirty yards away stands a simple, round, thatched mud hut. A trail of smoke spirals through the top. I walk forward until I am standing at the bearskin door.

"May I come in?" I ask. When there is no answer, I lift the skins and step inside. Sitting by the crackling fire is Helene Belefonte, wrapped in a long woolen shawl embroidered with a pattern of stars. She is tending the fire. Helene appears tiny, bent with age, her hair pure white, but her eyes still bright. I bow and sit down by Helene's side.

She is silent for sometime before she finally speaks.

"It always comes back to this, Lila Sophia, our simple relationship with the Earth. It is time for me to finally rest my bones in the ground. I have been waiting for this for so long"

She looks up at me. Her face is craggy and tired. I barely recognize her except for those deep brilliant black eyes.

"I am glad you are here, my sister and friend. I wanted you to see where it all started thousands of years ago. A simple hut in the woods, a fire on the hearth, the medicine bundles of my grandmothers, and the weaving spells of our sisters. Just like this." Helene's eyes get misty as she looks at the past. "I was scared you know, away from my family and great black

Hercynian Forest that was my home. I was the one chosen to fulfill my grandmother's dreams, her visions of a temple that would stand as a civilization rose—and ultimately fell."

"If you saw me then you would have seen a young woman—headstrong, determined, and dedicated—but I didn't really think I was up to the task. Not that I ever told anyone this. I have had so much time to work with my pride. I have needed it. The only thing that kept me going was knowing that there would come a time when the Goddess would not be allowed to show her face, a time when our sisters would be persecuted, when we would be forced to hide who we really are. I knew that I would need to prepare the Château Lumiere for those times as a sanctuary where our teachings and prayers could continue. The Goddess has never let me forget my duty, Lila. It has been with me every waking moment."

Madame Belefonte shivers, and I put another log on the fire. I don't want her to be cold.

She continues: "My life has not been an easy life. It has often been very lonely—especially when Dominique left."

"She was your great love?" I say softly.

"Yes, my great love. We know these things in truth when we come to the end. She is my Beloved." Madame Belefonte answers. Tears run down her face. "I should not have parted in anger. It cost me too much. Now who knows when I will be able to tell her that all is forgiven."

I know this is partly why I am here. There is a part of Dominique in me, a reminder to Madame Belefonte of what she holds dear.

The fire crackles in the center of the hut.

"The Château Lumiere will go back into the stars, the

elements, and the Earth. The cities of old are falling: Rome, Paris, London, Beijing. My work is done."

"You have given us so much, Mother." I place my hands together and bow low, looking deep into Helene's eyes. Their beauty and intensity pour into me like cool streams and molten lava. They pour into me as wisdom.

"We each do what we must do," Madame Belefonte replies. I can feel that her body is tired.

"It is important that you go and meet Theo. He has waited long for you. In the end you must go to him, not out of duty but out of love."

"And Rhea ... ?" I ask.

"Rhea may be here when the rest of us are all gone, and our planet Earth is once again only a dream," Helene answers. "She will be patient with you. She is, perhaps, the most ancient of us all. She watches the rest of us live and die. Even those like myself who live for thousands of years. Your love with her can grow slowly and deeply. There is no hurry."

"I have something for you." I reach into the folds of my cloth and take out a radiant gemstone the size of a goose egg. The stone is a deep crystalline blue with radiant fire coming forth deep from the center."

"This was Dominique's." I hold up the stone to the light.

Madame Belefonte lifts her head. "Ah ... the Phoenix Stone. This is generous, but perhaps you should keep it for yourself. You have a long journey ahead. The stone has powers that are useful," Helene replies.

"It is for you." I gently place the stone in Madame Belefonte's hands. The jewel glitters against her wrinkled flesh. Her once well-kept body now shows the signs of age.

"I gave the Phoenix Stone to your mother many centuries ago. It was a token of our love," Madame Belefonte says softly. "Thank you, Lila. It will be sweet to carry this with me as I depart. It will ease the passing. If for some reason you see Dominique again, tell her that all is forgiven and that I love her."

"But she is dead," I say quietly.

"As you well know, many of us reincarnate. You will recognize Dominique if you see her. If she has been successful with her manipulations of time, then you will eventually know this too. Tell her I love her." Helene says softly one last time.

"Thank you, Mother." I look into Madame Belefonte's face and take in her shriveled body beneath the cloak. She has been alive for thousands of years, and now she is ready to die.

"Lila Sophia, I want you to be the one who is witness to my passing to the other realm."

"You have been there at many of my births," I whisper. "It is an honor to be with you here at your death."

She bows, acknowledging my words.

"Know that I love you and that ancient streams flow through you. Your greatest gift is love, Lila Sophia. Remember this."

"Light the fires, child. Light the fires," she says as she motions to the hearth fire. Madame Belefonte's cragged face is brilliant as she speaks.

She wants me to light the hut ablaze. I take a deep breath.

"Do it, child. Now!"

Helene Belefonte lifts the Phoenix Stone upon her heart, and then, as though it always belonged there, the jewel merges with her skin.

I light a torch on the fire, step outside and then light the small hut from multiple directions.

The hut goes up in flames easily. In my mind's eye I see Madame Belefonte inside, radiant in her beauty and glory. Tears run down my cheeks, and they are tears of gratitude.

When I open my eyes, there is an aged tree growing where Helene had been sitting. The hut is gone. Her last act of illusion. There is only the forest. The rest of the park is empty except for a sliver of a trail that leads deep through the darkened wood.

CHAPTER
FIFTY-FIVE

*At some point, every Temple of Astera dissolves, for the
locations of our temples change through the millennia
as the energetic grids of our Mother Earth transform to
accommodate new creations, new civilizations, and new
forms of Life. The Wheel of Life turns through the ages.*

Gaia Codex: Node 333.43.71

I START TO WALK down the narrow path into the mist-
drenched wood. There is no color in the landscape only
shadows. I slowly turn back to look back to where the
Château Lumiere had once stood. There is nothing but a dense
forest with trees outlined in the mist and the nearly silent sound
of fog dripping down through the leaves.

"Lila Sophia," a voice echoes.

"Lila ..." It is Rhea sitting back against a tree. The scent of
rose petals, cinnamon, and lemongrass mixed with tobacco
wafts through the air. She is smoking an herb cigarette. Not far

from where Rhea sits, two muscled horses are tethered to a tree, quietly chomping the green grass.

"There you are." I am relieved that Rhea is here.

"You said your goodbyes to Helene?" Rhea asks as she slowly inhales the smoke.

"It is done," I reply quietly.

Rhea slowly stands up and then puts her arms around me as an ancient chant of beginnings and ends swells forth from both of us, reaching up to the skies and down deep into the Earth.

In the silence that follows, the vibration continues to move through the trees dripping with mist.

"It is done," Rhea finally says. We hold each other heart-to-heart, forehead-to-forehead. We have been here before, breathing in each other's breath, as one world dies, and another is born.

We take the horses' reins, continuing on in silence, leading the horses through the wood until we see the grey stone wall. The rusted gate hangs on its hinges—open and unguarded.

"We will need to move quickly once we are on the other side. Are you ready?" Rhea asks.

"Yes." I take a deep breath, and I don't look back as we move through the broken gate to the other side.

CHAPTER
FIFTY-SIX

When a population expands beyond its limits, many will die as a means of dynamic self-regulation initiated by Gaia herself.

Gaia Codex: Node 321.54.83

THE NEIGHBORHOOD WE enter is filled with trash and refuse: rusting abandoned cars, decomposed papers sinking into the muck, scattered broken furniture, broken glass, and piles of stone from buildings and walls in a state of collapse.

Stinking rot pervades the air, the scent of decomposing meat, vegetables, urine, and human defecation. My eyes water at the stench as I take in the sight of corpses scattered haphazardly through the streets. There are rotting limbs and half-eaten faces, gold and diamond wedding rings left on fingers, and expensive soft leather shoes exploding off of swollen rotting feet. Dogs gorge and roam in packs—finally able to feed after years of near starvation. Buzzards move restlessly, move from pile to pile, as if they find it hard to choose between the rotting bodies.

The windows of most shops are shattered, the doors left ajar, but much of the merchandise is intact. Street after street, boulevard after boulevard—and we see no living humans. Only the caws of the ravens, the howls of the dogs, and the steady, quick clip and clop of our horses fill the streets.

"We should move quickly. There have been plagues." I say this as Rhea nods.

My morpho markings are pulsing in response to the virus. This was one of the intended adaptive features of the Metamorphosis Project, my ability to take in poisons, viruses, and diseases in order to provide an antidote and panacea, to bring bodies into balance, to bring forth a state of healing.

Tears rush down my face, knowing that I can do nothing for all these souls who have already passed.

My reading of the disease comes as both a visual image and as quick pricking sensation. I feel it in my markings, but I do not take it into my body. The virus is unusual: it simultaneously eats the flesh and clogs the veins so blood cannot flow.

"What has happened to these people is what is happening to the waterways of the planet. It's a clogging or congestion. It is a system collapse. It takes a life very quickly once it reaches a tipping point," I say aloud.

"It's not just Paris, it's London and New York. People are fleeing the cities in light of the plagues," Rhea says quietly.

"You see this?" I ask. "Yes," Rhea answers. I pause for a moment and tune in. It is there, the terror and fear of billions of incarnate souls dying and in shock.

There are tears streaming down my face. It is exactly like my dreams and visions back at Hampstead Heath.

"You have seen death like this before, haven't you?" I ask Rhea.

She slowly nods her head. "It doesn't get any easier no matter how many times you see the collapse of a civilization or a world. Especially when it is because of our collective ignorance."

"We that remain are here to say prayers for those that have passed. Do you understand?"

"Yes, of course," I answer.

As we move through the empty streets, I see and feel Theo. It has become so easy to see him in my mind's eye. *Soon, my love.* I whisper, hoping that somehow he hears me across the distance.

It is good to have the horses, the knives, and the bow and arrows—as a deterrent, if nothing else. Desperation engenders dangerous actions, but we run into no other humans. The streets are empty except for the dead. We travel through the night, and then the next day when we finally arrive at the docks on the second night dawn has not yet broken.

"We are here," Rhea says. I see movement—a small rowboat with a single figure pulls up to the shore.

"Thank you," I whisper into my horse's ear, "May you be matched with someone who treats you well, feeds you, and needs you."

I have left food and water in the saddlebag, hoping it will help who ever finds it. I slap the horse's sweating rump as he gallops off into the empty streets.

"Ladies, let's move quickly," a young man with sandy blond hair says as he ushers us into the boat.

As we row out to sea, I look back on the desolation. Fires burning in an eerily calm sky.

"It may be the last we see of this land for a very long time," Rhea says.

May we all remember what we have done to you, Mother, and to each other. May we remember and not repeat our ignorance and neglect. Please give hope and nourishment and care to all children who have survived. May the seeds be planted for us, may we humans start anew.

I say my prayer to the winds as tears fall down my cheeks.

PART FIVE

Amazonia

CHAPTER
FIFTY-SEVEN

Planet Earth is the Water Planet.

Gaia Codex: Node 3321.4321

THE SUN IS rising as we climb aboard the *Phoenix Fire*, a sailing boat built by the five handsome sons of Mary Tullee, our Irish sister-priestess. There are other passengers on the *Phoenix Fire* as well, extended family and friends: children, young women, men, and elders. There are forty of us in total.

"So, this is Dominique's daughter?" Mary Tullee asks as we board the ship. Mary is a large woman with a stout face and keen, deep blue eyes. Her greying hair scatters to the wind.

"Yes, this Lila Sophia," Rhea answers, amused.

"Mary Tullee," I make a deep bow. "Thank you for having us."

Mary Tullee looks at me and then seems to sniff me with her nose.

"Hmm. You have a strange but beautiful scent, lady. Like

fresh wind, like …" she thinks for the moment, "… like flowers in a spring garden, like mother's milk and fresh black earth. My boys will adore you. You behave now, you here!" She pinches me on the cheek and looks me in the eyes. "We don't want any new ones until we land on solid ground. Got it?"

Rhea is smiling. I am blushing.

"I understand," I answer, and now I am smiling too. Mary Tullee's mirth is contagious.

In a lowered voice, Mary Tullee says, "I see you, priestess. You have the DNA we humans need. It is in your scent." She takes me in with her big deep blue eyes, and I hold her gaze and show her for a moment who I am—unveiled.

Mary Tullee nods. "And you have a soul too match. Good. Your parents' experiment appears to be justified. You will be guarded like gold while you are here, Lila Sophia. You are precious cargo."

"Thank you, Mary Tullee," I reply.

"Thank me after we have made it safely across the Atlantic," Mary Tullee laughs. We sail in uncharted waters.

"Boys!" With Mary's call, five strapping young men come running up the main deck.

"Boys, you know Rhea Sahar, but you haven't met Lila Sophia Nataraj," Mary says, sweeping her hands toward me. The boys bow.

"Tal, Tag, Radth, Gurth, and Ian. My lion, dragon, phoenix, bear, and tiger—all in one."

I catch my breath. Each of the brothers is more handsome than the next, and I notice that all of them are also blushing slightly … as was I. There is electricity in the air. Rhea looks on, amused at it all.

"Mama, we need to set sail now. The trade winds are rising that will take us out to sea," golden-haired Tal says. He towers over his mother, but I see that he, like all the boys, gives Mary Tullee deference.

"I just want you boys to make sure you have met our precious cargo. Now, all of you promise to behave. Her mother was a friend of mine." And with that we are off—moving westward across the sea.

The terror of the plagues has not left me, and in those first nights, my eyes fly open as I smell the sweet rot of flesh that accompanies death. I hear the pleas and prayers of those who died too quickly. Many of these souls are still in shock, wandering in limbo somewhere between here and there. Tears stream down my face, and prayers flow from my lips.

Mother, please help these souls pass into comfort, rest, and clarity. May they find rebirth in auspicious circumstances. May we all understand the fruits of our actions and know that we always reap what we sow. Mother, may we be wiser in future times and understand that tragedy like this does not need to be happen. I pray to the soul of our species and to you, Mother Gaia.

On these nights Rhea holds me tight, rocking me back and forth as my tears flow, soaking the clean cotton sheets and our shared soft skin as we lay together. I am happy for the solace of her arms.

CHAPTER
FIFTY-EIGHT

The stars guide the seafarer across ocean waters and
celestial seas back to our place of origin.

Gaia Codex: Node 44.32.1.845

AS WE CROSS the Atlantic, my days are filled with sweet play and a merriment I haven't known in a long time. Radth, Tag, Gurth, Tal, and Ian daily seek my attention with their flirting and courting, their playful games and overt displays of prowess.

"You would make a wonderful wife, Lady Lila," Tal Tullee says as he presents me with gifts: an apple, a polished stone, and a bracelet carved of birch.

"I can see the children already, tousled, rosy cheeks and golden haired," Tag agrees.

"I second that," says Gurth. "She will be our mother's favorite."

"We will build her wonderful houses—don't you think, boys?" adds strong and muscled Ian.

Radth just looks at me from across the deck of the ship with his smoldering eyes that say *I want to kiss you a thousand times* and offers me books I might like to read or describes the use of rare herbs the family has collected on their travels.

The Tullee boys, despite their flirting and teasing, are courteous and gentlemanly. They pull out my chair and make sure I have everything I need. They carry my bucket if I am helping with chores.

Rhea watches it all with amusement.

I accept the boys' presents. I dance jigs with them under the moonlight and sing the songs given to us by our mothers, songs of ancient lands and of our ancestors. We laugh until we cry. We make bets. The boys show me their woodworking and metal skills, their knowledge of agriculture and astronomy. They wrestle each other to me show me their strength.

And after several weeks, on a full moon night, golden-haired Tal bends down on his knees.

His eyes are not laughing. They are beautiful, kind, and strong. "Lila, Lady Lila, will you be my wife?"

I am not surprised by the question, but it still takes my breath away

"I am asking you to marry me, Lila Sophia," he says again—in case I did not fully understand.

I take Tal's hands in my mine and look deeply into his eyes.

"Tal, I am promised to another."

"Where is he?" Tal asks quietly.

"Tal … look at me." I hold his hands tightly. In my mind's eye I see Theo, in the forest with the Tree of Life. I feel the ancient promise and the circles of my sisters at the Château Lumiere.

I hear Rhea, Helene Belafonte's, and Old Woman's counsel. *The ancient promise. I have made a vow to Theo in my Heart.*

"Do you understand, Tal?" I ask. I know that like his mother and the priestesses, he has the gift of reading thoughts.

When he finally speaks, Tal does not let go of my hand. "I understand, Lila Sophia. You are the Goddess-Priestess who offers herself to the King and then journeys with him to the underworld so that the Earth may be reborn. There are ancient songs about you, Goddess. But is it what your heart wants? Can you answer that for me?"

"I am going because I choose this. It is my destiny," I say quietly.

"Are you sure about that?" Tal asks quietly.

"My heart calls me, Tal." I say this, and it is true, but they are also difficult words to say to him.

Tal looks at me for a long time. His golden hair is silver in the moon.

"We would have beautiful children, you and I. Precious off-spring for a new world to come. Our Mother will love you as her own daughter. It should be a simple choice to be with me, Lila Sophia."

"And your mother should know that I am promised to Theo. The Priestesses of Astera have promised me to Theo. I have promised myself to Theo." Suddenly there are hot tears stream-ing down my face. It is crazy being promised to a man I have never seen—a man I have only seen in dreams. *It would be a happy life with Tal Tullee and his brothers.* Happy, joyous, and boisterous. We would grow sweet in old age. Our grandsons and granddaughters would be the foundation of a civilization of new tribes who would celebrate life on Earth. It is all so clear. But if

I took this choice, this life with Tal, something else could not happen. Something I cannot fully see right now. Something connected to a world not yet born and to Theo, who I am so intertwined with that that I do not even feel the origin of our first meeting, it is buried so very deep in time. Something would die within him, within me, within us—perhaps within the world—if I choose Tal Tullee.

"Tal, I can't marry you." There are tears on my face as I say it. "I need to follow the path I am on. I can't fully explain it, but it is not only about me."

"I know," he says quietly, gently placing my hands back into my lap. "It never is, Lady Lila."

We are both silent for sometime before Tal finally speaks, "My mother said you would say 'no' even though you love me … and the rest of my brothers." He smiles sadly.

"Your mother is a wise woman," I reply quietly.

Tal is silent. His eyes shine under the stars. I feel his sadness.

"Don't cry too hard, Lady Lila," he says, "just enough to know what you have lost and what you have gained. Our choices have more power than we often know." And with that he kisses me quickly and sweetly on the lips. He is sweet to the touch.

Tal leaves, and I am alone on the ship's high deck under the stars. Tears continue to stream down my face as we sail into the night.

Mother, please guide me to my highest path. Please guide me to that which is in highest service to all Life. And Mother, may I be with Theo—soon.

The prayer falls off my lips. Tonight Theo feels far away.

CHAPTER
FIFTY-NINE

*Every moment offers choice. There are ten thousand paths
to take. There is one to choose. Listen deeply for that path
which takes you home.*

Gaia Codex: Node 3321.832.01

"SO, YOU PASSED the test of the Tullee boys?" Rhea
asks the next morning.

"What do you mean?" I answer grumpily as I slowly
sip my morning tea out of a scracked porcelain mug.

"Last night, the birth of worlds spun on the choice of a young
woman with an ancient soul. Who would she love? Who would
she choose—to bear his children, to carry his seed? Perhaps in
the end, there isn't a right or wrong choice, for the creation, the
Mother, is infinite in her variation. Or perhaps there was a right
choice for the young woman, the priestess with the ancient soul
was able to again listen to the deepest calling of her Heart."

"Yes, it was something like that," I sigh. "It is not a choice
without regret."

"Don't look so heavy, love. The Tullee boys will find willing, wonderful wives that will bear children to lead wise tribes. Mary Tullee knows that your vows have been made. She was only encouraging you—and her boys—to see if you were serious. Though I am sure she would have adored you as a daughter-in-law. Come, let's help make soup for lunch." Rhea jumps up and strokes my face softly and then kisses my forehead. *Again the rush I always feel with her.*

"I always feel it with you too, Lila Sophia." Rhea whispers, reading my thoughts. "Every time we touch, it's like a first kiss." She then grabs my hand. "Come, my love, let's chop potatoes." I get up and follow her still feeling both the weight and the possibilities of my choices.

Days turn to weeks. There is much storytelling on the boat and many dreams of what is to come. There are many collective prayers for what has been. The scale of death has shaken us to the core. Everyone on the *Phoenix Fire*, except Rhea and I, will continue on around Cape Horn to Patagonia. Rhea and I will go up the Amazon.

"We will start anew in Patagonia," says Radth, who is studying his mother's medicine craft and had trained to be a doctor before the collapse. "Mother sees it clearly."

"Do *you* see it clearly?" I ask.

"The dreams, the visions have been coming, Lady Lila. We do have our mother's blood. We have also been preparing for this since we were children. At first it was the big adventure that we would set forth on when we were young men. That's what Mama told us, and then we started to see for ourselves the signs that the collapse would truly happen."

"How did all of you escape the plagues?" I ask.

"All of us didn't," Radth answers quietly. "There were twice as many of us in our tribe when we first set off on the *Phoenix.*"

"Mother had been seeing and feeling the upcoming plagues for years. She always said that when a culture is out of balance, plagues and destruction follow. About eight years ago she put us on a diet of her special herbs. She also trained us to create adaptogens within our bodies."

"Was your mother a taskmaster?" I asked.

"She is a taskmaster," he laughs.

"Her methods sound similar to what the morpho markings show me."

"How does that work?' Radth asks.

Everyone on the ship has been curious about my morpho markings. There were lots of questions and, with the children, lots of touching. Some of the girls and boys started to paint the marks onto their bodies—in play.

"Well, I feel the contagion when it comes in contact with me. The marks will start to change color, and then I receive a flow of images that shows me how to transmute the contagion. It's always different, the antidote, and often, of course, our bodies do it automatically, but I am being shown the mechanics of it."

"Interesting. Sometimes death is the only way for life to continue or flourish," Radth says.

"Like the plagues, right? They are tragic yet allow for something new to arise."

We are both quiet for a moment, pondering the implications.

"Yes, like that," I answer quietly.

"You know, my brothers and I wish you were coming around the Horn with us."

"And you know that I can't." My voice is firm. I pull my wool cloak closer around my shoulders.

"I am glad that Rhea is going with you," Radth finally says.

"Me too," I answer.

"She will make sure you reach your destination," Radth adds.

CHAPTER
SIXTY

Inside every cell a universe resides.

Gaia Codex: Node 3321.231.1

"THE STARS ARE beautiful," I murmur. It is few nights later, and Rhea and I are up on the decks lying in two hammocks the Tullee boys have strung up for us. It will be an early morning moonrise. Right now the sky is dark except for the arched dome of infinite stars.

"They are," Rhea answers back. "Remember the story of the Egyptian goddess Nut who swallows the sun every night and gives birth to it everyday. Her body was made of stars if you remember. Our bodies are made of stars, Lila."

I feel the night sky penetrate our bodies as we hold hands, swinging back and forth in the hammocks.

"See Scorpio up there. It means we are below the equator. We are getting closer," Rhea says.

"You know, Dominique had this crazy training where she would have me memorize different constellations at different latitudes as they move through time. We would practice in a planetarium she set up in one of our homes—the Star Temple she called it. She said that it would be useful as a means of locating where I was both in space and time. I guess she figured that since I have a photographic memory I would be able to track these things. I still don't know exactly what she meant. It was as though she expected me to travel through time."

"Perhaps Dominique was on to something," Rhea laughs.

"Rhea, did you ever run across my parents—in the past or in the future?" I ask.

"I can't physically travel to the future," Rhea answers. "I can only move forward sequentially in time. Your mother, though—well, there were moments where I sensed she was experimenting with something usual, as though she could move backwards and forwards in time, or more specifically through the web of time. I say this because I did see her and Raj at points that seemed out of sequence from what I know about her incarnations. I saw her once in Paris in the eighteenth century and another time in Japan during the Heian period, both times she tried to hide like I wasn't supposed to see her. It was decidedly odd."

"Was she always like this?" I ask, "inventing, manipulating, creating, pushing the edges of possibility?"

Rhea laughs, "Always, you should know that. You have spent time with her Lila."

"My mother did not lend herself to being easily defined or understood." I answered.

Since leaving the Château Lumiere and embodying the Codex, I have remembered many more of my connections with Dominique through time … our incarnations together. Usually we were friends and sisters, although it seemed that we often exasperated each other as much as we loved one another, vexed ourselves as much as we were devoted to each other.

There are still missing pieces in my memory of my past incarnations. My condition is odd: I have an impeccable photographic memory for the events of this life but my incarnational memory is more mysterious and elastic. I feel the larger web of connections through time—both my personal lineage lines and the genetic lines of the species—but even though I have many specific personal memories, it is as though each moment reveals another nuanced layer of both past connections and future potentials. It is not static but instead a living breathing web of emergent experience.

I wonder about Dominique's ability to time-travel. Is it true? Or to just another one of her conundrums that she has left as bait for those of us with overly curious minds.

A warm wind is blowing. I look up at the stars and then back at Rhea.

"Is your fate difficult?" I ask.

Rhea continues to look at the stars as she answers. "I experience time differently than most, as you know, and of course it is hard to see those you love die while you remain."

"And without getting older ..." I add.

"Yes, this is often the strangest part, Lila. Sometimes I simply wish to grow old, to experience the fullness of the cycle of birth and death. Instead, I only get to experience aging through others."

"For me, the unfolding of time is tied up with Theo," I say quietly. Rhea and I haven't been talking about Theo much on this journey, but I think of him every day. The plan is that Rhea and I will go up the Amazon and then trek through the jungle

to the borders of the Hriya land where Theo is supposed to be. I often can look, with some accuracy, into a possible future and at least get a few glimpses, a premonition or two, but when I think of what might happen with Theo, oddly, I see nothing. It doesn't look bad. It doesn't look good. I just feel that everything will change, and with each passing day I feel my passion and desire rising. The thought of him is a heady wine.

"Is there more that you can tell me about Theo?" I ask Rhea.

"He is the mystery, isn't he?" Rhea probes. "There are ancient tales that some day he will be released from his vow to carry and heal the ills of the world and that humanity will have a new chance—the wheel turns, and the world will be reborn. These are the stories passed down in many cultures, but you know this tale, Lila. I know that Theo can only be released through love. Luckily your heart, sweet sister, is vast."

My heart opens because of what you have taught me.

Rhea is the one who has helped me remember this love that deepens and flowers over time.

The ship sails at a steady clip. The night is calm, the breezes gentle. Rare conditions on these open seas.

"The other thing I can tell you," Rhea says softly, "is that he is my twin brother."

"Your twin brother?" I turn over to look at Rhea. "Truly?"

"Yes," Rhea says, "Theo and I are forever joined as souls. We were born tens of thousands of years ago to the same mother, a Priestess of Astera named Theanna. She never incarnated again but left her legacy in both of us, her only son and daughter. My twin brother Theo, as you know, went on to become a mighty leader, a once-respected king, who, in the end, through his voracious, crazy desire for power, destroyed his kingdom."

"Theo was not born to the throne, for our mother was the courtesan lover of our father, King Aran. She was not his Queen. But Theo took what he felt was rightfully his by secretly killing King Aran's firstborn son and proving himself a mighty and charismatic leader. When King Aran also died of mysterious causes, Theo became king … with King Aran's deathbed blessing. They called Theo the Lion, and, for a while many loved him, but he got greedy, and well, you know the rest of the story. The conqueror who cannot stop."

"When his people were dead and the fields filled with blood, when that civilization, Urtha, which is no longer even in the annals of recorded history, when it collapsed, Theo was broken. It was then that Prometheus the wizard wise man saved him and taught him and then put the curse on him that bound Theo to the Earth."

"A curse?" I ask.

"Well, in part", Rhea answers, "Theo agreed to the fate and the spell. He offered himself both to right his past wrongs and also to bring into balance humanity's plunder of our Mother Earth."

"And you?" I ask.

Rhea continues. "My mother, Theanna, took both my brother and I away into the forest after our father, King Aran, sired us. Many said it was for our protection but it was to teach us. For you see her true love was not King Aran but Prometheus and they had conceived a plan that would unfold over tens of thousands of years. Theo and I were at the heart of their mechanizations."

"So my brother went to take the throne and I was trained in the ways of the Priestesses of Astera, although our numbers were few in those days. My task was to roam the earth for eons

and teach those women who were to come after me, to spark the fire inside them, and to lead those who had forgotten back into the folds of deeper memories, into connection with the Codex itself."

"So in some ways, my fate is not unlike that of Helene Belefonte, except, as you know, I am bound to the Earth, not a temple. When my brother Theo's fate became evident after his fall, I vowed to stay with him. I could not bear for him to be alone for eons. But then, dear Lila, we realized that we could not be in the same physical space because of what we are. When Theo and I are together there is too much power and it is not a gentle power by any means: tidal waves, eclipses, ice storms, and earthquakes occur. So we both try at all costs not to cross paths. It took Theo and I time, indeed many centuries, to realize that we had perfectly played out Theanna's and Prometheus's vision."

As Rhea speaks, I see my lives with her together over time. "You have been training me through our love and friendship to be with your brother Theo."

Rhea smiles. "Yes, in a way you could say that, Lila, but it has been out of love and because I wanted it to be you who would be with Theo. I am happy that you will be his consort, Lila. You are the medicine he has needed for a very long time. Lila I am sorry that I have not told you sooner but it had to be the right time and now, I believe, dear sister is the right time."

"I understand." I answer softly. Timing is

"Has it always been certain that I would be with him?" I ask.

Rhea looks at me. Her eyes are penetrating. She is reading the Codex.

"No. There were many specific choices along the way, Lila that brought you to this place. Your choices, my choices, Theo's choices, Dominique's choices, Helene's choices, and so many choices of other people as well. Our fates and our Mother Earth's fate could all have been very different at many different junctures. They still could. Only time will tell. Nothing is certain. And no, dear sister, not even you and Theo are a certainty, but I hope and pray that it is so—for all of us and for our Mother Earth."

I am startled by Rhea's revelation. She and Theo were born from one womb, these two souls whose hearts and fates are so deeply wound up with mine. It settles my heart and at the same time brings me further to the edge unknowing.

That night Rhea and I fall asleep under the dome of stars as we sail westward into the night. We hold each other tight.

CHAPTER
SIXTY-ONE

Some say many Earths exist simultaneously.

Gaia Codex: Node 334.21.321

IT IS TIME for goodbyes. We are at the mouth of the mighty Amazon, where Rhea and I will continue on a smaller boat up the river. The Tullee family and the rest of the crew will continue sailing around Cape Horn. The boys gather around me in circle and hug me all at once. There are tears in all of our eyes.

"We won't forget you, Lady Lila. We will toast you and your offspring at the coming of every spring," Tal says as he gives me a kiss on the forehead.

"We will be praying for you, Lila Sophia. We will be in prayer for all of us," Mary Tullee says as she hugs me.

"Mary Tullee, I have something for you." I hand Mary Tullee a deep wine-colored scarf that I have woven on the journey. In the center is a red rose, surrounded by five golden rings matched with seven silver rings, and at the bottom is a cornucopia filled with the abundant fruits of the Earth. "For you, Mother Tullee, in honor of your children and your children's children."

"This is beautiful, sister." There are tears in Mary Tullee's eyes as she takes the scarf into her hands. "You know, I wish that fate was different and that you were travelling with us around the Horn—and I know that it is not to be so."

I wonder when, and if, I will ever see the Tullee family again.

Later that day, from our small riverboat, we watch the *Phoenix Fire* sail off into the horizon. Most of the communities here in the lower Americas have been reverting to simpler ways of living for decades, so the fall has not been so harsh here, and the plagues have not hit as hard.

As we move up the Amazon, my dreams are filled with Theo. Yet it is usually only his voice in the darkness, whispering in my ear: "We will soon be together, Ma." In these nights I do not see his face.

I also know that every day we get closer to Theo, my time with Rhea becomes shorter.

She and I have agreed. She will lead me up the river and into the jungle, but then we will say goodbye.

"Have you spent time with the Hriya before?" I ask Rhea as we slowly move up the Amazon River.

"I try to see them every few hundred years. They are older than the Priestesses of Astera, much older," Rhea says. "We are babies compared to them."

As we move up the river, my self-doubt also rises, like a noisy mynah bird chittin' and chattin' inside my head.

"It's normal, Lila," Rhea says as she watches me fidget restlessly, swatting mosquitoes off my skin. "Let all your mental

chatter run its course and then center here." She touches me gently between the heart and solar plexus. Her fingers bring all my energy back into my body. "You have been preparing for this for many lifetimes, my love. It will be like breath for you. But remember not to hold anything back when you are with him."

Rhea's touch comforts me, but I am still on edge.

For everything there is an ending. After weeks of travel Rhea and I stand at the water's edge. Waiting to say goodbye.

"I don't know when we will see each other again, Lila Sophia. It is not always easy to find each other—it is not always certain that we can—but please know I always carry you in my heart," There are tears in Rhea's eyes as she speaks.

I bring my forehead to hers. "I love you, Rhea Sahar," I say, looking deep into her eyes.

"And I love you, Lila Sophia," she says as she gives me one last kiss. *I will miss her.*

A few hours later, as I watch Rhea's boat sail down the Amazon River and into the last light of day, I place my hand on my heart as tears of thankfulness—for my sister and dear Beloved—run down my cheeks.

CHAPTER
SIXTY-TWO

It is said that within the tens of trillions of cells that compose the human body we have the memory of every form of Life that has ever existed–terrestial as well as celestial. Inside us are the imprints of the first ferns in primordial Carboniferous forests some three hundred and fifty million years ago. Inside us are the furthest reaches of the stars, suns in galaxies far from the spiral of the Milky Way.

Gaia Codex: Node 444.85.211

I HAVE FIRE-MAKING TOOLS and a swinging hammock made of sisal fiber to string up in trees. In addition, I have my buck knife, machete, and bow.

My camp is next to sweet water. It is a protected space in a jungle that can devour. The voices of Old Woman and of our collective human ancestors who have remembered how to live with the land all run through me.

First, you find the source of water, and then you listen. Listen to the land, to the plants, to the animals. Let them know that you are there in service to them. If you listen carefully, the plants and the animals will let you know what can be harvested or killed, when and how, and then you can partake. Yet remember: for everything you take you must give something back. This is the law of Life. When we break this law, all Life will suffer.

Alone, I am unbound. Here, in the depth of the rainforest, my memories of past identities—of Lila Sophia, a Priestess of Astera, daughter of Dominique and Raj—even my memories of Rhea and Theo, both so present in my heart and mind, all become but tiny bubbles that float, emerge, and submerge on a vast ocean. I am this ocean. Here amongst the flora and fauna, my morpho markings become even more dynamic. I feel each marking on my skin as it pulses and transforms until my body is covered with multiple eyes that not only see, but feel, taste, touch, and hear a full sensorium.

The jungle enters into me, and I into it, and through it all a prayer wells up from deep in my heart, falls from my lips in languages and tones I never formally studied but that I deeply know. A prayer for all beings, a deep chant for the well-being and vibrancy of Life in all its forms. There is an ancient knowing inside of me as a woman, a soul, and a priestess, as a reflection of Mother Earth herself. It is my calling to embody, feel, and help transmute this suffering and pain that has been part of the human condition. I will offer myself again and again.

The world I have come from feels increasingly far away, as though it somehow existed in another time—one thousand, ten thousand years past—or forward. Yet if I listen very carefully, I feel the pain, shock, and sorrow, as well as deep relief in many cases, of the passing of millions of souls from one realm to the next as plagues and famine devastate the human populations of our Mother Earth. Alone here, I hear their calls of fear and their release. One world dies as another is reborn.

CHAPTER
SIXTY-THREE

There have always been those who have lived outside the lines of time. They are said to reside in hidden valleys, deep jungles, on mountain peaks, or in those liminal realms that are only seen by those with the eyes to see. As for the Hriya, they are as old as the rainforest itself. At the beginning and the end of a world, the Priestesses of Astera send one of their own to the Hriya to partake in the Rite of Renewal.

Gaia Codex: Node 33321.8541

DAPPLED LIGHT FALLS on my skin and the sound of howler monkeys echoes into the edges of my dream—a dream where the veins that carry my blood are the tributaries of rivers that flow downward to the sea. I am she, and she is I. The Earth calls me home.

I feel her first. I slowly open my eyes. She is staring at me with a persistent intensity. Her eyes are dark and black. Her soft breath falls upon my skin. Her scent is the rainforest itself. She has short, cropped black hair, and her face is painted with broad stripes of bright blue. She stands directly over me.

"It is time you go to him." Although she does not move her lips, her words sink easily into my mind. "I'm Anka."

I repeat her name under my breath as her intense black eyes continue to penetrate me. She is exploring me with her mind, but gently. She reminds me of someone, of something, a distant echo of a memory ten thousand, twenty thousand, and hundred thousand years into the future—or in the past.

I reach my two hands out to her, palms forward. Mirroring me, she places her two palms in mine. Her brown hands are warm, and they are pulsing.

"Come," she says silently. It is both a question and a directive.

I get out of the hammock and begin to take down the camp. Disassembling my small thatched hut, putting out and covering the traces of my fire, and removing any sign that I was here. It is more of a ritual *thank you* than a necessity, for eventually the rainforest consumes all.

An hour later we are walking together, following a trail as thin as spider silk deeper into the verdant green. Anka moves before me. She wears nothing but a loin cloth and what appear to be subtle painted markings: tiny points of luminescence on her dark skin that appear like stars within the sky.

Her breasts are bare and exposed. Soon I follow her example and strip off my thin cotton shirt. *The flesh is another organ for experience; it sips in the smells, sees and tastes the vibrations.* My markings pulse as we move deeper in. This is ancient jungle that at its heart is some fifty-six million years old. When I remember

that *Homo sapiens* has only spent some two hundred thousand years on this planet, I begin to laugh. *So young are we.*

A whistle. A click. The sound of cascading bird calls. The rustle of wind.

Anka does not talk. She just makes these sounds, and as we walk together, our perception and experience meld. Her vision, her taste, and her touch become mine.

Each plant, tree, and insect has a unique chemical texture, a color, or a scent that imparts information about what it can be used for: if it is toxic or beneficial or both. Many of the plants emit a low hum, a vibration that guides you on how to interact with them—if you listen closely.

As we walk, Anka occasionally stops and picks up a few leaves or berries and before she puts them into her pouch, she hands them to me: to smell, to taste, to feel.

A plant will communicate everything you need to know. How to use its roots and leaves, when to harvest it, how to best cultivate it when it seeks cultivation, who its animal allies are, and what plants it can "marry" and mix with. The plants themselves are our most powerful and direct teachers in these matters. It is best to let the forest completely absorb us—until it is only her that we touch, feel, taste, and see. It is then she reveals her secrets.

Anka shares with me in wordless communication. Her eyes are deep and black—it is hard to see where her pupils begin and irises end. Great intelligence is reflected in their luminosity. They are warm and heartfelt, but they do not feel wholly human.

Finally after some days, I ask aloud, "Are your people human?"

"Yes and no. You will see," Anka answers with a click of the tongue.

As we walk, I put my hands on my belly. It is damp with perspiration, and I see and feel a glimmer, a vision of what is to come—the flower of my womb.

CHAPTER
SIXTY-FOUR

We priestesses remember those who wear the universe of stars in the curves of their skin and in the hallowed chambers of the temples of their bodies. We remember those who live in both heaven and earth equally.

Gaia Codex: Node 75.854321

ANKA IS A steady guide, and after some days and nights, we arrive at the village of the Hriya. As the morning mists lift from the leaves, she moves towards a thickening of vines. With a movement of her finger, a subtle parting appears. The air has the viscosity of water. As we step into a clearing, the momentary opening closes behind us. On the other side, rushing waters mist the air as light shines through in iridescent rainbows. Parrots caw and flap in a crescendo of ruby, sapphire, brilliant yellow, and emerald green wings. Waves of butterflies flicker through the trees. A rush of voices follows and a patter of bare feet on muddy ground. I gasp.

"You are home, Lila Sophia. Welcome to Hriya." Anka

gestures towards the concentric circles of men and women of all ages. *The voices, the wind, the birds, the rustle of leaves—all rise to meet and greet me.*

Like Anka, the Hriya people are ornamented with intricate luminescent tattoos that capture constellations of stars, and like my own markings, mimic those on butterfly wings.

An elder woman who wears a crown of magnificent macaw feathers approaches and breaks the silence. She speaks swiftly in a language that mimics the song of birds and the flow of water and is punctuated by soft velvet clicks of her tongue.

"Welcome, A-ma, we are happy." *I understand her.*

Instinctively, I bow deeply to the ground in front of the elder. When I finally rise up, the members of the tribe have circled around.

Then they come up and touch my skin, dozens of hands playing over my body.

My markings light up. They know how to read them, how to take in the information of where I have been, what I have seen, what I have stored and transmuted. I, in turn, am learning from their touch. I am receiving information: a flow of images, textures, and words.

We are the Hriya. We are Stars, and we are Earth. For us, they are one and the same. As the hands of the Hriya run over my skin, I experience the rainforest expanding and contracting over hundreds of millions of years as millions of species emerge and then die off.

We are Hriya. We have been here since the beginning.

And I am a Memory Keeper. In every cell in my body my DNA carries information. I have known this, but here it is coming alive. *We are the Gaia Codex.*

This continues for some time, and then suddenly the circles disperse, the hands fall away, and I am sitting in the middle of a circle looking deep into the eyes of the Elder Mother.

"Mother," I bow to Elder Mother. I am not separate from her. We sit still for some time, the two of us taking each other in.

Finally Anka beckons me out of the circle. "Come, see our village." We walk a short distance to a few open huts—a long-house and several elegant structures built at varying heights in the trees, moving up into the canopy through a series of swaying bridges. Herbs are drying on racks.

I notice that the simple objects of daily life—bowls for eating and water, tools for hunting, and the structures of habitation themselves—are grooved and lined with intricate designs that mimic and reflect the forest. As my eyes slowly adjust, patterns appear: engraved lines form into butterflies, hundreds and thousands of them, in all stages of metamorphosis, caterpillar, chrysalis, and butterfly. Or maybe this is inside me. The line between inside and outside is very thin. The drawings and carvings are very fluid, a breath of the jungle, metamorphosis in motion.

"How long have the Hriya lived here?" I ask Anka.

Anka looks at me with her dark eyes. "By your count, hundreds of millions of years. For us, we have always lived here. Simple. Time is different for us. It is unbroken."

"But you understand our sense of time?" I ask.

"We have read your marks," Anka replies simply.

"Where are the Hriya, your people, from?" In answer, Anka turns her back towards me and lets me gaze once more at the tiny marks on her skin. This time I see constellations clearly as I look deeper into the luminescent marks on her dark skin.

"You see, A-ma?" Anka asks again without moving her lips.

"We Hriya are of stars and earth. We live there, and we live here at the same time." Anka touches the earth and then looks up to the sky. "For us there is no separation. The stars on our skin are also the stars of the universe. They are inside us."

"It's beautiful," I reply.

"Yes, A-ma. Beautiful," Anka replies.

"Do you die?" I ask.

"Yes, of course. Everything lives and dies. But we are also our ancestors, and our ancestors live in us. It is very simple. They are We, and We are They. The Soul of our people is unbroken for millions of years." Anka pauses for a moment. "When the Soul of a people dies, the people die. This is why your people come to us, for renewal."

CHAPTER
SIXTY-FIVE

Many of the sacred plants of Mother Earth provide
a doorway to the stars and to subtle realms of
consciousness. Many of Earth's tribes have known this
since the beginning of time.

Gaia Codex: Node 4444.321.8541

IT IS LATE afternoon when we sit down on mats woven of yucca plants. Some hours ago we had shared a light meal of palm hearts, manioc, and a sweet tender catfish. Now we imbibe a liquid concoction, an infusion of complimentary herbs and roots, harvested from the rainforest, and served in a gourd. Wild honey drips slowly.

Hriya women and girls of all ages surround me, chanting as they braid flowers through my hair. Fragrant sweet blossoms, the velvet petals of orchids—deep magenta, pristine white, brilliant yellow and luscious violet—and bright orange and red passionflowers. The women mix thick paints, red from the brilliant ruby-colored seeds of the annatto tree and black from the fruit of genipa tree. There are also pastes of luminescent sapphire blue, emerald green, and dark amethyst that come from flowers and succulents that are beautiful but unfamiliar to me.

Anka, who sits next to me, whispers softly in my ear, "Today you go to the GEA. Today you go to Him."

"The GEA …" I murmur as I think of the talisman Theo gave me in the dream.

Anka touches me. Her answer is a flow of images and words that sing inside my head. *The GEA is where worlds are born and die. It is where the stars meet Mother Earth. We Hriya understand the GEA to be the center of the rainforest that through hundreds of millions of years has never died. It is where you will meet the Theo.*

"The Theo is trapped waiting for you, waiting for the A-ma," she says aloud.

"Trapped?" I want to hear their knowing of what they have seen.

"Yes, only the A-ma can set him free," Anka replies.

Garlands of roughly cut diamonds, sapphires, emeralds, and rubies are strung around my waist. I feel the unique vibrational essence of each jewel. My breast and my belly, my arms and my legs are painted. The women paint the constellations of the luminescent stars, all the while singing songs of evocation.

You are Sun, and You are Moon. You are Mother who births us, protects us, and nourishes us. Mother, who consumes us back into her womb, where all things return—bones, flesh, blood, and stars.

The soft, caressing, healing hands of the women cover and touch my body in blessing. The songs are of an ancient telling. Gentle and nourishing. Evocative. As I sip the tea, soon I am also singing this chant of chants.

As the light fades from the land, the Hriya star markings begin to shine bright on my body, constellations mixing with my morpho markings. I am pulsing.

"A-ma. You are ready." It is a statement and not a question, voiced by Elder Mother as she gives me final blessings with her hands.

I bow deep to all in the circle.

"Thank you." I say the words aloud. I feel such deep gratitude for Life, for what has come, for what has been given and lost.

"A-ma, A-ma." This name, my name, here in this circle, is spoken as a wave that rises and falls. Several young women lift me to my feet and lead me down a soft mossy path that shimmers in the night. The leaves of the forest shimmer as my morpho markings pulse in response.

The night forest shimmers with light. The plants, the leaves, the trunks of the trees, the night-blooming blossoms all pulse.

There are three Hriya women, including Anka, who accompany me. As we walk into the forest their hands never leave me. As they touch me I receive a constant flow of communication passing from their fingers. Together we are breathing with the forest and its ancient histories and then, suddenly, their hands leave my body.

"We are here, A-ma. We leave you now." The eyes of the women shine in the night, reflecting a thousand stars. The night pulses with our collective breath, and then they are gone.

CHAPTER
SIXTY-SIX

The Center of the World. The Tree of Life. Axis Mundi.
Mount Kailash. The Garden of Eden. Strewn throughout
myth and human history there are clues of these places
where creation begins eternally anew. It is also said that
the origin of creation is in every breath we take. It resides
in every moment. If your good fortune brings you to
a sacred spot of origin, if you pass between the veils of
illusion, if you experience within yourself or deep within
the eyes of another this Eternal Garden of the Soul, say
yes and surrender everything.

Gaia Codex: Node 444.76.541

I AM SITTING IN a gentle valley of soft moss. Everything shimmers under a lucent blue moon. The plants and flowers glow, the ground is covered with numerous crystals and scintillating gems. The air is fragrant with nectars.

The growth patterns in this valley spiral towards a center where a plant grows some nine feet tall and again as wide. The plant has a single bloom. The petals, not yet opened, are luminous and translucent. It breathes in gentle shudders that mirror the rhythms of my own in-breath and out-breath. *This must be the GEA.*

A waterfall flows, glimmering in the moonlight. I am naked, yet I am neither cold nor hot.

I feel the pulsing heart of my sister-priestesses run through me. Their prayers caress me as I enter this sacred wedding: of matter and spirit, man and woman, past and future. My body is not my own. It has never been fully my own. I am here as a sacred vessel and temple. I wait for Theo and wonder, after all this time, what it will be like when he finally caresses me, when we gaze into each other's eyes.

I close my eyes and wait. Breathing in and out.

Time passes.

❧

I hear his voice first. "You are here, Ma," he says as he walks across the soft valley floor.

My eyes open slowly to take him in. He is tall and muscled, with wavy dark hair. He is a man in his prime, and I wonder if my dreams of sickness have been mistaken.

He sits down beside me. His eyes are brown, green, gold, and black with a hint of sapphire blue. They are alive and deep. His lips are soft and full. Power ripples through his limbs.

"I am," I answer, as my eyes meet his. My voice is strong and full. The Goddess fills me.

The energy that runs between us is palpable.

"We are here, Ma." His voice plays through my body, awakening every cell. It is velvet. It is deep.

In Theo's presence, as we sit together, I feel a deep

calm—peace radiating from the very core of my belly as it moves through my heart and flows through the top of my crown. As I look into Theo's eyes, and he into mine, there is release. All that I have been carrying for so long, the worry, the tension, the promises, the vows, my hopes and fears, the weight of a thousand lifetimes—it all falls away. Everything is gone, except pulsing living light that is in the center of every cell and at the center of creation itself, the luminous vibration that connects all creation. It flows between him and me, through our hearts, and each of our vital organs. It flows through the energy centers that run up and down the spine.

I finally speak. "I thought I was coming to heal you, but it is you who are healing me."

I look into his radiant face. So handsome. So beautiful. The mirror of my soul. The heart of my heart.

"Together we heal each other, Sophia. This is our gift together," Theo says.

Theo is my Beloved, the deepest reflection of my Soul. *It is has ever been so as our bodies, hearts, and souls once again join as One.*

In-breath and out-breath—after the stillness, the movement arises. Kundalini, Shakti moves up my spine. As our flesh touches, I feel in my Beloved's body the rivers of blood that are clogged up with pollutants, the organs that are being eaten away. They are our shared human legacy. I feel his pain—our pain.

"I am here, my love," I whisper.

"… And for that, Sophia, I am thankful." He lies back as I softly kiss—each ache, each pain, each suffering. As I gently let my heart and lips caress him, our ignorance, our cruelty and the greed that both he and I have rendered in lifetimes past,

that humanity has perpetuated for millennia, is touched, felt, acknowledged, and healed.

"They are our shared wounds, my love," I whisper to him softly. "You will never have to carry them alone again." "I knew you would be the one, Sophia," Theo whispers in my ear as he holds me close.

"We are here to finish what we started so very long ago. The completion of the circle," I say as I touch his skin softly.

I let the intelligence of my morpho markings work and as new DNA moves through our bodies, reconfiguring our human blueprint. A seed of light ignites, and I feel Mother Earth rest inside the alembic of my womb. *Anima Mundi—the Soul of the Earth.*

As his heart pulses, my heart flowers, ten thousand petals opening as his maleness moves inside me penetrating me deep as golden light. Healing the wounded part of our shared feminine Soul: the rapes, the degradation, the silenced voice of generations of women who feared to speak their truth, and the imprisonment of the radiant force that is the Goddess. She who is both Death and Life. As he moves and kisses my lips—he heals, and I heal, and when I peak, when we climax together, the flower blooms, resonating out, waves of light rippling without end, across that ocean which has no shore.

CHAPTER
SIXTY-SEVEN

*In the Hindu tradition, it is said Shiva and Shakti spend
eons together in a lover's embrace on the crystal peak of
Mount Kailash. Others say that Shiva and Shakti leave
the mountain to walk the world in human form. Few will
recognize them when they do.*

Gaia Codex: Node 444.521.76

WE SPEND DAYS, weeks, months, and years in this
garden, or maybe it is one single night. I lose track
of time as Theo and I play, as we converse on the
birth of stars and planets, the most beautiful hues of color, taste,
and touch that we have ever experienced, of how a soul awakens
through lifetimes–or in a moment. Being with him feels infinite,
as though a boundary of soul and heart, pleasure and the
universe itself, is ever dissolving, expanding and again arising.

When the sun finally rises, I wake to the flutter of butterfly wings—thousands of sapphire iridescent morpho butterflies
are draped over my body and across the green velvet moss. The

sensation of their tiny legs and of the flutter of their wings is exquisite. They are part of my DNA, my origin.

The sun is high in the sky, after a long moonlit night. The GEA is some ten feet away from me, its last huge velvety petals falling to the ground. It has bloomed.

I look around. I do not see Theo. I still feel him in my body, in my cells. His scent is on my skin. I close my eyes and call out to him. "Theo …"

As the sun arches into the noonday sky, the butterflies flutter away. I am human. I am female. I notice a woven basket full of fresh mangos, papayas, and bananas. Next to it is a gourd of cool water. I let the cool water wash down my throat. It is fresh and rejuvenating.

"Sophia." Theo's voice caresses my ear. He is right behind me.

I open my eyes and turn towards him. My heart skips a beat in release.

"Theo." Instantaneously, we come together: forehead-to-forehead, our eyes nearly touching, taking each other in, our lips kissing softly. I am sitting on his lap, my arms wrapped around him. He is strong.

We continue kissing, stopping only to look deeply into each other's eyes.

It feels so natural. Like we have always been like this and that what came before was only a dream.

Theo places his hand on my belly. I feel the pulse under his hand—a child, our child, growing in my womb.

We felt her soul descending, igniting, and rippling through my womb as we made love. It is a radiant soul—she will incarnate female, she is one who has travelled the stars and who knows Earth. Her heart pulses, sweet, open, and wide. This I see.

"I don't know if we have met her, Theo, this soul, this child who grows inside me, but she is beautiful," I softly say as I hold my belly. I see and feel the cells dividing, the embryo being formed.

"She is," Theo replies, kissing my womb and then kissing me on the lips.

I look up and see the beginnings of a new luminescent bud on the GEA plant.

Theo kisses me deeply—and then again. His lips are soft and warm upon mine.

I remember the talisman Theo gave me in the dream. It all seems so long ago, tales from some ancient time, and yet it is so close. I feel the folds in the fabric of time that make the past and present become one.

CHAPTER
SIXTY-EIGHT

When the GEA blooms in the deepest forest, the world is
born anew.

Gaia Codex: Node 444.8541

THEO IS WATCHING me intently as I weave a garland of velvet orchids to string around my belly. I know the beauty of the flowers will inspire our daughter-to-be. Most of my thoughts in these days are about her: her well-being, her health, who she will be as she enters the world. What her soul has to say to mine. My child, My teacher, My friend. My sister.

Theo continues to watch me.

Finally, he speaks. "We must go, Sophia. It is time. The GEA flower blossoms once every ten thousand years. It has bloomed. I am released. You have freed me," Theo says.

"We have freed each other, Theo," I reply.

I feel our child and the pulse of the Mother in my womb, I feel
every cell in my body connected to Mother Earth.

"We must go together," I say softly.

"Yes, we will go together, Sophia." Theo kisses me on my forehead. I feel the strength of his protection and his love.

We leave the next morning as the first rays of light penetrate the forest floor. As Theo and I walk down the narrow path, we enter a denser cloud forest with trees that extend up hundreds of feet into the sky. The flora and fauna is transformed. How long have we been inside the garden of the GEA? It feels like eons, but perhaps it has only been one night. I truly don't know. Time and experience are like a palimpsest rich with many layers when the center is still.

Some things are certain. Theo walks beside me. His hand is firm and strong in mine. Our child grows in my belly.

When we finally enter the village of the Hriya, children circle around, laying their hands on us as they call out in greetings of clicks and birdcalls. At first glance, the village looks the same: the subtle living structures still stand, the children and adults with their star-marked bodies are tending to their tasks of weaving, sharpening bows, and drying herbs. But as I look closer, there is no one I recognize. No sign of Anka or Elder Mother.

I pause, close my eyes for a moment, and look deeper. Time has passed. I feel it, and I see it, for a moment. Every event that has passed through time is here to read, like rings on a tree. The realization comes to me that I have been gone a long while.

"The A-ma has come," one of the young girls calls out in clicks and birdsong. An older woman approaches me. Like the Elder Mother before, she wears macaw feathers and a necklace of raw cut gems, jaguar teeth, and precious seeds—the regalia of her position—but she is a different woman.

"You have returned, A-ma. The world turns, and you have brought the Theo with you." She looks up and down at Theo. "He is healthy." She smiles and then laughs. There are now many of the Hriya gathered round us. Men and boys with their spears and bows, and mothers with their babes nestled into their breasts.

"We are happy," the Elder Mother speaks for all in the circle.

The children cannot keep from touching us. The adults wait.

"Is Anka still here?" I ask.

"Anka?" Elder Mother pauses as she runs through a tree of memory and family lineages. Finally, she answers. "No. She has not been with us for many generations, but she is here."

Elder Mother nods towards a majestic trumpet tree with red blooms. I remember that the roots of this tree were used to heal wounds and that the Hriya believe that the soul of an ancestor often resides in certain trees.

"Anka," I whisper under my breath, and the brilliant red blooms on the tree shudder. Instinctively, I put my hand to my belly.

The men and boys look at Theo with curiosity.

The man in the tree. The man wed to the GEA. First Father. His story had been both an initiation for young Hriya men as well as a tale of warning.

To break the tension, Theo walks up to the group of men and boys and starts to make jokes with them in their language. Soon the men and boys are laughing, and as Theo squats on the ground, drawing figures in the dirt, they share stories. I smile. Theo's muscled body shines in the sun. It is good to see him like this. He feels human.

That night there are stories, songs, and feasting. Garlands of scented orchids are placed around Theo and I. After the feasting, we gather in circle. The men hold the outer circles with a steady resonant chant that mirrors the pulse of the Earth, as the women touch my markings and my belly with their hands, giving blessing to the child within.

At the end of the night, Elder Mother and I stand together. I look into her flickering eyes. Each flash is an input: plants, insects, mammals, stars, waters, and sun—the collective soul of Hriya through millions of generations.

"You are us, and we are you, A-ma. May this be forever true."

"We breathe the same air and watch the rise and fall of the same sun. This, I will never forget," I answer.

I am old, and I am young. In the depth of my belly, I feel my child, my daughter growing: an illuminated soul descending into matter.

The next morning, a young Hriya woman hands me garments made of soft woven cloth, subtle in color and weave, strong yet feathery light to touch.

"These are for your journey," she says.

It will seem strange to cover my nakedness. Pores breathe differently when skin is covered.

"Wear them when you come to the river," the Hriya sister says simply as if reading my thoughts. "You will need them there."

"Gentan will be your guide," Elder Ma says. A young man of the Hriya tribe stands next to her waiting. We will travel light: a bow and arrows, a spear, a pouch of dried berries, and gourds of water.

"Thank you. I bow to Elder Ma and Elder Father." I bow low

to the soul of these people sustained through millions of years. They are our teachers.

"Please give our greetings to your sisters—the Priestesses of Astera. Tell them they should be honored to have a true daughter," Elder Ma says.

"Thank you." I bow low once more. "It is I who am honored."

The Priestesses of Astera. My sisters. Where are you now? I call silently in my mind, but in this moment there is no answer.

Theo has given the boys and men pieces of his hair and special bows and arrows and spears he has made.

"You will both be in the heart of Hriya for generations to come," Elder Father says as we prepare to leave.

"As the Hriya are in our shared heart," Theo replies.

I watch Theo's face. It is so calm, as though leaving the forest is completely natural.

I still wonder who this man is. Perhaps such things are always a mystery. Early the next morning we leave the Hriya village.

PART SIX
Gaia

CHAPTER
SIXTY-NINE

You can never step in the same river twice.

Heraclitus

Gaia Codex: Node 3321.41

THE RETURN JOURNEY is slow and steady. My eyes take in the shifting vegetation. Trees stretch up into the canopy, everywhere are oversized ferns and vines, monkeys, and flocks of fluttering macaws. There are also plants and animals that look almost familiar, but not quite. Flying mammals with glistening feather ruffs and orchid blooms as large as a small one-room house. Nature, I know, is always evolving, always changing. I wonder when we are, where we are. Does anything remain of the world I once knew? Theo walks beside me, but I keep these thoughts to myself.

After some weeks, we come to the edge of the mighty river. Word of our arrival was sent by messenger, by runners who know the forest trails like lines in the palms of their hands and who move much faster then a woman in her fourth moon of pregnancy.

The boat that greets us is made of graciously carved and joined hardwoods, and born along by majestic sails of many colored silks: emerald green, cobalt, saffron, and ruby. There are beautiful carvings on the sides of the boat and on the mast-head—jaguars and anacondas, majestic macaws and swirling dragons.

I grab Theo's hand. I am emotional, perhaps it is the state of pregnancy, but tears are streaming down my eyes. "It's beautiful." I recognize the ship. My childhood notebooks—now long gone—included pictures of such vessels. I wonder whether I will find other elements from those musings where we are going: the technologies, the cities, the poetry, and the stories.

"Sophia, I am glad you are happy." Theo takes my arm and carefully guides me up into the boat.

The ship's crew is dressed in colorful hand-woven clothes.

"An Theo!" Many call out as though he is known here. This is strange.

Both the men and the women wear their hair long and braided, with stones and talismans woven through. The crew appears to be a fusion of nationalities so refined that I could not say whether they were Caucasian, Asiatic, African, or Indigenous. Their eyes are shining, and I notice the subtle morpho markings on their skin, markings like my own.

"An Sophia, welcome. We have prepared a chamber for you." As the captain, a tall, dark-haired woman, speaks, she holds her hands over her heart and looks me in the eyes.

"Sister," she continues. "I am Kee." She speaks an unknown

language, but I understand her. Her transmission language skills are strong. *Sister*, I silently reply.

Her eyes reveal to me things I have never seen. Her genetic code is different from mine and yet somehow familiar.

The spoken language is soft, rhythmic, rich, and full of the elements themselves.

"An." I take it is a name of care and respect. We are given a quick tour of the boat. I meet many of the crew—young men and women with names like Hetru, Urab, Tean, and Skosh.

The crew doesn't ask questions, but many greet Theo with hugs and bows, or by showing him sketches and instruments and newborn children as though he is familiar to them. *How curious.*

"Come, let's get you settled in," Theo says, taking us into the chamber that was prepared. Inside, the bed is a soft nest, lined with gossamer, silk, cotton, bamboo, and hemp. The textures feel sumptuous. There are large octagonal windows that open to let the air in on either side or close for privacy at night. I lie there, resting, feeling the child in my womb.

Theo pulls the curtains of emerald green and purple over the window, and we curl up together.

"I love you, Sophia," Theo looks deep into my eyes as he speaks.

I kiss him deeply, softly taking in his scent.

"I love you, too, Theo." As I say this, my heart pulses warm like liquid golden honey. "Wherever we are, I know this is where I want our child to be." I say softly into his ears.

"Me too," Theo says as he wraps his arms around me.

"It is good to be a simple man again. With a beautiful wife soon to have a new child to bring into the world," Theo laughs.

"I don't think you will ever be a simple man," I laugh as I give him another kiss on the cheek.

"No, probably not," he laughs. "But in your arms at least I know I am a man of extraordinary good fortune."

"This is true. We are deeply fortunate," I reply.

As I fall asleep, I hear each of our hearts—Theo's, our child's, and mine—beating together in unison.

That night, I have a dream that catapults me back. I am in ancient Egypt on the Duat, the River of the Dead, where souls pass to the afterlife. Within the dream, I wonder if my new life with Theo, my time in the GEA, this sweet perfection is all but dream—and whether I died somewhere back in the Amazon rainforests, or during the plagues of Paris, and I am now simply passing through the underworld, moving into the next life? I am shaken.

I try to wake myself up, once, twice, three times, and finally, I feel Theo's strong arms around me, his sweet breath on my neck.

"Theo … I am scared." I pull him closer.

"It's okay, love," he says as though he has been awake waiting for me. "It takes time to adjust when we move through the dimensions and move through time. There is no hurry, Sophia. You are here now. Know this."

I turn over and cuddle closer, feeling the steady movement of the river, and as I fall asleep, I take in his scent to make sure I am truly here.

Some days later I am on the ship's deck, watching the edges of the river and the unbroken jungle. There are occasional vessels

that pass us: long canoes and other sailing ships like ours—made of wood, beautifully decorated—that seem to move with the smoothness of the crystal technologies that guide our vessel. Conch shells are blown, and sometimes goods are exchanged in the passing.

Above, in the sky, there are occasional elegant flying vessels, silent dirigibles and some other type of sailing ship, one that appears to float effortlessly in the winds. I am still getting a sense of where and when we are.

"Betee, do you know about the Egyptians?" I ask one of the crew as she comes down from rigging a sail. My dream from several nights ago is still present in my mind.

Betee crinkles her face. "I don't think so. But there are myths of ruins of ancient stone pyramids at the bottom of the Sea of Sahar. Does that ring a bell?"

"Yeah, it does a little bit, thank you," I answer.

I want to ask her questions. Lots of questions, but I don't want to startle her. I begin to gently look at her mind when she stops me gently.

"An Sophia. It was a very long time ago. They say hundreds of thousands of years ago. Does that help?" Of course she has the gift of telepathy. Perhaps all of these people do.

She is kind, and I see that she wants to be helpful.

"Yes, I think so. Thank you, Betee. I am still acclimating."

Betee leans in closer.

"An Sophia, there are some who know who you are, but we understand that you and An Theo will want to tell your story in your own time. Our crew is simply here to help with your safe passage."

"Thank you," I reply.

"You're welcome." Her eyes are warm, her skin cinnamon brown.

She is turning to go, but I have one more question.

"Did you meet An Theo before we joined your voyage?" I had to ask.

"Yes," she says it matter-of-fact as though I should know, but then she sees my puzzlement.

"He came here a few months ago to say if all went well, he would be returning and bringing you, and we should be ready."

"I see." The news is both comforting and unnerving.

How had Theo been so certain? How had he come here before? How had he been able to travel to me so clearly, appearing in my dreams and on the streets of Paris? All had somehow seemed self-evident in the garden of the GEA, yet now these questions begin to bother me.

I feel into the web, looking for my sisters: for Rhea, Helene, and Dominique.

I do not feel them directly, but I feel their seeds and spirits woven into many bodies, connected with many souls who are living, here and alive on this planet. I miss them. I miss Rhea and wonder if we will see each other here in this new place—this new world.

How far have you travelled, dear sister? I whisper it to the wind. *Know that I haven't forgotten you.*

I had eventually told Theo of my love for Rhea. He had only smiled and said: "That makes two of us who love her." Nothing more, but I am still curious. I will ask him again in time.

And Dominique? What is known of her fate? I am now at peace with her disappearance, but I still have questions.

Surely, now, after all this has come to past, you can finally

show your face, Dominique? The winds of the Codex seem to have no answers.

I also wonder what happened to the world I was born into, a world that was on the brink of disaster so long ago. That world where there were places like London and New York, and people drove cars and used computers. I feel that the tragedy was transformed, but how long did it take? Were there centuries of suffering and forgetfulness, or did we humans quickly make the transition and rapidly build a new world from the ashes of what came before? I do not know and when I search the Gaia Codex there is a block around the information—at least for now.

"Sophia." Theo has come up from behind me and given me a soft kiss on my neck. "Kee has something to show us." I am feeling a bit nauseous with the baby. It comes and goes—elation and ecstasy and then the heaviness of pregnancy.

"Theo, I need to know how you were able to visit me in Paris and so clearly in my dreams."

Theo sits down beside me. "I am surprised you never asked before," he says.

"When we were in the Garden of the GEA, time was different," I reply. "The past and future seemed to melt away. I was just present with you. But here I feel the threads of my past again, and I wonder about our future. Where are we, Theo? Where exactly are we in the web of time?" I ask.

Theo looks at me intently as he softly runs his fingers through my curls. "As I said the other night, Sophia, it takes time to calibrate when we move our physical body through dimensions. It is a process of tuning into a specific location in space and time. Time, for some, is navigable. Be gentle with yourself. I have long had the ability to move and appear through time, but it was a glamour and illusion of sort. When I saw you in Paris and at the banyan tree in Kew Gardens, I was not fully physically there. Does this make sense?"

"It does," I reply, thinking of my experiences and trainings with the Priestesses of Astera.

"As for where we are in time—come with me to see Kee." Theo puts his arms around me as we walk up towards the captain's cabin.

"Yes!" Kee opens the carved cabin door. She is over six feet tall with jet-black skin and pale aquamarine eyes. Her morpho markings glisten midnight blue on her dark skin.

"An Sophia, Theo thought you might enjoy looking at some of our technology here on the ship. Plus, I wanted to spend some time with you both. Have you found your quarters comfortable?"

"Wonderful," I reply.

"Good," Kee smiles. "That's thanks to Suxsie. She creates the beauty."

I have seen Suxsie around. She is a beautiful creature with morpho markings colored like the fragrant flowers of an abundant garden.

"She is Kee's lover," Theo had whispers in my ear as he gently caressed my bottom. Theo is flirtatious with me, and our chemistry seems to have only heightened here on the ship. It is delicious. The tortured man of my dreams is gone.

Kee walks to the center of the room and gently spins a luminous globe with her finger. It appears as a hologram, but is hanging from an elegantly wrought brass stand. "This," Kee says, "is a globe of Terra Gaia."

I had heard the name Terra Gaia used by some of my sister-priestesses long ago.

"Earth, Aearth, these are name we have called our Mother Planet in the past," Kee continues. "In common speak in these times, we call her Terra Gaia."

"This is Earth right now?" I ask. The sphere shows a planet with many islands and archipelagos. Many of the continents I had known—Europe and Asia and Africa—have shifted or are partially underwater.

"Yes, we have always been a water planet, but now much of our land mass is underwater. But there are, as you can see, some vast tracts of land—like here in the rainforests or over here in Dumar." Kee points to a portion of the planet that looks like parts of Asia and Africa merged.

"How many people are on the planet right now?" I ask.

"Around four million," Kee answers. "We naturally stop having children if the population gets higher than that. It is in our genetics, so we don't kill ourselves with overpopulation. We listen deeply to the rhythms of Mother Nature."

Kee continues to spin the globe. As she does, I see aerial views of cities and human establishments, but they appear to blend in with the landscape.

"We live under the sea as well." Again, Kee answers my unspoken question. "There are some tribes who seem well suited for that and even have trained their morpho markings to grow gills as needed."

"Does everyone have morpho markings?" I ask slowly.

"Most, but not all," Kee answers as she looks at Theo, who does not have morpho markings.

I have so many questions. "Do you have contact with other planets?" I ask.

"Yes, of course," Kee answers. I think for a moment of the

moon missions, and the clumsy spaceships that existed some seventy years before I was born in the middle of the twentieth century—so long ago.

Kee starts laughing. "No, not like that. The ancient arts of interdimensional travel have been reclaimed. It is more elegant and takes fewer resources."

"You read minds quite well," I laugh.

"Yes, of course," Kee answers. "Can't you read the thought streams of others?"

"Yes, but we kept such skills hidden where I came from—at least in polite society."

"Sophia is still adjusting," Theo adds gently. "We both are." As Theo says this, I wonder if he is just saying this to comfort me, for when I observe him, it's like he's always been here in this new world. More at ease than I have ever seen him.

"I am catching up. The past, the present … the future." I touch my hands to my belly, to the child growing in my womb.

"We honor our ancestors who made wise decisions so we can be here. We honor you and Theo," Kee says quietly.

"So this is our world," Kee continues, "and this is some of our technology." Kee tunes a few machines based on crystals and delicately stringed harps.

"Zero point energy," I say under my breath.

"What do you mean by that?" Kee asks.

"The energy it takes in is in balance with the energy it produces," I answer.

"We don't create technologies that destroy Terra Gaia," Kee says simply. "We humans learned our lessons on this a long time ago."

I let out a sigh. Theo looks back at me, amused. I had of

course told him of my visions as a child, my dreams, and my drawings, and he knew of the inventions of the Priestesses of Astera.

"You are here, Sophia … you are truly here," he says softly.

"You know of the Priestesses of Astera?" I ask Kee. I need to know.

Kee puts her hand on mine, and as I do, I see the circles of my sister-priestesses long ago at the Château Lumiere. "Every culture has a creation story, Lila Sophia. Sometimes they are true."

CHAPTER
SEVENTY

Through multiple incarnations, there is one place we call our true home.

Gaia Codex: Node 3321.41

"SOPHIA, WAKE UP, love." Theo gently kisses the nape of my neck. "Get dressed, we are approaching Lev-Li-Sea." I roll over and look at him. He is dressed.

"Already?" I ask. I could easily sleep a few more hours.

"Come," he says. "You don't want to miss the approach into the port."

Ten minutes later I am up on deck. Theo hands me a warm cup of the ginger tea I have been drinking in the mornings to settle my stomach.

Ahead of us is the port. Hundreds of ships are in dock, each with jewel-colored sails floating in the wind and beautiful carved mastheads. Above the port, the city rises: terraces upon terraces that look like they are sumptuously carved into the cliffs, dotted with lush hanging gardens and the occasional glimmering glass dome. Nearer, I can see markets, hundreds of brightly colored stalls and vibrant markets.

"Welcome to Lev-Li-Sea, An Sophia." Kee and Suxsie are standing with us looking at the sight before us.

"This is where we can rest, Sophia." Theo puts his hands gently on my swollen belly.

"There will be lots of family here and many midwives."

The baby kicks my belly. I laugh.

"She agrees," I say.

"We all look forward to meeting you little one," Suxsie calls out.

And then it all flashes before me. Soon I will raise my child, my daughter, to the stars and the seas and give thanks for her birth. Soon I will whisper her name in her ears just as my mother, Dominique, whispered in mine those many years ago. The cycles of Life will continue here on our Mother Earth.

The End

ACKNOWLEDGEMENTS

A book is born from many sources of inspiration cultivated through loving nourishment and seminal conversations. In the case of *Gaia Codex*, it is also informed by a body of wisdom sustained through generations.

My own initiation into this mythic lineage of women and has come through many sources: deep conversations with women and men all over the planet, written and oral records of many cultures, and the guidance and love of profound teachers. *Gaia Codex* was the book that I "had to write." It could not have been done without the love, support, and inspiration of many extraordinary individuals.

I am deeply thankful to have the guidance, prayers and deep teachings of Rinpoche Thewang Sitar, Lama Pema Tendzin, and Amma (Amritanandamayi).

Gaia Codex was also born of the blessings of many dear Sisters and mentors who have helped bring to life the intimacy of sisterhood and the path of the Sacred Feminine as a living, breathing tradition.

Osprey Orielle Lake, thank you for your deep love, sisterhood and mentorship—your embodiment and mastery of the timeless path and deep rooted earth wisdom. Lynn Augstein, your Gift of love, nourishment and deep visionary seeing has made Gaia Codex possible. My dear sister, you have my deepest gratitude and love. Cynthia Jurs, thank you, Goddess-Sister-Tara, for being such a radiant champion for Gaia, a mentor, beloved friend, and dear sister of my Heart. Lissa Rankin, dear one, you are an amazing catalyst. Our walks and conversations over these last years are woven deeply through the pages of *Gaia*. I treasure our friendship and our shared journey of Awakening–over time. June Katzen, thank you for your love and inspiration, for feeding me yummy food and inspiring my soul with your archetypal wisdom and guidance. You are the treasure. Nina Von Feldmann, when you came into my life everything changed. Thank you for sharing your brilliance, vision, wisdom, and our sisterhood through the ages. Dear, wise, ancient priestess. I love you. Elizabeth and Catherine Scherwenka, I love you both so much. Our shared journey of unfolding into Oneness over the last ten years has been my teaching and treasure. Samantha Sweetwater, our friendship over the decades is an extraordinary, Gift of Awakening. I love you. Magalie Bonneau-Marcil, I continue to be amazed by our journey of love and heart, thank you for the continued inspiration and sisterhood. Christy Brown, the place where we meet always takes me H(om)E. Thank you for our sisterhood, communion, and that ancient connection born in the deep yogi cave, the in-breath and out-breath. Ann Hughes, you are magic, light, and incredible evolution in motion. I—and so many others—have been blessed with the gift of your love. Carla Kleefield and Celeste Worl, thank you for your love, support, and the most amazing celebrations of Sister-Mother-Magic beautifully born of your LOVE.

To Ashawna-Shawn Hailey (October 1949–October 2011). In many ways, dear one, this book is the fruit of our journey together, both in inspiration and with your generous support. I miss you and you are with me every day. You have been one of Life's great Gifts. Kim Hailey, my continued deep gratitude to you.

Sally Kempton, thank you for your deep wisdom, transmissions, and teachings. For your embodiment of the Sacred Feminine and your wonderful book *Awakening Shakti*. Our conversations and your sage council over the years have been extraordinary.

Susan Griffin, our conversations have been seminal during this creation process. Thank you. I honor your wisdom, vision, courage, and groundbreaking offering of *Woman and Nature* so many years ago, a gift for so many of us.

Kimberly and Foster Gamble, thank you for your friendship, vision, and deep support of *Gaia Codex*. Kimberly, our walks, lunches, and your sage council from your own experience of the path less travelled have been seminal. Thank you for so graciously and radiantly embodying lucid courage, visionary intellect, joy, beauty, and deep kindness—the Living Goddess.

Marta Salas-Porras, thank you for the gift of your exquisite, ever-unfolding, creative intelligence—a living treasure. Dorka Kheen, you are an inspiration, my dear, an amazing catalyst and I so honor and delight in our dance through the years. Myra Jackson, thank you for your lucid consciousness, catalysis and magical connection through time.

Michelle Grenier, Chandra Hines, Elisabeth Manning,

Laurie Magaritonda, Erica Rand, Claire Savage, dear ones, you have each inspired and shaped *Gaia Codex*. Our communion, your love—the extraordinary expressions of your souls are woven through these pages.

Joanna Hartcourt-Smith, thank you for your radiant loving embrace. Erika Harrison, thank you for your love, support, and sublime intelligence. Linda Adams, Zen Cryar-Debruke, Wyolah Garden, Christian Leahy, Leslie Meehan, Ginny McGinnis, Christy Sweetland, Gabrielle Schwibach, and Anna Molitar. Thank you for your teachings, your commitment to our Mother Earth, to women, and to evolutionary consciousness. I cherish each of you.

Bonnie Bell, thank you for your radiant, deeply forged wisdom and insight. For planting seeds that nourish many over time. Tosha Silver, Goddess-Ma, what a delight it is to continue the dance together. Here and now.

Amy Logan and Trista Lee Hendren Løberg, sisters, I celebrate your courageous, visionary voices in taking a stand for women and the sweet communion of heart. More to come! Jacqueline Wigglesworth and Julie Bridgham—your deep artistry, global intelligence, and ability to shine light on beauty and tragedy are extraordinary. Shannon Biggs and Atossa Soltani, thank you for your continued visionary dedication to our Mother Earth. You inspire me. Neema Namadamu your courage and voice is our inspiration. Thank you for awakening the spirit of the Congo and the brilliance of the the feminine voice in our hearts. I am thankful for our time together in Circle.

Amore Vera Aida, Lis Addison, Katherine Amer, Amy Ima Banasky Jacqueline Chan, Tracy Collins, Sher Katz, Michelle Klink, Erica Linson, Mellie McAyle, Megan O'Grady Green,

Lisa Smith, April Sweazy, E'lana Solaris, Julia Weaver, my gratitude for to each of you, for your vibrant evolutionary catalysis, your deep embodiment of feminine wisdom, and the amazing creations you are each bringing into the world at this time. You inspire me.

Cynthia Simon, magical seer, *you are* the *Codex*. To commune with you is divine. Sienna Rankin-Klein you are a blessing–one thousand years in an eight-year-old body. Sedena Cappannelli, thank you for igniting such fluid connection and beauty. Debra Giusti (Lioness), thank you for your visionary catalysis and divine timing.

Bonnie Gray, thank you for your love, nourishment, and gracious alchemical embodiment of Earth wisdom. Beau Takahara, your embodiment of grace and beauty through the decades is a continued inspiration to me—a blessing. Jodi Evans—fierce radiant love goddess—when we talk universes come alive. Rachel Bagby, you are living, breathing poetry in motion: social catalysis at its core. Thank you for shining your light on me and on so many beings—a Gift.

Thank you to the extraordinary circles of women in which I have the honor to participate: Earth Treasure Vase Circle, Rosebud Circle, the Flaming Mystic Circle, and the Summer-Winter Solstice Circle. Dear Ones, you each inspire. I am blessed to weave with you, to learn, to evolve, and awaken with you over time

Nina Simons and Kenny Ausubel, our personal conversations over the last years have been alchemical and have planted seeds of true inspiration. Nina, I honor your deep groundwork laid for the next generation of women, exquisitely and powerfully mapped through the microcosm of your personal journey.

Your work is heartfelt, powerful, and "now." Kenny, your mercurial intelligence delights me: worlds-within-worlds. The legacy that both of you have created is deeply rooted and I sense it will shape the course of many generations to come. Thank you.

Christopher Miles. The journey with you through the birth of *Gaia Codex* has been amazing. Our sessions together and your ability to catalyze the soul's birth through deep metamorphosis is truly a blessing. You are a master at what you do. Thank you.

David McConville, I have so delighted in our conversations and explorations over the years—the unfolding of universes and the exploration into the cycles of birth and death, the visions of emergent cultures, and the synthesis of technology and consciousness. I treasure our friendship.

David Abrams, our conversations, your encouragement, and your living body of wisdom and wildness continue to touch me deeply. Mother Gaia is reborn through your writings, your magic, and enchantment. Thank you.

Lou Hawthorne, I treasured our journey together with Sacred Agent and continue to delight in your amazing wide-ranging intelligence. Thank you for the continuing conversation.

Hugh Wheir, thank you for your deep support of *Gaia Codex*—my *Avataṃsaka Sūtra sangha* brother.

Robert Thurman, our conversation and interview on the *Avataṃsaka Sūtra* some years ago was a turning point for me. I offer you my continued deep gratitude.

David Shearer, our early and continued conversations over the last decade on metaphysics and awakening are woven

throughout *Gaia Codex*. You are a precious soul and I cherish you.

Brian Weller, you are living evocation of the timeless tradition. *Satsang* with you is a blessing. I am so thankful for our friendship. You and Freddi are precious.

Paul Hawken, thank you for our teas, illuminated conversations, and your encouragement throughout the writing process. You are Living Treasure for me… and for so many of us.

Nion McEvoy, my deep appreciation for your consciousness, mercurial intelligence, and timing.

My deep appreciation and love to Andrew Aungerleider and Gay Dillingham. Jim and Suzanne Gollin, Annie Frans and Tom Van Dyke, Suzanne Bohan and Glenn, Carol Misseldyne, Thomas and Theresa Banyanca, and Allan Badiner. I have so enjoyed brainstorming and playing with all of you through the writing process—in the company of Hurricane Hayes. Thank you for your insights, love and support. Dal LaMagna and Jackie Wildau, thank you so much for your inspiration and support. A blessing.

A special thank you to those who have helped shape my DNA, this path, and my journey through the years. Kirston Leigh Mann, who struck a spark in my heart of the timeless sisterhood way back when we were teenagers, I love you, and I have not forgotten.

Robert Barnhardt, thank you for believing in me early on and for your continued heartfelt connection. You are a blessing to me and so many. To Alex Conn, for magic and connection.

Alison Kennedy, thank you for being an extraordinary, magical mentor to a young woman birthing into the ancient traditions of the feminine. So many doors were opened under your tutelage. You have my deepest gratitude.

Dr. R.G. Stienman, thank you for your friendship and for awakening the heart and mind of a young freshman. You are a gift and an expression of a life authentically and courageously lived. I carry you and Freddy in my heart.

Dr. Linda Hesse, thank you for your skillful guidance at U.C. Berkeley in helping me begin to translate "the Ineffable experience" into words.

Dr. David Stronach, I am forever grateful for your generous sharing of the deep roots of history and archeology. Our long talks over wine were formative.

Dr. Lawrence Stark (1926–2004): it was a blessing to have our numerous conversations over dinner and wine at Chez Pannisse. You changed how I perceived the world and my understanding of where technology and metaphysics meet.

Donald Karl, your wise legal counsel and especially our magical connection around the essence of the redwoods, so many years ago, was seminal. Thank you for keeping in touch.

Philip Glass, thank you for our auspicious meetings and your words of encouragement to a young artist. You hold the soul deeply.

John Perry Barlow, you have continued to bring extraordinary magical connections into my life for decades now. So many of my favorite people have come into my life by way of you. I love you in all your brilliance … and your cragginess.

Koichi and Hiroko Tamano, my time studying Butoh under your tutelage and performing with Harupin-Ha was the secret teaching. Thank you.

Michael Naimark, our friendship through the decades

has been an extraordinary gift. Everything changed when you invited a young Butoh dancer to Cyberthon.

Kathelin Gray, sister, you are deeply woven into my heart. Thank you for decades of love and inspiration. More to come! John Allen, I celebrate your brilliance, your courage, your cosmic origins, and your humanity. Our continuing conversation through the years is a Gift. Deborah Parrish Snyder—dear Tango—thank you for your courage, connection, and vision.

Alfredo Sfeir-Younis, thank you for your encouragement and blessings through the creation process. Taiun Matsunami-San, thank you for your deep welcome some twenty years ago and the gift of living Zen.

David Ulansey, your generosity with your scholarship and our many long conversations over the last few decades and years helped establish an academic foundation for the more visionary aspects of *Gaia Codex* in its very early stages. Drew Dellinger, you are a living inspiration and activation.

Charles Ostman, thank you for your friendship and generously sharing your evolutionary intellect.

To Jeffery Pudwell, thank you for opening up the U.C. Berkeley libraries to me. I am forever thankful for your generosity in helping me follow my obsession in its nascent stages in the early 1990s.

Thank you to Ken Goffman—you are deep in my early DNA of metamorphosis. It is precious. Eric Gullichsen, in appreciation of your brilliance, pioneering ingenuity, and a life uniquely, unapologetically lived. Padma Prakash—wisdom and learning comes in many forms. Stephen Olsson, I so enjoyed seeding the early stages of the creation and writing process with you over wine and long conversations. Angel Ilyas—you arrived at exactly the right moment. You are a Gift. Mark Dippe—thank you for your Golden Heart. William Brooks Cole—thank you, dear one, for your generous heart and magic muse. Thank you to Heide Foley and Irina Michalova—to learn and love together over time is an unfolding blessing. Suzie Senk and Marlene Deel, thank you, dear sisters—I love you. Brock Foxsworthy Hanson—you are the Spark—may it ever be so. Gail Kennedy— Dear One, you are a blessing. I love you. Vessica, you have my gratitude and love.

Erik Spicard and Victor Sagalovsky—dear cosmic brothers. I adore both of you. So many journeys started with our laughter and the play of our imaginations.

Karl Gadjusek, how lucky were we to enjoy the fruit? Carlos Seligo, I am forever thankful for our play, creations, and explorations as undergraduates at U.C. Berkeley... through you, so many worlds were opened to me. To Robin Gadjusek (1925– 2003): I love and cherish your poet's soul. Thanks to Victor Friedberg for being a courageous wrangler of wild horses and to William Skyzniarz for saying "yes." Thank you, Rick Fujii, for our extraordinary spontaneous mystical moment together so many years ago. Hayato Kitaoka. I have not forgotten. Warren Stringer, for your deep muse and radiant soul. To Alex Theory, you have my gratitude. Mathew Klien–to your strength and pure heart. Malcolm Casselle, your timing is magical, thank you for bringing fortuitous opportunity into my life in exactly the right moments. Dennis Couwenberg–to your courage and beautiful soul. Aswin Wattanapramote and Marena Wattanapramote. Thank you for your hospitality and sharing your precious elixirs. Navin Kulshreshtha, thank you for your generous, auspicious connections.

Dwight Loop, thank you for creating inspiring music for our book trailer and the "soundtrack of life," also my gratitude to the amazing muse-musicians of Tropozone.

Maya Rock (www.mayarock.com), thank you for your editorial expertise on *Gaia Codex*. Jannon Stein, thank you for your generous, masterful copyediting. It has been a blessing to work with you both. Thank you, Dustin Lindblad (www.abedovia.com) for your vision and artistry. Damon Za and Benjamin Carrancho (www.damonza.com), thank you for your beautiful cover design and book layout. Laurie Rausch (www.codediva.com) for fabulous help with customizing our websites.

Randall (Randy) Hayes, thank you for your grounding wisdom throughout the creation process and for inspiring me every day with your vision and deep dedication to our Mother Earth. I love you. You are a precious Blessing in my Life.

To my wonderful nieces, Nicole Drew, Paige Drew, and Gretchen Drew, you have inspired *Gaia Codex* since your birth. I love you. To my brother, William Drew, and dear sister-in-law, Anna Drew, for your continued, amazing generosity of heart.

To my dear Aunt Susie (Ether Long): thank you for believing in me.

To my cousin, Susan Klingaman Estilaei, thank you for your loving spirit. You are a blessing.

To my mother, Katherine Drew, thank you for being such a beautiful, wise, expression of womanhood. I love you.

To my younger sister, Ann Kathleen Drew (1969–98), you, dear one, were my first sister in this life and you are never far from my heart.

This book is dedicated in memory of my father Joseph Coleman Drew (January 21, 1940 – April 9, 2014). I love you,

I miss you, and I carry forward your teachings—of humanity's deep connection to the web of life, of the wisdom of nature, of the inevitable cycles of civilization, and how a soul incarnates through time. I honor your vibrancy, humbleness, integrity and deep dedication to the journey.

Finally, there are many others who are inscribed on my heart and who have been instrumental in the creation of this book. If your name is not here, know that I hold our connection deeply even if it was ever so brief, for our lives are indeed a tapestry of many threads.

ENDORSEMENTS

Sarah Drew's *Gaia Codex* bears the ring of truth disguised
as fiction. As many more become aware of our true nature,
of the interconnectedness of all things, and of the illusion of
form to which we have attached ourselves, it feels plausible
to think that, like Lila Sophia, we might all shimmer with
energy, communicate telepathically, see the future, read the
past, remember past lives and recognize reincarnated souls,
and find hope in the Divine Feminine. This post-apocalyptic
tapestry of a tale, woven with lush language and ornate
imagery, offers the possibility of metamorphosis, the chance
for redemption, and the promise of what can happen when
we stop harming the natural world and start nourishing it
instead. Gripping in pace, urgent in its message, and rich
with relatable characters, *Gaia Codex* transported me to
a world so radiant that I was disheartened to come back
to reality after finishing the book in one bed-ridden day.
Yet even in my disappointment about how many of us
have tragically lost touch with our Divine nature and with

Mother Earth, I am filled with hope that one day, such fiction might become real life.

Dr. Lissa Rankin, MD, New York Times bestselling
author of *Mind Over Medicine: Scientific Proof
That You Can Heal Yourself*

At this critical time in human history, an essential navigational instrument for our way forward is the renewal of our stories. *Gaia Codex* is an exquisite novel transmitted as a long-forgotten text and incantation reconnecting us to our living Mother planet and feminine wisdom, while opening our hearts and minds to different ways of knowing and ancient memories. As you read this wonderful story, you will see it emerges unexpectedly as if from our own dreams, yet spoken through the ages. Transformative and beautiful.

Osprey Orielle Lake, Founder of Women's Earth
and Climate Caucus and Award Winning Author
of *Uprisings for the Earth*

Gaia Codex is truly a *terma* (a sacred found text) for our times. Brilliant. Moving. Captivating. Enchanting. Illuminating. Fabulous.

I laughed, I cried, I was transported into an altered state where every word echoed through my cells and awakened knowings and memories of the ages. The world you have imagined resonated in the very fabric of my being. It is not imagined. It is a dream reawakened. It is ten thousand lifetimes remembered and retold anew.

So much came to me in the reading. Much insight catalyzed. At times I wept in the deep recognition and the sheer beauty. When it was all over, I had tears coming out of my eyes for several hours although I was not actually crying. I was just so touched. And energized.

Thank you for this Gift.

Bowing deeply … It deserves to be distributed widely and adored by many.

> Cynthia Jurs, Sacred Earth Activist, Teacher,
> Founder of Earth Treasure Vase Project and
> Alliance for the Earth

Sarah, I am FULLY ACTIVATED from reading *GAIA CODEX!!!* I am blown away … truly astonished. A blend of *Avatar, The Red Tent,* and *The Mists of Avalon,* it reads like a movie. I feel deeply transformed after reading this book and I feel that any Human Being that comes in to contact with the *Gaia Codex* will be forever changed and fully activated in their truth and power to continue forth on this journey of the Great Mother. It's as if you are calling forth all of us that have been asleep … Thank You!

> Catherine Scherwenka, ONENESS International
> Teacher and Trainer

Gaia Codex is a deep journey into the past and future to discover how we could live right now. Sarah Drew reveals not only the beauty of nature, but the better instincts of human nature as key. *Gaia Codex* will deepen your love of this living planet and commitment to the great work ahead.

Randy Hayes, Founder Rainforest Action Network

Gaia Codex is beautifully woven and deeply reminiscent of an ancient wisdom time and space, rekindling the Circle of community, prayers of connection with the Earth and the return of female empowerment.

Dr. Carla Kleefeld, PhD, LPCC-Board Member,
Women's Donor Network

I LOVE this book! *Gaia Codex* is a brilliant, timeless history of the Divine Feminine and provides an empowering map— to better understand where we have come from and where we are going. I believe all ages and inclinations will be fed by your offering. I am grateful for what you have done. It is exquisite. Thank you!!

Kimberly Carter Gamble Producer, Director,
THRIVE and CEO, Clear Compass Media

Consider our world, if men and women truly understood the role and power of the feminine and its relationship to the Earth. *Gaia Codex* truly invites the reader to experience this. I couldn't put this book down. The language is rich, the story inviting and I recommend that you read it.

Bonnie Gray, wife of John Gray (author of *Men
Are From Mars, Women Are from Venus*)

Gaia Codex is more than just a novel. It is a languorous immersion into a clear, cool stream of consciousness—a journey into something ancient and protean. Ms. Drew's deft prose marries the genomic and supernatural to the indigenous and urban. Something revelatory emerges from the chrysalis and by the final chapter, it feels less like a work of fiction and more like a Movement.

Christopher Miles, Astrologer and Energy Healer

From the moment I picked up *Gaia Codex,* I felt my cells responding with a deep primordial urge to activate something inside of me … something I had assumed was already working at full throttle. My love for Mother Earth has been strong and solid throughout my life, but this shifted me into a new place of knowing. A familiarity … a longing … I can't even articulate the full scope of what I felt as I traveled deeper within its pages. I felt my DNA changing, guided by Lila Sophia, a metamorphosis into my own soul remembrance of every lifetime I've experienced on this amazing and magnificently loving planet. What a gift this is to the world. Thank you, Sarah Drew, for creating this written sentient being which left me feeling fluent in the language of Mother Earth.

Kristy Sweetland, MTP, ACC-Founder of
Coaching to Come Alive

Once in a while a story wakes you up. I began reading Sarah Drew's *Gaia Codex* late one evening in early January

2014 and finished it as the dawn rose over the redwoods of Northern California. I saw the world through new eyes. The *Codex* is a breathtaking tale of timeless love woven by a woman who knows and lives the divine. Our world has been waiting for The *Gaia Codex*. Don't wait to read it!

Brian J Weller, Educator, activist and business development specialist

There is a gift that is shared among women and men throughout Earth's evolutionary history. To receive it, one listens with the silent center of the heart. It is made of sacred substance that gives archetypal shape and form to all creation. The gift awakens us and opens portals into spiritual dimensions of consciousness.

Gaia Codex is such a gift as a novel. Received by Sarah Drew's heart and transmitted through her devoted writer's soul into text. Gaia Codex is a powerful love story for this potent transformative moment in time. Through her mythopoetic storyteller's weaving, novelist Sarah Drew illuminates a divine feminine wisdom path of radical awakening, species maturation, and planetary evolution.

Gaia Codex is a "Must Read Novel" not because it is an elegant story of feminine initiation, healing and awakening, it is essential reading because Gaia is calling us all to remember the truth that is hidden within the sacred chambers of our heart. We are Oneness expressing itself as Gaia again and again and again.

June Katzen, Archetypal Psychologist and

I am filled with immense gratitude for *Gaia Codex*. This poetic tale has served as a guide on my path in the most profound and sacred ways. *Gaia Codex* is a deep transmission that meets my heart's deepest desires. The time has come for this story to be shared and to be spread to many.

Magalie Bonneau-Marcil, Social Change Artist
and Founder of Dancing Without Borders

Gaia Codex is an eloquent gift and guide, an elegant weaving of skillful storytelling and sacred ancient wisdom teachings in reverence of the divine feminine, humanity's ultimate potential for intuitive and intelligent action, and to the Earth herself, whose survival in its natural state depends on the awakening of the global collective consciousness.

Christy Brown, Yoga and Meditation Teacher,
Founder Christy Brown Yoga

From the very first words on, I knew *GAIA CODEX* was a magickal text written for me, for my heart, and the knowing and remembering that resides within all of us. Instantly connecting us through these memories, this *Codex* is truly a Living Book. At once fractal—as the words transmit and accelerate transformation within my own being—and also a beautiful sharing of the greater Being, this larger process of transformation we're all in together. The wisdom being gifted through these codes are a promise straight from the heart of our Mama, passed on to each other over eons. Whispered through the wind and the scent of the earth herself. These codes coming to light, in this way, are a powerful sign of our times and what's possible right now.

Nina von Feldmann, Founder Dreamdanz Global and Co-Producer WaterSines

To find yourself at the intersection of nature, and history, and magic is to step into the world of *Gaia Codex*. Reading this delightful book is like taking a journey not only into these worlds, but also into your own soul. In the end you will discover yourself initiated, and courageously renewed.

Claire Savage, educator and author of *Older and Better, Super Confident Women at Mid-life and Beyond*

This brings tears to my eyes!!! WOW!! *Gaia Codex* is a masterpiece, here to be part of a huge shift in consciousness and in the world. It is a key, a transmission, a code to awaken the Divine Feminine in humanity. It is a deep reflection of so many of us on this planet at this time who are moving into our greater mission. *Gaia Codex* will be a valuable teaching text in our workshops for Mothers and Daughters in the path of the Divine Feminine. It is a book not only for women of all ages but also for men who want to more deeply understand the women they love. Thank you for this Gift!

Elizabeth Scherwenka, Teacher-Coach, Oneness

A Gita for the Goddess, *Gaia Codex* delivers me into a world I already know as my own, a world that knows itself in the burden and the blessing every woman's carries. To read it is be wrapped in a fabric of memories my soul has known throughout time, memories I hold in my blood, bone, and breath, memories woven into every love and loss that has touched my life, into the love-song I walk with the earth and the More-Than-Human world. Gaia brings this inner knowing into vibrant, poignant, and holy detail. I believe it can be this for all women, young or old. I believe it can be a bridge for mothers and daughters, teens and elders, sisters and friends, unlocking a deeper communion and purpose than we believed possible. The book is an invitation know ourselves as carriers of the evolutionary impulse of humanity. May it travel to hearts and souls far and wide.

> Samantha Sweetwater, Founder of Dancing Freedom

Waves of laughter and tears with rich and luscious imagery transport the reader into a world of magic and creative promise, awakening our awareness and guiding us towards a future worth creating.

Reading *Gaia Codex* inspires the reader into a journey, awakening the imagination with depth and insight filled with magic and possibility.

This Journey clearly references our current time, revealing

the most likely outcome if we continue this path of unconscious management of our resources without regard for the future of our species.

It is a transmission of wisdom, sensory awareness and consciousness for cultivating our relationship to the Mother Earth.

Sarah's writing draws us into a luscious new world and I was unable to put the book down, waiting for moments when I could continue reading. When I finished I was left wanting more.

Gaia Codex is an important, timeless book that has great wisdom for people of all ages.

Lynn Augstein, Dimensional Light Artist and Designer

I'm enthralled with *GAIA CODEX!* Sarah Drew has crafted a beautiful work for us all; guiding us to reawaken to cellular memories of magnificent connection and alignment with Mother Earth. This book is so hopeful and timely. I savored each of the rich, unusual descriptions and the otherworldly characters. Nuances from lifetimes of memories are coming alive for me. The *Codex* itself is so fresh and rife with meaning, history and insights. I feel as though I'm remembering a much deeper part of myself and every page provides a key to greater understanding. Sarah, thank you for shining your beautiful soul through each page … this book is a true Gift so well written, so rich in detail, story design and the deepest of interwoven meanings. *Gaia Codex* is a book about redemption that Awakens Life Within.

Sedena Campanelli, Co-Founder of Age Nation, World Council of Wisdom Keepers, and Award Winning Author of *Don't Go Quietly*

Thank you with my whole heart for the *Gaia Codex*. I lingered over each word, each codex, in this book of re-membering. As I read the novel, ancient hopes and new visions within the very bones and cells of my being were awakened. For me, the *Gaia Codex* is a luminous evocation of all that we have forgotten and all that we have always known. It is a call ever deeper to that which we may have only encountered in the dreamtime or in the wild. A call to nothing less than a 'resouling' of the collective within both our individual bodies and the body of our Mother Earth.

Christian Leahy, Founder of Studio Poema: Illuminating the New Story, Writer and Earth Activist

ABOUT THE AUTHOR

Sarah Drew is a passionate explorer of culture and consciousness. She has traveled extensively throughout the world, from the plateau of Tibet to the jungles of the Amazon. She studied Zen as a private student at Ryosen-an Temple in Kyoto, Japan—and has the honor of studying under the tutelage of Bhutanese lamas. Her professional background is as a creator of innovative media and technology. She loves fashion, design, evolutionary biology, and taking long hikes in the coastal redwoods near where she lives in Mill Valley, California.

Explore the *Gaia Codex* at
www.gaiacodex.com

61746411R00210

Made in the USA
Middletown, DE
14 January 2018